The Ice Bridge

**A suspenseful murder mystery set
on Mackinac Island**

By Kathryn Meyer Griffith

~

*For the loving memories I have of
and the beauty of Mackinac Island where
my husband and I spent our
twenty-fifth and our fortieth wedding anniversaries.*

The Ice Bridge

by Kathryn Meyer Griffith

Cover art by: Dawné Dominique
Copyright 2015 Kathryn Meyer Griffith

Other books by Kathryn Meyer Griffith:
Evil Stalks the Night
The Heart of the Rose
Blood Forged
Vampire Blood
The Last Vampire (2012 Epics EBook Awards Finalist)
Witches
Witches II: Apocalypse
Witches plus bonus Witches II: Apocalypse
The Calling
Scraps of Paper-1st Spookie Town Murder Mystery
All Things Slip Away-2nd Spookie Town Murder Mystery
Ghosts Beneath Us-3rd Spookie Town Murder Mystery
Witches Among Us-4th Spookie Town Murder Mystery
What Lies Beneath the Graves-5th Spookie Town Murder Mystery
Egyptian Heart
Winter's Journey
The Ice Bridge
Don't Look Back, Agnes
A Time of Demons and Angels
The Woman in Crimson
Four Spooky Short Stories
Human No Longer
Dinosaur Lake (2014 Epic EBook Awards Finalist)
Dinosaur Lake II: Dinosaurs Arising
Dinosaur Lake III: Infestation
Dinosaur Lake IV: Dinosaur Wars
Dinosaur Lake V: Survivors
Memories of My Childhood
Christmas Magic 1959 short story

Prologue

January 2008

The evening sun was setting and the Straits of Mackinac, blanketed in a rapid moving winter fog and frozen over since the first day of January, was a path of glittering cold ice—six feet thick above the frigid waters. The amethyst shadows, a snow twilight that was not quite night but no longer day, had drifted in and the whiteness of snow and frozen water wreathed in mist created an eerie landscape that seemed like no place on earth.

Mackinac Island sat to the right of the straits between Lake Michigan and Lake Huron. The island's lights were flickering on as the day faded. People were closing their shops, locking the doors and going home for the night. The tiny houses lit up the snow.

Looming behind the island like a monstrous sentinel, Mackinac Bridge, a five-mile structure of metal and concrete, connected the lower and upper peninsulas of Michigan. The Canadian winds caused the bridge to sway fifteen feet in opposite directions. It was decked out like a carnival with strings of gleaming ruby, emerald and white lights.

Though the inhabitants of Michigan appreciated the bridge and its convenience, many travelers were wary because it moved so much. Some refused to drive across it. Even macho truckers sometimes gave up the wheel to a bridge attendant, a braver soul, and let him drive the rig across for them. On the other side, the truckers would reclaim their truck and go on their way, never telling anyone they'd been too frightened to do it themselves.

In the late winter when the ice of the straits froze solid, not everyone used steel bridges to get from one piece of land to another. Some used another kind of bridge—a bridge of frozen water.

That night in the dusk, a solitary figure on a snowmobile was chugging across the ice, from Mackinac Island towards the mainland of St. Ignace, and staying in close to the curve of cast-off Christmas trees that had been stabbed into the frozen surface. The ice bridge, as the islanders called it, was a narrow path stretching three-and-a-half miles across the straits that separated Mackinac Island from the St. Ignace mainland. To the locals the ice bridge meant freedom to come and go for up to two months a year without paying ferryboat or airplane fees. It meant freedom to go day or night, on no one's schedule, to the mainland to seek entertainment, visit friends, and bring back the supplies they needed. Or it meant freedom to go for a late rendezvous.

The snowmobile was building speed, zipping across the ice, sure of the course in the misty light. A quarter of the way across, the driver noticed a slushy area and swerved off the path to the right. A soft snow had begun to fall from the night skies and the lone traveler, from a distance a larger pale blur among the smaller ones, became more difficult to see.

Someone who fidgeted in the woods impatiently watched from the trees on the north side of the island with a pair of binoculars and saw everything the rider did. The man, bundled in second-hand clothes and a shabby coat, observed the snowmobile's progress with cold calculating eyes. He dropped his smoldering cigarette from a shaking hand, and stamped his feet to stay warm as his breath puffed out in pale wisps between the trees. He noted the exact moment when the snowmobile veered off the trail.

Then with a vindictive smile the man knelt down, pushed a button on a box by his feet, and eagerly observed, as far out on the path the ice cracked and gave way beneath the snowmobile's treads.

That'll teach you, he thought smugly. *You've always had it so easy. Not anymore. I warned you, didn't I? But you wouldn't listen. You wouldn't give me what's mine, so now I'll just take it. There.* He chuckled spitefully. *Rest in peace. You got what you deserved.*

The heavy machine sank swiftly into the frigid waters, pulling its rider and one of the evergreens into the hole with it.

There was only time for one scream to drift up from the tear in the ice, but with a ghostly echo, it haunted the night for a brief time and then, like the snowmobile and rider, it was gone. The darkening dusk was silent again. The ice that covered the water—water nearly two hundred feet deep at that spot—folded over the fissure and began to refreeze into a tomb of ice.

The shadow person in the woods laughed gleefully and picked up the box, tucked it beneath his arm and went in search of warmth and food. He was tickled that he'd accomplished what he'd set out to do. Proud that, for once in his wretched life, he'd been brave and clever enough to do what he'd had to do. *Mother, you old witch, wouldn't you be proud of me? It's a shame you're not alive to see it—a real shame.* This time his laugh was softer and full of some strange satisfaction only he understood.

The man left the woods and began the hike back across the straits. He knew it would be a long walk and he'd be frozen by the time he climbed into his junky car and headed home. He didn't care. He smiled the whole way through the snow and hummed an old song his mother used to sing to him when she wasn't too drunk or out of it. He hummed and plotted his next step and it kept him warm.

A few evenings later, the missing tree and the frozen-over hole where the straits had swallowed the snowmobile were discovered by two other islanders on their way back from St. Ignace in the middle of a snowstorm.

They reported the anomaly and the next morning at dawn island police were called in to investigate. The storm was nearly a blizzard by then, but one of the policemen was insistent that they examine the ice immediately. He believed someone might have fallen through, but if so, past experience pointed to an accident. People had gone into the water before while crossing the ice bridge and it was tragic but not unheard of. It happened and sometimes, as awful as it was, it was the cost they paid for using the bridge. Often the ones who fell in managed to get out or were yanked out; were rescued, but not always. One time fourteen years earlier a man had gone through the ice, and by the time they'd dragged him out he was dead from the frigid water. It'd been a long time ago, but accidents did happen.

That January morning the police chopped into the ice, dredged the water below but couldn't locate a body or a snowmobile. They knew they might not find either until the spring thaws, if they ever found anything. They discovered a mitten, though, embedded in the ice, and someone recognized it as belonging to one of the full-time residents of the island—a woman. They noticed the slushy spot nearby that had already refrozen and speculated as to what might have happened. In the end, the chief of police had to write it off as an accident because, as he put it, who'd want to harm the victim? No one any of them could think of.

"The ice bridge has only been in use a few days and the victim's only been missing, that we know of, for about the same time," the chief spoke aside to his lieutenant. "It's easy to see how there might have been a weak spot in the ice this early. She went off the path to avoid what she thought was an unsafe stretch and, instead, hit a real bad patch. It broke beneath her and sucked her in.

"Poor thing. At least she died quickly. Drowning in freezing water isn't the worst way to go, Lieutenant. I don't need to tell you that."

"I know," the other officer replied. "You lose consciousness and fall asleep about the time you run out of air."

"It's pretty quick." The chief snapped his chubby fingers in the air. "Terrible thing. But nothing we can do for her now except keep looking for the snowmobile, her body, and fill out the forms. We'll speak to people and investigate further, but I'd wager a week's pay it was accidental."

His lieutenant didn't think so. He had nagging questions and was determined to get them answered. There were things at the scene that hadn't looked right to him. He'd never convince his superior of that. Chief Bill Matthews was a pragmatic kind of guy. If it looked like an accident, then it was—simple as that.

Yet at his lieutenant's insistence the chief let the other officers circle the site in yellow crime tape, so people would avoid it, and afterwards, the ice bridge was reopened. Everyone who used it swerved to the left and went nowhere near the scene of the accident. Many made the sign of the cross over their chests as they passed the spot where the woman might have disappeared, or they said a swift prayer so the ghost of the dead woman wouldn't appear to them.

People on the island were superstitious that way.

Chapter 1

October 23, 2007...two-and-a-half months earlier

It'd been a long time since Charlotte had been to Mackinac Island. Nearly fifteen years if she wanted to count them.

Her Aunt Elizabeth, whom everyone called Bess, lived there and owned a modest house on Lake Shore Road, down past the Mission Point Resort. It contrasted sharply with the rich people's huge cottages that were sprawled across the island. Charlotte used to spend summers with her aunt when she was younger. They'd been happier times she needed to revisit.

Now, as she stood on the top level of the Star Line's ferryboat and shivered in her jacket, her eyes fell on the island as it came towards her across the choppy water of the Straits of Mackinac. She remembered how much she'd once loved the place, how she'd ride her blue one-speed bicycle with the dented basket all over the island, and how she'd chase the seagulls or stare at the boats droning in and out of the harbor for hours.

She remembered how she'd adored the horse-drawn carriages, equine taxis, that transported people along the miniature asphalt roadways to Fort Mackinac or up West Bluff Road towards the Grand Hotel for lunch or high tea.

She remembered how the beauty of Lake Huron's waters contrasted against the milky sky with thick swirling clouds and how the Round Island Lighthouse and the Round Passage Light beamed their lights off shore. Memories brought back the awesome magnificence of the Mackinac Bridge as it spanned the waters between St. Ignace and Mackinac City. At night, it reminded her of Christmas with its long expanse covered in multicolored twinkling lights.

Most importantly, she remembered how she'd loved the island because it was where she first realized she wanted to be an artist or a writer. But how could she not have become an artist of some sort—on an island with Mackinac's natural beauty of rocks, shore and water, and the picturesque boats and woods full of wildlife around her? Then there'd been the vivid skies above the island and the straits where the waters were beautiful with swirling shades of green and blue. It made her smile just to look at it again.

Oh, Mackinac, I'm so happy to be back...why did I stay away so long?

The island was a little piece of land eight miles in circumference that didn't allow motorized vehicles, except snowmobiles in the winter. They'd outlawed cars in 1901 saying the island was too small to accommodate them and that they made too much noise and fouled up the air. Mackinac was a throwback to a simpler world of Victorian cottages, horses and interlacing bicycle trails-1,800 wooded acres dotted with historic national landmarks and most of it under federal protection. It was a place where police officers patrolled on ten-speeds and people walked through a quaint village filled with fudge shops, souvenirs and artsy crafts. It was the home of the Grand Hotel, a sprawling structure famous long before the movie *Somewhere in Time,* starring Christopher Reeve and Jane Seymour (featuring Mackinac and the hotel) came out.

Her Aunt Bess had worked at the Grand for over thirty years, waiting on tourists who came to the Grand Buffet. Though she was tired of the job, she loved the hotel. She said it was like being in another world filled with antique opulence and old ghosts.

Her aunt loved the island, too, and would never leave it as her sister, Charlotte's mother, had done so many years before. Charlotte's mother had been looking for a different, better life on some mainland far away. She'd found it and never returned.

But Charlotte, her eyes puffy and red from crying, had returned, older and wiser and with a damaged heart. She should have been on her honeymoon out in the Caribbean somewhere sipping strawberry daiquiris and spending passionate nights with her new husband, Lucas Sanders. But she wasn't.

Instead, she was running away from a world in which her fiancé had waited until a day before their expensive wedding to send her an e-mail—one of those pesky ones that made you accept them right away so the sender knew you'd received it—saying he wasn't going to marry her. He was already married and on the dream honeymoon that should have been hers...with her now ex-best friend Rachel.

Shock wasn't a strong enough word to describe what she'd felt when she'd read that e-mail. After all, she'd been engaged to Lucas for five years. And to break up with her in an e-mail? The least he could have done was telephone her and tell her in his own voice. Well, it was over.

She fought back tears as her thoughts touched on her doomed wedding. Her eyes hurt and her hands clenched on the rail until her knuckles were white. She shook her head, mumbling in a low voice. He'd taken a chunk of her life, a lot for a man to steal from a young woman. *Oh, she hated him. Hanging would be too good for him. Electrocution would be too good. She wished she could....*

"Miss, are you all right?"

She turned her head and met the eyes of a tall man standing behind her on the boat. The angry tears in her eyes kept her from seeing him clearly. Young, she registered, and though not excitingly handsome, his face was kind.

She glanced around. She'd been so preoccupied with her sorrow and dreams of revenge that she'd been leaning over the railing. Her cheeks were wet with tears she didn't recall shedding. He probably thought she was going to jump or something.

No man was worth that. Not even Lucas.

But she would have liked to throw her ex-fiancé over the railing into the chilly waters below, him and Rachel. She almost smiled at the thought of the two thrashing around in Lake Huron like abandoned baby dodos, the ferryboat chugging away as she waved goodbye to both of them.

She'd teach them to hurt other people—to hurt

her. "*I'm* fine," she sighed, composing herself, as she turned to face the stranger. No doubt she'd had that murderous look on her face before, the one her mother warned her would scare off Santa Claus. "I just had some unpleasant thoughts on my mind, that's all."

She wiped her eyes and looked at the man again. He was around her age, somewhere past thirty, had brown hair that the lake spray had ruffled into unruliness and brilliant sky blue eyes that smiled when his lips did, as they were doing now. He wasn't as handsome as Lucas, but attractive in a healthy puppyish kind of way. He looked sure of himself and casual in his lemon-yellow shirt and faded jeans.

Lucas, on the other hand, had been short, dark-haired and lean with cold gray eyes. Eyes that only smiled when he knew he had something other people wanted or when he was thinking about money. She wondered if those shark eyes were smiling now and the thought that they probably were made her sad.

Ooh, what did any of it matter now? Lucas had betrayed her. Lucas was gone and she had to move on. *Move on.* That was the healthy thing to do.

It'd be a long time before she trusted a man again.

"Miss?" The stranger was staring at her, his hands lifted as if he was ready to catch her should she try to jump.

"I'm okay, really," she replied softly. "Don't worry about me." She felt the tears coming on again and swung away from him.

The ferry was pulling into the dock and the boat was bucking beneath her feet. She checked her wristwatch. Eighteen minutes. That's how long the ferry ride had taken.

Now she had to face a new life and she was ready because she'd given the old one away. She'd sold everything she owned back in Chicago, quit her job, and had agreed to spend the next six months with her aunt, who was lonely and needed her.

At least someone needed her.

"Are you sure you're okay?" The man was still behind her. She'd almost forgotten him. His hand gently touched her arm, but she shook it off.

"Please, just leave me alone," she whispered, trying not to cry. She must look awful, and she felt worse. Was there a sign on her back saying: *Loser. Fiancé just dumped. Needs help. Sign up here?*

"Sorry if I bothered you. It's only that, well, you remind me of someone and at first I thought I knew you. You looked like you needed someone to talk to, that's all." His voice was so sympathetic she nearly spun around and apologized for her bad manners. Not a good idea.

She didn't want him to see the misery in her eyes and didn't want to talk to anyone at that moment, especially a man. Not when another man was the cause of her unhappiness.

A little time was what she needed. That's all.

Without another word, she brushed past him and pushed through the crowd off the boat like the rest of the lemmings. She was anxious to get where she was going and away from the stranger's unwanted attentions.

Gathering her bags from the cart, she collected the blue one-speed Murray bike she'd brought along to ride on the island. After years forgotten in her mother's garage, she'd been surprised to find its wheels still went round and round. She'd rescued it and put a larger basket on the front, knowing she'd need it to carry things, and because the old basket had rusted off. Bikes were gold on the island. A person either walked, rode a bike or a horse. She favored the bike because it ate less, didn't pee in the street and never had to see a vet. And she loved feeling the wind in her hair and on her face.

A messy pile of what was left of her previous life, her bike, the clothes in her suitcases and bags, surrounded her. She had no idea how she was going to carry everything. She'd left her car on St. Ignace, as some of the islanders did, in a guarded parking lot. She'd use it for shopping and errands when she returned to the mainland every week or so.

Standing there trying to decide how she was going to get the luggage and the bike to her aunt's house she spotted her kind stranger again. He had an overnight bag slung across his shoulders and was headed straight for her.

Oh, no.

"Looks like you need some help, Miss. What hotel or bed and breakfast are you staying at?" He acted as if she hadn't brushed him off a few minutes ago. He was smiling and helpful and it gave her another twinge of guilt because she was going to have to turn him down again.

"I don't need help, especially from someone I

don't know." Charlotte shoved her long chestnut hair behind her ears and stuck her chin up like a petulant child.

He put out a large hand for her to shake. "Well, I'll introduce myself and then we'll know each other. I'm Lieutenant Maclean Berman of the Mackinac Police Force. You can call me Mac."

Oh, darn, he was being so nice. How could she stay mad at half the population when she couldn't usually stay mad at even one person for more than a minute? She couldn't.

"You're a cop?" She blurted out, her hand leaving his. "That explains it."

"Explains what?"

"Why you're so nosy. Wanting to know about me and wanting to help and all." She tried not to smile, but one slipped out anyway. So he was a man, but she didn't have to be rude. "My name's Charlotte Graham. And no, I'm not going to a hotel or a bed and breakfast; my aunt, Elizabeth Conners, lives down Lake Shore Road. I'll make it there fine by myself."

She wanted him to go away.

"That's at least two miles." The cop was grinning. "Now I know why you looked familiar to me. I know Elizabeth Conners. She works at the Grand Hotel. About fifty, a tiny woman with blue eyes and hair the same shade as yours. Independent and spunky, like you? You two could be sisters you look so much alike."

She disregarded the independent and spunky remark. He was trying to make friends and she wasn't biting. "Sisters? I'm nowhere near fifty."

14

She was trying to load as many bags from her shoulders and into her bike's basket as she could cram in. Hopeless. She still had three sitting on the dock. It'd been easier getting them on the ferry from her car when she'd had a porter to help her unload them.

"Well, you're definitely the much younger sister." Without asking, Mac easily grabbed the three bags up from the ground and took one off her shoulders. He seemed to handle the burden with no problem.

"Well, I'm going to help you whether you like it or not, Miss Spunky Independence. Elizabeth would never forgive me if I didn't. In a way, related to an islander as you are, you're an honorary islander yourself. We don't treat other islanders like strangers. We help each other out because we're a close-knit bunch. You'll see."

Realizing she had no choice Charlotte accepted his help and they aimed themselves towards the street. "Lieutenant Berman, are you a year-round resident here?"

"Yep. I'm one of the crazy ones. Winter, too. I work all year long for the police department and live with a friend in an apartment above the Mustang Lounge."

A friend? It was most likely a woman because he was too good-looking and eligible to be alone.

"You know where that's at?"

"In town," she answered. "I used to spend summers here as a kid. The Mustang's one of the places that stays open all year round for the locals, right? I know not many people remain on the island through the winter because my aunt swears it turns into Alaska here after November."

"That it does. Only about five hundred islanders actually stay through the winter months, not just because of the cold but because it's too expensive to get supplies to the island when the waters freeze and the ferries stop running. Prices in the winter, as if they aren't high enough, skyrocket."

"So my aunt tells me." It was practically November and she'd never been on the island this late in the season. She'd never spent a winter on Mackinac, merely summers. If she stayed this year, it would be her first one.

"Yeah, it gets cold enough to freeze a dinosaur around here. It feels like the winds are made of ice at times. But I like the island in the snow and through the holidays with the decorations strung from light post to light post. Like the huge Christmas tree in the center of town. I enjoy riding around on a snowmobile and skimming across the ice bridge to the mainland, bundled up in two coats and three pairs of gloves. I like not having much to do. You know, winter's the only time we get the island back to ourselves."

"After the boatloads of tourists leave, hey?"

"Yeah, after the *fudgies* leave." He smiled at her as she sidestepped a pile of horse manure in the middle of the road.

A horse and carriage rattled by, bikes whizzed around them and it was as if she'd never left. She was twelve years old again running wild around a place that'd been magic to her. Her tension was already easing away.

She looked up and took in the stately Victorian homes that lined Lake Shore Road with their skillfully painted exteriors and their elaborate flower gardens that were now beginning to wilt. She'd always dreamed of owning and living in one. Now? Fat chance. Only princesses and millionaires could afford one of them. Oh, well. Perhaps someday.

She lowered her head and watched where she put her feet. A puddle of what appeared to be water but wasn't, cascaded down the gutters behind a horse taxi with a covered roof and four speckled white Clydesdale horses pulling it. The beasts whinnied and clomped their hairy hooves, looking around as if they were bored. It would take her a while to get used to the pungent horse odors again, she mused, but, eventually, she would, as she had when she was a kid.

"Fudgies," she said, as she pushed her bike, "they still call the tourists that?"

"Still do. As long as they come, buy and eat so much fudge, I guess we'll always call them that. They're our bread and butter, though, so we can't complain. The islanders wouldn't have jobs; I wouldn't have a job, if not for the tourists. Their money pays the bills."

Charlotte nodded, knowing he was right.

They passed by the village shops: Professor Harry's Old Time Photos, Dockside Inn, Island Bicycle Livery and further up the road, Ryba's Fudge Shop and the Mercantile. They continued walking past Marquette Park, where the horse and buggies for rent were lined up waiting for customers, and past Mission Point Resort with its lavish gardens and white wooden chairs snuggled up to the water's edge. The Mission Point had a whole complex of shops that included one of the best bakeries on the island. Charlotte recalled the Cheese Danish were heavenly.

Charlotte wished she were riding her bike instead of pushing it. Yet it was a lovely fall day, cool and sunny with a strong breeze and it was nice to be leisurely strolling, kind of a nostalgic journey, through the quaint town she'd left behind so many years before.

Not much had changed. Some of the houses were fixed up and the crowds in town, though it was the last week of the summer season, seemed larger. The tourist business apparently was thriving. All in all, the island itself felt smaller but everything else seemed the same.

For a while she was a child again, hopeful and full of awe for the future. Free. As if anything were possible. It'd been a long time since she'd felt that way and it felt good.

She caught Mac watching her and there was a friendly interest in his eyes. She hoped he wasn't getting any romantic ideas. Just the thought of it, made her fall silent.

There wasn't any more conversation between them before they arrived at her aunt's house. If he started to say something, she'd walk ahead faster, pretending she hadn't heard. She knew she was being unfair, but she couldn't help herself. Underneath it all, she was unexplainably drawn to him and it was unnerving, so behaving distantly was better than breaking down and dumping her sorrows on the man. That'd scare him off quick enough all right.

He seemed to accept she wasn't in a talkative mood and didn't push it. When they got to her aunt's door, though, he did ask, "If I'm not being too bold, what were you mad about on the ferry anyway?" The smile he gave encouraged her to confide in him. He would have made a good priest.

He'd been kind to her and he was a friend of her aunt's. Since she wanted the subject closed once and for all, she told him in as few words and as dispassionately as she could about her aborted wedding and absconded bridegroom and her traitorous best friend. She made it brief and when she was done, she could see the usual pity welling up in his face and was instantly sorry she'd said anything at all. That'd teach her.

"Charlotte, I'm so sorry. I didn't mean to pry. How could anyone do such an awful thing to you? All I can say is that he wasn't much of a man or a human being to end it that way. You deserve better than that. I want to apologize for all my gender." There was compassion in his words. "No wonder you're upset."

"Yeah, well, I imagine he had his reasons for what he did and the way he did it." She waved her hand in the air in an I-don't-care-gesture, her face emotionless. "The way I look at it, at least he didn't marry me first and then run off with my friend. So, looking at it that way, he did me a favor."

Lt. Berman studied her for a moment with

perceptive eyes. She had the feeling she wasn't fooling him one bit, and he said, "Well, things will get better for you here with your aunt on the island. Mackinac heals everything, even heartache, you'll see. I'll bet you in a few weeks you won't even remember that guy's name. Take care, now."

She didn't know how to respond. He actually believed that. The island would heal her.

Without saying another word, she turned and knocked on her aunt's door. She'd had enough of people's sympathy. He was right about one thing, she did want to forget Lucas and go on with her life.

For now she wanted to be left alone.

"Thanks for helping me, Lieutenant Berman," she murmured before the door flew open and Aunt Bess, looking older and wearier than she'd last seen her, welcomed her inside.

When Charlotte stole a look over her shoulder, her bags were sitting on the steps behind her and the friendly cop was gone. Walking down the street towards town, he swung around and waved to her and her aunt, leaving them alone to get reacquainted. Not for the first time since she'd met him, she thought he was considerate as well as kind. Or perhaps he was just being a good public servant.

She wiggled her fingers back at him.

"Well, child, it's good to see ya," her Aunt Bess declared, hugging her so hard she thought ribs were going to crack. Bess claimed a couple of suitcases and pulled her niece into the house. "Leave your bike out on the porch, no one will take it."

Ah Mackinac, innocent island where everyone trusted everyone else.

Once inside, Charlotte dropped her luggage and purse. "It's good to see you, too, Auntie. You're looking–"

"Tired and older, I know," her aunt finished for her. "I've turned into that middle-aged frumpy fat woman I swore I'd never be.

"But," she added quickly, "I'm going to begin exercising again. I'm going on a diet. Now that you're here, I'll get into shape in no time. You'll see. You love to walk and I'll walk with you. That'll do it."

Charlotte was going to protest her aunt's self-description but the other woman didn't give her a chance. Truth was, Bess did look haggard. Her blue eyes, so like Charlotte's except for the hint of gray, were lackluster, and her aunt's brunette hair was gray-streaked. Her face was lined, especially around the mouth as if she'd been frowning too much. She'd put on more than a couple of pounds.

Charlotte hadn't seen her aunt in years and in those first moments realized that it'd been longer than she'd thought. It was amazing how fast people aged when a person didn't see them for a long time. It didn't help that her aunt was wearing a frayed and baggy sweatpants outfit. Something like an old woman would wear. Her aunt had once taken such good care of herself, had dressed in the latest fashions and had been so pretty. What had happened?

Bess had been married young at age sixteen to her beloved Charlie. After fourteen years she'd lost him and had now been a widow for the last two decades. Charlie's dying had been hard on her, but she'd overcome it. She'd overcome everything in her life that had been put in her path. Or she used to. Charlotte had always thought of her aunt as a strong woman.

Now Charlotte's mother, Isabel, Bess's younger sister, was a different story. Though the two sisters were close in age, Charlotte had to admit her mother looked fifteen years younger. Her mother dyed her hair to cover the gray, worked out at a gym four days a week and had a husband of twenty-five years who adored, babied and cherished her. Her mother dressed in chic clothes and bright colors, spent money on herself and would never be caught in faded torn sweatpants.

Apparently, Aunt Bess had no one to pretty herself up for.

"But you, Charlotte, you're looking good, under the circumstances. You remind me of your mother at your age. Prettier. Don't ever tell her I said that, though. Is she still as vain as she always was?"

Charlotte laughed at that. Her mother was forever saying that Aunt Bess was the vain one. If her mother could see her older sibling now she wouldn't say that, but the two sisters didn't see each other very often. They lived in different worlds. Once they'd been close, when both had been young and had lived on the island, but that had been before Isabel had moved so far away. Now they exchanged birthday cards and Christmas presents and little else.

"Just as bad, perhaps worse. Mother can't stand that she's on the downhill slide to fifty and tells everyone she's barely forty."

Aunt Bess chuckled. "Ha, I guess I'll just keep on getting older while she gets younger. Eventually I'll die of old age and she'll be a baby again." Another good-natured chuckle left her lips.

"Come on let's get you settled into your room, Charlotte. I'm giving you the upstairs loft for as long as you're here. You always liked it for the privacy and the view so I fixed it up as cute as I could in appreciation for you coming to stay with me."

Her aunt was right. The loft had the best overlook of the Lake. Sunrises were breathtaking and when the windows were open, there was usually a cool breeze coming in off the water that found its way into the room.

Bess led her niece through the hallway to the steps and up to the room Charlotte remembered so well. Once the walls had been a sick yellow but now they had a fresh coat of mauve paint. Crisp white curtains with lilacs sprinkled across them hung at the windows with a matching quilt on the full-sized bed positioned beneath the window. It didn't look like the same room. It was lovely.

Bess dropped the bags on the bed. "I see you already met one of our most desirable bachelors."

Relieving herself of what she'd been carrying, Charlotte looked at her aunt, confused, and then got it. "Oh, you mean Lieutenant Berman? He was only helping me get my stuff here. I had more than I could handle and he was being nice. I met him coming over on the ferry."

"Lucky you. He's a sweet guy and a real catch. Did he know you were my niece?"

"Not at first. Then after we introduced ourselves, I mentioned who I was going to meet and he said I looked like you."

"So he offered to help you before he knew who you were?"

Why all the questions? "So?"

"So, he doesn't normally push himself at a woman. Any woman. Not since his girlfriend died a few year ago. He's basically shy."

"His girlfriend died?" Charlotte had the feeling she didn't want to know more but that she was going to hear it anyway.

"It's a sad story...even sadder than yours, Charlotte. Mac Berman was born and raised on the island and had a childhood sweetheart here. Melissa Wittiker. She taught second grade at the island grade school. Mac and Melissa had been saving and planning for their wedding for years, it was going to be a big affair at the Grand Hotel. But two weeks before the wedding Melissa was out sailing with some friends and fell overboard.

"She drowned or so they thought. They never found her body. Mac went into a long depression. He almost gave up his job on the police force and left the island, but in the end, he didn't. Good for us. He's an excellent cop and a better human being.

"Rumor was, he almost attempted suicide at one point. He loved Melissa so much. He's never been the same and he's never dated since. I know him pretty well and I can say he's the best the male world has to offer. He's caring, smart and honest. If I were twenty-five years younger, I'd go after him myself. I wonder why he didn't say hi to me and come in? We talk all the time in town or up at the Grand if he comes in for something. We go way back."

"I have no idea." But she did. Inside she was cringing, recalling the way she'd treated him and the way she'd whined about her own tragedy. Being left at the altar was nothing compared to what he'd gone through. She hadn't loved Lucas near enough to want to kill herself.

Oh, well, what was done, was done. She'd probably see little of Lieutenant Mac Berman unless someone perpetrated a crime against her aunt or her. On Mackinac Island, there wasn't much chance of that. Crime on the island, according to her aunt, was as rare as unicorns.

"You look tired, sweetie." Aunt Bess's eyes were on her. "You should rest for a bit. I'll rouse you for supper and you can give me the whole sordid story about what that creep Lucas did to you. I never liked that man. From what you've told me he only cared about fattening his financial portfolio and what other people thought of him. If he had ever loved you he wouldn't have run off with your best friend. Good riddance to bad rubbish, I say." She shook her head. "There's no excuse for what he did. None whatsoever."

Charlotte smiled weakly at her aunt. "A nap might be just the thing, Aunt Bess. The last couple of days I haven't slept much. Been too busy." Been too upset. Leaving her job, putting stuff in storage and packing. Running away. "Perhaps now, here, I can."

Outside the window the water was a flat endless

crystal of turquoise, and the wispy clouds were gray and cherry tinged. The chilly air rushing in made her peacefully drowsy. How many nights as a girl had she lain in this bed, head in the window, gazing out at the lake and sky, or sleeping in the soothing breezes? More than she could count. It'd always calmed her.

Suddenly she was so exhausted she could barely stand. There was time enough later to explore the island. Time enough to get out into the world and crash back into a life without Lucas, Rachel or her job. Right now sleep was what she needed. She'd sleep away the old life before she began her new one.

"Then you take a nice rest, sweetie," her aunt said, "and I'll wake you for supper. I'm making homemade stew and biscuits."

"Sounds delicious." Charlotte yawned as her aunt closed the door and left her alone with her thoughts and her gloom. Nevertheless, Charlotte found herself happy to be there with her aunt and free of the sadness that her Chicago life had become.

She was never going to return to Chicago. She was never going back to the corporate world of crowded skyscrapers and the breakneck pace of making big money. She didn't need money anyway. Not her. Not much. She could live on air. Ha. Whom was she fooling? She was broke.

Perhaps she'd stay on the island in this house with her mother's sister the rest of her life. She'd never get married, simply work in one of the tourist's shops selling fudge to the *fudgies* and riding her bike around the island—hiding.

She could be happy, couldn't she?

After she unpacked, she stretched out on the bed and drowsily watched the boats trolling the lake. She watched the seagulls flying over the shoreline. Eventually their swooping and soft crying lulled her to sleep and she rested better than she had in weeks. A deep comforting sleep that helped to wipe away the past and nudge her into the future. She had no nightmares of Lucas rejecting her or of Rachel laughing at her because she'd run off with her almost husband. No nightmares of slaving away in a cardboard cubicle with deadlines she could never seem to meet. Or of crowded narrow streets full of angry cars, towering metal buildings that blocked out the sun and hot summer pavements. She had no dreams of her old life. There was only welcoming blackness because she was finally home.

****

Charlotte awoke to the aromas of meat and freshly baked biscuits. By the absence of light in the room, she guessed it was around seven or eight. It was so chilly she shivered. Late October on Mackinac was already a lot colder than Chicago.

Outside the sky would remain illuminated by the sun's reflection until after eight-thirty even this late in the year. She checked the clock on the nightstand. It was eleven minutes after seven. She'd slept six hours and felt better for it yet there was still over an hour remaining before darkness fell.

Enjoying the outside view, she breathed in the sweet air, then got up and went downstairs to the kitchen. She'd put on a heavy sweater and jeans. It would get downright cold on the island after dark. After supper, either they'd take a long walk along Lake Shore Road into town or they'd sit on the porch that ran the length of the front of the house. Catch up on each other's lives. So she'd be dressed warm and ready. Her mother said she was a freezy-bug, but she just liked to be warm.

"You look much better now that you've had some sleep, kiddo. It agreed with you." Aunt Bess put out a second plate of warm stew on the table and sat down across from her. There was a basket of fluffy biscuits in the middle and a crystal dish full of butter.

"I've been feeling better ever since I got here." Charlotte gestured at the scenery showing through the windows. "It already seems as if Chicago was another life. That it was only a dream that ended badly."

"Oh, that other world existed, all right. But for a while you can forget about it and take a vacation. Have some fun. Be good to yourself. The world will always be out there waiting for you when you're ready to go back.

"Now," her aunt let out her breath, as she took a bite of stew, "tell me exactly what happened with you and Lucas. I mean if you want to. I won't force you into talking about it before you're ready."

"You're not. I'll tell you everything and then we won't speak of it or him again. Ever. You agree?"

Her aunt nodded her head. "If that's the way you want it."

"That's the way I want it."

Charlotte told her everything and Bess listened.

When she was done, her aunt said, "You're better off, believe me. I always knew he wasn't the man for you. Things happen for a reason and I'm sure you weren't meant to marry Lucas. Your true love is out there waiting to be found. Now you can start looking for him."

"Not for a while. I need to concentrate on myself right now. I have no idea what I want anymore."

"That's okay, too. You'll figure it out. You're a smart girl."

Charlotte finally smiled. "I want to thank you for inviting me, Aunt Bess." She didn't say a thing about staying there forever. It was too soon for that and she hadn't decided yet. For now, Bess only believed she was there for a rest and a change of scenery. She'd leave it at that.

"Ah, it's purely selfish on my part." Her aunt patted Charlotte's hand. "I've missed you." She hesitated and finished, "Truth is, I've been lonely and your being here is an answer to a prayer."

"For me, too." Charlotte had been looking around as they ate. The kitchen hadn't changed much since she'd visited last. It was cramped but cheery; had wooden floors that had been scrubbed and polished so often they were worn down to the bare wood. The room's windows were old so they stuck halfway up or halfway down when it was warm outside and dropped like guillotines when it was cold. In the summertime, her aunt propped them up with wooden sticks.

Over her head, there was an ornate but dusty ceiling fan. On her right along the wall were oak cabinets that had been there since her childhood and were filled with familiar plates and mementoes. Her aunt was a collector. Among the curios were sparkly rocks, wind-smoothed pebbles, delicate feathers she'd found on the beach, and tiny figurines in glass, shell or quartz she'd found at yard sales or on end-of-the-season clearance at the shops in town.

On the walls there were original paintings of Mackinac by local artists bought for pennies before the artists had become famous...of seagulls, lake scenes and horses pulling carriages in front of the Iroquois Hotel on the waterfront.

The kitchen walls were covered in lilac-themed wallpaper and the curtains were lace panels. Bunches of dried lilacs, the official Mackinac flower, were everywhere. They were big business on the island and in June, the Lilac Festival brought people from all over the world. Charlotte never saw or smelled lilacs that she wasn't reminded of Mackinac.

After they finished supper, her aunt suggested a walk.

Charlotte patted her tummy. "Sure. I need the exercise after that meal you made me." She was surprised, but relieved, that her appetite had returned. Though she could afford to lose a couple pounds, starving herself, as she'd been doing, wasn't the way she wanted to lose them. "Can I take along a couple of these biscuits?"

"For the seagulls, huh?"

"Yeah. It's been a long time since I've fed a seagull."

Bess sent her a sideways grin. "You haven't changed much, have you?"

"Not really." Charlotte's expression was wistful as they went out the door and headed towards the village. They'd taken their jackets along. After dark it would really get cold.

They strolled through town, talking about their lives as Charlotte peeked into the closing shop windows and marveled at how little the town had changed since she'd been there last.

Some of the shops she remembered were no longer there but others, full of expensive or tacky souvenirs, homemade crafts, candies and pastries, had taken their place. Restaurants. Bars. An old-fashioned grocery mercantile. Entertainment establishments geared towards the tourists.

"In a week, after Halloween, most of these stores will close." Bess stopped in front of Ryba's Fudge Shop. "The season will end and the summer tourists will be gone until next spring. Hallelujah. My tired feet are applauding. And we'll get some peace and quiet."

"And freezing temperatures and a ton of snow."

"You got it. So enjoy the crowds, shops and fair weather now because in a few weeks they'll be gone."

The women stood on the ferry dock as Charlotte had so many times as a child. The shadows of the coming dusk hovered, and Charlotte tossed out pieces of biscuits. Hanging in the air before her eyes, the birds fearlessly fought for the crumbs she offered. They screeched and called to their other bird friends to come and join them as they snatched the snippets out of her fingers.

Some islanders didn't like the seagulls. They considered them a noisy, messy nuisance. She loved them. To her, they were graceful and lovely as they flew about her head like huge feathery butterflies. Some were bashful, some aggressive, and some hung back, eyeing her with suspicion; while others nearly knocked her over to get at the food.

She and her aunt resumed their meandering.

It was dark by the time they'd turned around by the tree where Christopher Reeve's character had first met Jean Seymour's in *Somewhere in Time*.

They'd just passed the Haunted Theatre when they ran into Lt. Berman. He was perched on a crimson ten-speed Schwinn and was dressed in his police officer's gray-blue uniform, dark pants and jacket. He rode past them and doubled back.

"Darn, he's seen us," Charlotte muttered under her breath.

Bess stopped and spoke to him first. "Hi Mac. On patrol tonight?"

"Uniform gave me away, huh?"

"Yep."

"Night shift." The police officer tipped his cap at Charlotte. She nodded, and glanced away embarrassed to meet his eyes, as she reflected on the things she'd told him earlier and what she now knew about him.

"I see you're reacquainting yourself with our little village." He was talking to her.

"I am." She met his gaze. The dark had fallen as if someone had dropped a night curtain over everything. In the glow of the quaint Victorian streetlights, Lt. Berman's face was softened and shadowed. She thought he was smiling at her. "It's been awhile."

"How long?"

She told him.

"That's a long time." Mac slid off the bike, his hands on the handlebars. "How come you haven't been back in so long?"

"Been busy." She couldn't look him in the face.

"I didn't say anything when I met you this morning, didn't get a chance. But I knew more about you than I was letting on since your aunt brags on you a lot. She talks about how well you are doing as an artist in the big city. She's so proud of you."

His kind words touched her and she smiled at him for the first time in the lamplight. "I want to apologize, Lt. Berman, for my rudeness to you earlier today. This hasn't been the best of weeks for me. Can you forgive me?"

"Apology accepted. I knew you weren't angry with me this morning. I know what being left behind feels like. I didn't hold it against you. Oh, and call me Mac, remember, everyone else does."

She put out her hand for him to shake and he took it. "Well then, let's start over, Mac. Hi, I'm Charlotte Graham. Call me Charlotte. I'm here to visit my aunt for a bit, enjoy the peacefulness of the island and—" she didn't know why she said it but she did and her words surprised her "—maybe do what I've wanted to do for years...try to write a book."

"A writer, too? Your aunt never told me you

write as well as being an artist." Mac exchanged a look with Bess who shrugged her shoulders.

"I don't. It's a daydream of mine, that's all. Computer art was my job in the city but writing is my secret passion. One I've thought of doing for years, but never had the time. With the tranquility of the island and the isolation of my aunt's loft, I thought I'd give it a go. The worst I can do is fail."

Her aunt had moved on ahead, pretending to be interested in what was in the shops' windows, but Charlotte knew what she was up to. Leaving her alone with Mac. Playing matchmaker. She shouldn't have bothered.

The shops were closing their doors and the people in the streets had thinned out. The village was usually a ghost town by ten o'clock except for the taverns and restaurants. The last ferries of the day had left for St. Ignace or Mackinaw City and the overnight tourists were heading to their B&Bs or their fancy hotels for the night.

Only a few stragglers remained, mostly shop workers, who came from around the globe to work there. They were going home on their bikes through the dark wooded streets to houses and apartments in the center of the island. Tiny bats flew around them searching for night bugs or for places to roost beneath the shop rafters. Some of the human stragglers were heading for Patrick Sinclair's Irish Pub, Horns or the Dockside Inn to party and listen to the Irish, pop or blues bands. The locals would patronize the Mustang Lounge or The Pink Pony.

Mac's eyes were roving the roads and storefronts as they chatted, alert for trouble, or as much trouble as a nearly deserted small tourist town could dish out. "What kind of book do you want to write?"

"I don't know yet. I'm still thinking about it. Fiction. I've always thought I might write what I like to read."

"And that is?"

"Anything mysterious or spooky."

She was talking too much, revealing too much about herself that she'd wanted to keep to herself. Her gaze took in Mac's uniform with the holster and gun. Remembering from her younger days that the island was a peaceful place, she changed the subject. "Does the island have much crime?"

"Sure, can you imagine a mugger jumping on his horse or bike to escape after he's accosted some old lady tourist? He wouldn't get far. The island's small and there's no way off except by boats or airplanes."

"So you're saying there isn't much crime?"

"Oh, there's crime, just not the real serious kind. Sometimes tourists come up with missing items, not much of that, though, for the thousands of *fudgies* who stream through here every day. There are domestic squabbles, especially in the winter, when people are trapped in their houses together for long periods. Or the summer kids get into mischief, get too drunk or rowdy after working hours. We give tickets to drunk drivers here, too, you know, even if they are on a bicycle. The biggest problem we have is bike borrowing." He chuckled, but she knew what he meant. "And really lately there hasn't even been much of that. The island is a fairly tranquil place.

"Except," and here he paused for effect, "we're always taking reports of weird occurrences and ghostly sightings."

She thought he was mocking her after what she'd told him about the kind of book she wanted to write, but he wasn't smiling.

"Ghostly sightings...you're kidding, aren't you?"

"No, I'm not. You wouldn't believe it but we have a lot of strange happenings, particularly in the winter when the island's practically empty. It's not spoken of much because it'd scare the tourists something awful to know things sometimes simply dematerialize on the island or someone's seen a civil war apparition at twilight up by the fort. Let me tell you, people have seen them."

The fort was Fort Mackinac that sat strategically high above them at one hundred and fifty feet on top of a hill in the middle of the island. The fort was used to guard the straits during the War of 1812 and later in the Civil War. Live soldiers had long ago abandoned it and since the 1900s it'd become a rustic historical site, a museum and a huge tourist draw.

"Ghostly sightings, huh?" she repeated softly. She'd had an unnatural interest in supernatural happenings her entire life. Call it morbid fascination or love of things that couldn't be explained but whatever it was, she loved a good ghost story.

She believed in ghosts. Sort of.

When she'd been twelve years old she'd seen something strange on the island one summer in Ste. Anne's Church on Huron Street. She'd been riding her bicycle and appreciating the sunset. It'd been the most unusual shade of orange streaked with indigo and half the skies had been this odd overlapping cloud pattern. The design was so symmetrical it had looked unreal, but breathtaking. It had been around dusk and the old church had been empty.

She'd stopped and wandered into the building that had given her eerie vibes whenever she'd been there for Sunday mass with her aunt. She'd often heard whispery voices behind the priest's pulpit when there wasn't anyone there. Bibles would be at their side one moment and in the pew behind them in the next. Once someone tapped her on the shoulder and she'd twisted her head but no one had been there. Weird things like that. Nothing so unnerving that she'd been afraid. Not then anyway.

That evening she'd gone into the church and at first she'd been alone. The last of the sun's rays shone in through the stain glassed Jesus and Mary windows. The whole place had been bathed in muted colors. It was a lovely old church. If only its stone walls could speak, what a story they might tell.

Getting ready to leave, she'd spied the woman in the front pew crying among the dancing shadows, cloaked in a translucent pearl white mist, and it'd been hard to see her until Charlotte moved closer. Startled, she noticed the woman was dressed in a billowy Victorian gown of chocolate brown with lace trim, gloves and a bonnet. She clutched a Bible to her chest. Her head was down and she was weeping. Charlotte could hear her sobs, low and heart wrenching. Echoes slowly subsided into the air and drifted away; they were the saddest sounds she'd ever heard.

The woman had stared up at her with a tear stained face and pleading eyes. Eyes with the same look in them as Great Aunt Janet had had after her two sons had died in that car accident the year Charlotte had turned eleven.

Soul sadness.

Then the woman had vanished. Just like that, she'd been gone. Frightened, Charlotte had gotten out of there as fast as her tennis shoes could take her. She'd never told anyone, they would have thought she'd made it up. Later she convinced herself she'd imagined it. She was a daydreamer.

She'd shoved the experience out of her mind and hadn't thought of it in years until that moment. Being back on the island and the mention of ghosts had dislodged it.

Had it really happened? She still wasn't sure, but it'd make a good story.

Mac was rattling on. "Oh, in my time I've heard plenty of ghost stories from people hereabouts. I've never seen a spook myself, though. But there could be something to it if so many other people on the island claim to have seen things. I can't tell you all the spirits that are supposed to haunt this patch of land surrounded by water."

He paused, an earnest look on his face. "Now that would be an intriguing topic for a book—ghost sightings on Mackinac Island. You could talk to the residents that have experienced unusual or weird incidents, and take down their stories. It'd make for interesting reading, now wouldn't it?"

"It would." Her mind was churning the idea over.

Ghost stories of the Island. It was a great premise.

"Do you think there are enough stories to fill a book?"

"From what I've heard over the years, I'd say probably more than enough for two books."

Charlotte was thinking out loud, "And as you say, I could interview people and collect their true stories. People love talking about the supernatural. Reading about it. That sort of thing. Real experiences given by real people. Or I do anyway. I could lay the book out in chapters and have each chapter be an interview with the person relating their encounter. It'd be a way to get to know the town folks, too."

"It sounds like a plan. I know I'd buy and read such a book if someone wrote it. I like spooky stuff. You could compile the tales and being an artist...you might consider illustrating it. Draw the settings, and the ghosts, as you think they looked."

"That's another good idea. I'll think about it. The book and the drawings. Thanks for the suggestions." Charlotte smiled.

Her aunt had reappeared at her side. "Are you two done chatting?"

"I guess I should resume patrolling," Mac said. "This island is a lot bigger than this main street and the shops here. Right before I saw you both I had a report of someone jumping out of the woods and scaring the bejesus out of a young Russian hotel worker when she was riding home. I have to go and talk to her about it."

Before he got on his bicycle, he spontaneously reached out and squeezed Charlotte's hand. "Good night, Charlotte. I'll be seeing you. On an island this size we're sure to bump into each other again before long. Keep thinking about that book. Sounds like a winner to me."

He waved at Bess as he rode off and Bess blew him a kiss.

As he'd held her hand and smiled at her Charlotte had thought: *He's attracted to me. Too soon.* She wasn't ready to be hurt again.

Mac rode away into the darkness and she caught the amused glance her aunt gave her.

"Don't get any ideas," Charlotte told her firmly. "I'm sure he was only being sociable."

"Yeah, sociable. He's smitten with you, my girl. Admit it. Even I can see it."

Charlotte shrugged and started walking again. "It's late, it's gotten so cold, and my face is numb. You ready to go home?"

Her aunt caught up with her. "Ready. I keep forgetting you're not used to this cold yet. You think it's cold now, just wait until December and January. You haven't felt anything yet."

"I can wait. One summer I overheard a tourist asking a clerk at the Mercantile why she didn't live here year round and I can still see the flabbergasted look on the girl's face. It was so funny. She said, 'Do I look crazy to you?' in a shrill voice and launched into this hilarious story about a friend who'd stayed for a winter. He said he almost turned

40

into a two-legged Popsicle one weekend. He ran out of propane and snowmobiled over to a friend's empty cabin but by the time he'd built a fire he thought his fingers and toes were gone for sure. He said the air was like dry ice and froze his breath in two seconds. The snow never stopped from November until April. He couldn't get off the island to get supplies and ran out of everything. That was one of those rare years that the ice bridge never solidified, so the price for everything went high as a kite. By the end of the winter, her friend ended up half-frozen, starved and broke and vowed he'd never do it again.

"The clerk said she'd listened and learned. She wasn't stupid and you wouldn't find her here when the flakes started flying because she was a sunbird herself. Give her warm days and cool nights and none of that bundling up like an Eskimo. She went home in the winter to where it was habitable and the cold wasn't a death sentence. I remember it so well because of the comical expressions on her face, the thing about the frozen toes and her being a sunbird. I liked the way that sounded.

"So, Yeah, Aunt Bess, I can't wait until December when icicles are hanging from my nose. That's going to be fun," Charlotte said sarcastically. "You know how I dislike the cold. My blood must be water."

"Not all years are that bad. Usually we have the ice bridge, snowfall is tolerable and you get used to the cold."

"I doubt it. I'll have to get a heavier coat. One of those parka things with the furry hood and some of those big fat mittens that make your hands look like the Pillsbury Dough Boy's."

"Funny."

Charlotte grinned, though she could tease about it now, it wouldn't be so funny when the ice age came. Maybe she would get used to it. She hoped so.

It was almost November and the tourist season was a week away from being over. Most of the *fudgies* would be gone and the Grand Hotel would lock its doors, signifying the end of the season. It wouldn't reopen until the following May. With its closing, most of the B&Bs, hotels and businesses would also board up for the winter, except for a few that stayed open for the locals.

The lights in the shops were winking out. There were only a few people milling around. The storefronts were going dark like the woods around them. It was shadowy beyond the streets. The wind rustled secrets among the surrounding trees and hushed as they moved past. A radiant half-moon glowed down and bathed them in soft light. In the distance, the seagulls and loons called to each other and settled down on the water until morning. They were sounds Charlotte found she'd missed. She took in a deep breath of chilly air as they walked along the abandoned sidewalks.

"You know it's so nice being here again," she confided. "Coming back to the island's like coming home."

Her aunt hugged her close as they walked. "It's your home, Charlotte, as long as you want it to be. You know, you can stay with me as long as you'd like. Forever, if you want. I wouldn't mind the company."

Charlotte heard the loneliness behind the words and the guilt returned. Bess had been like a second mother to her. Ever since Christopher, her younger brother, had died when she was six. Her mother had fallen into a grief she hadn't climbed out of for years afterwards. But Aunt Bess had been there for Charlotte and given her the attention she'd needed. Her parents had loved Christopher so much and Aunt Bess had loved Charlotte. She and her aunt were alike, both artistic dreamers and both loved the island.

Bess had taken care of her that first awful summer and after that, Charlotte had spent most summers with her aunt until she was twelve. Then her family had moved again and they'd lived too far away for Charlotte to visit easily.

As a teenager, not spending summers on Mackinac had been a disappointment. But she was there now and she needed her aunt and her aunt needed her. Charlotte didn't know what was wrong in Bess's life or why she was unhappy, but she knew she had to stay and find out. In time Bess would tell her everything because neither one could keep a secret from each other.

They passed Mission Point.

Complete darkness had laid its hand on the island and the air was filled with old memories. She imagined yesterday's tourists strolling the same path and felt as if she were on another world, one heavy with velvet mysteries and soft echoes of past times and people.

Her mind filled with ideas for her ghost book as she gazed into the night crowding in around them. There seemed to be things lurking in the gloom, murmuring and scurrying about out of eyesight beyond the trees. It was easy to conjure apparitions in a place so silent and deserted.

She'd forgotten how spooky the island could be at night. Yet Charlotte wasn't frightened. For her the island would always be safe.

****

Inside her aunt's kitchen they made cups of cocoa.

"Put that jacket of yours on again, Charlotte, and we'll sit on the porch and chat like we used to. I hear Mars is closer to earth than it has been in fifty thousand years. In an hour or two it'll be the brightest star in the heavens; amazing, you have to see it."

They lounged on the porch in their chairs, cradling cups of warm cocoa between cold hands. Charlotte could hear waves further out crashing against the rocks. The moon's glow lit up the scenery around them. Bess's face was faint but visible and the night shadows had washed away her cares.

"What do you plan to do now?" Aunt Bess shifted in her seat. Cold blooded, she wasn't wearing a jacket, only a bulky sweater.

"Go through some of the shops before they close next week. I have to buy some writing supplies, paper and extra printer cartridges. Long term? Take some time to regroup. Decide what I want to do with the rest of my life. Start preliminary research on that book I was telling you about. The one Mac gave me the idea for."

"That Mac, he's more than just an island cop, you know. He has hidden talents. A great guy. I bet you could get him to ask you out without trying hard at all."

"Not interested. It's too soon for me to think about dating anyone. Right now I just want to live my life and find out who I am. That's all. I have a lot of thinking to do."

Bess patted Charlotte's arm. "All right. No more about Mac or any other man. You're going to write about the island's ghosts. Wonderful topic. Intriguing. I say go for it."

"Do you believe in ghosts, Aunt Bess?"

Her aunt was quiet a moment, then replied in a guarded voice, "Funny you should ask that. Up until a couple years ago, I would have said no, I didn't believe. Now I'm not so sure."

"What do you mean?"

"It'll sound silly."

"I won't laugh." When her aunt hesitated further, Charlotte pressed, "Come on, please? I'll be collecting tales from people and I'm not going to have a book if everyone's like you and won't tell me their stories."

"Okay, I have seen something spooky. But if I tell, you have to promise not to laugh at me or think I'm bonkers."

"I won't laugh. Tell me." Charlotte experienced a twinge of excitement. It would be the first ghost story for her book. Second, if she wanted to include her weeping church lady.

"Some nights I go out there along the shore to walk." Bess pointed towards the water that shimmered under the moonlight. The waves were rippling beneath the murky sky and the stars were glittering tiny spiked lights. "And I see ships—far out on the water. Sometimes there are as many as five or six Yankee Clippers. I suspect they're smuggling vessels from another century, coming from the northern horizon. They're all masted ships with their rakish sails billowing. I can hear the muffled shouts of their sailors on the night air. They come closer to shore until I can almost see them, but they're misty—see through. Not real. When they get to shore where the water is too shallow to support their size, right before my eyes, they begin to dematerialize. I swear to God. Their sails first, then their rigging and finally the lower parts of the ships. Soon they're nothing but smoke hanging all around me.

"First time I saw them I thought I was hallucinating. I do have a drink now and then. But I've seen them a couple times now. Usually in the dead of winter before the straits freeze."

"Ghost ships. Wow. Aunt Bess, that's some story. Can I put it in the book?"

"I don't know. If the book gets published and you use my name my neighbors will think I've gone round the bend into crazy land for sure."

"I could say it's from someone who wants to remain anonymous."

"Then you can use it."

"Great. Can you remember anything else about the sightings?"

Bess recalled a few more details and Charlotte listened. She couldn't wait to go upstairs and key it into her laptop. The book had taken firm root in her consciousness and she'd decided she was absolutely going to write it.

When her aunt stopped talking about the ships, they talked about other things. The wind had picked up and the cold had begun to gnaw into Charlotte's skin. She couldn't believe it was only October.

After a while, she said, "I want to pay my way while staying here, so I've been thinking about getting a job, something fun that won't tax my brain. The book won't take all my time and I need to get out and mingle with people; get my mind off my old life. A job would do that for me."

She'd seen the sparse groceries in her aunt's cabinets and refrigerator. She'd seen how run down the house was and seen the stack of unpaid bills on the table right inside the door.

"You don't have to do that," her aunt objected. "I don't need any money from you. I've got a good job at the Grand and–"

"By what I can tell since I've arrived, it doesn't pay enough."

"No, it doesn't. Not anymore. It's an hourly wage and the hotel doesn't allow tipping. What with the rising costs of everything on the island there's never enough money these days. As hard as I work I can't make enough. I get so tired. I guess my age is catching up to me. I make do, child. Always have, always will."

"I'm going to help."

"But there's no graphic art jobs here like you're

used to, Charlotte. You'd have to go off the island to get an advertising job. Are you willing to go to the mainland every day?"

"No. For now, I don't want a graphic design job anyway. I'm not interested in making a lot of money. I can always return to the big city for that. I'm going to work on the island. If I'm going to get those ghost stories, I need to fit in and win the trust of the townies."

"What else can you do?"

"I can do anything I set my mind to. A cashier. Or I can be a waitress at one of the open-all-year restaurants. I want to contribute my share of the household expenses, that's all. Pay my way." Charlotte had already told her aunt that she had no savings left. She and Lucas had lived an expensive life style and the wedding that never happened had taken whatever she'd had left.

"You know," her aunt remarked thoughtfully, "I heard the other day that Letty, the owner of the Market Street Inn, is looking for someone for the front desk. The inn stays open year round. It's a mom and pop establishment, more of a bed and breakfast, with eight or so rooms.

"The hours are from eight in the morning to two in the afternoon every day but Tuesday and Wednesday. Letty's husband, Herbert, isn't in the best of health and she wants him to rest more. Most of the townies, after working all summer, don't want to work through the winter. There won't be a long line for that job. Tell Letty I sent you. You'll get it."

"That'll do. I'll go speak to her tomorrow."

Charlotte stopped rocking. A night bird was calling somewhere out over the water. "If the season ends in a week and the Grand closes does that mean you take off work for the winter?"

"I can't afford to. The last few years I've been working off-season as a bartender at the Mustang Lounge. It's night shift, though. I hope you don't mind. I'll be home most evenings until eight and we can have supper together before I go."

Charlotte was thinking ahead, she could work at the Inn during the day and, with the house all to herself nights, work on her book then.

A smile hovered around Bess's mouth. "Are you going to ask everyone who wants a room at the inn if they've seen a ghost?"

"Something like that. Maybe the inn is haunted. That would be great. I could ask Letty. Hmm."

"Just don't scare the fudgies away. We need their money."

They both smiled in the dark.

When they were getting ready to go in Charlotte finally asked, "Aunt Bess, do you want to talk about whatever's really bothering you? No, don't deny it. You're not your usual optimistic self. You don't seem happy." Charlotte could have mentioned the extra weight and sloppy clothes but she wouldn't hurt her aunt's feelings for anything. "What is it?"

"I don't want to lay my problems on you."

"Why not? I've dumped mine on you. Come on. I'm not leaving this porch until you tell me what's wrong and I'm freezing. I can't feel my nose. Have pity on me."

"It's a man."

"It isn't still Charlie after all these years?" Charlie had been her husband for a long time. When he'd passed away so young, of a heart attack, Bess had nearly grieved herself into the grave with him. They'd had a happy marriage, even without the children they'd wanted so badly. Charlie had lived for Bess and Bess had lived for Charlie. They'd had that rare kind of love that Charlotte had been trying to find her entire life and hadn't so far. She'd been young when her Uncle Charlie had died, but she remembered how much her aunt and uncle had cared for each other. She'd felt their love.

"No, it's not Charlie. Charlie's only a sweet memory now...a ghost." Charlotte could see her aunt looking towards the water, her eyes gleaming in the moonlight. "I'll always love him but he's no longer here. I needed a flesh and blood man." She paused.

"Remember I'm not leaving this chair until you tell me everything."

Her aunt's form was very still in her chair. She sighed. "All right, I need to talk to someone. I've kept it secret for so long. I'm tired of covering up and lying. Deception eats away at the soul."

"Go on."

"There's this man, Shawn Sheahan. I love him. He's worked with me at the Grand Hotel for the last twenty years. He's a carriage driver during the summer months. Irish with a brogue, he has wavy hair the color of night, and the most amazingly tender eyes that always seem to be laughing. I guess, in a swarthy way he's handsome. Tall. He's got a wicked sense of humor and a wicked smile.

But he's also caring and gentle. So much like Charlie used to be." She stopped speaking and gasped softly as if talking about Shawn hurt her in some way.

"And?"

"He doesn't belong to me, Charlotte. He's married and has a wife and three kids back in Ireland. John, who is seventeen, Amy who is fifteen and Teddy, who is about twelve now, I think. Shawn goes home to them every November first. So I only have him for the tourist season.

"Now I suppose you want to know if we've been lovers?"

"I wasn't going to ask."

"No, not in the physical sense anyway. I love him, have since the first time I met him; but he's taken and like me he's a good person, a Catholic. Adultery is a sin so our relationship has been purely platonic. We spend our free time together. He's my best friend."

"Oh." Suddenly everything about her Aunt Bess's solitary life made sense. There was a reason she'd never remarried, didn't date, and had never left the island. She'd stayed here, alone, in this house to be near the man she loved. A man who couldn't reciprocate her love the way she wanted. Charlotte was stunned. She'd never had a clue. No one had.

"Does he know how much you love him…and does he love you?"

"He does and he does," Bess answered without faltering.

"If he loves you why doesn't he get a divorce?"

The older woman tilted her head and rocked her chair. "Because, he's an honorable man. He loves his family, loves Katie, his wife, and refuses to run out on his responsibilities and commitments. I respect him for that. I'd never ask a man to leave a wife and family who need him as much as they do. It wouldn't be right. I'm no home wrecker."

Unlike Rachel.

"How did Shawn come to be working here if he's Irish?"

"He came to the island years ago when a friend told him that the Grand Hotel was hiring carriage drivers who knew how to train and take care of horses. His friend told him that the island was fantastic and so were the tips. Shawn came because there weren't any jobs as good where he lived and he needed a lot of money at the time. One of his children required special medical care, an operation or something. He loved the job and ended up returning every spring.

"I accepted from the beginning that he could never belong to me but I didn't care. I had him every summer. Does that make any sense and does it make you think less of me, Charlotte?"

"No." Though the confession surprised her. Her aunt had fallen in love with a married man she could never have. It was no wonder she was so sad. Poor Bess.

"I know what you're thinking.., a married man, how stupid of her. But I met him, became friends and we slowly fell in love. We couldn't help ourselves."

Charlotte reached over and laid her hands over

her aunt's. "So, it's been twenty years and you've loved a man who can't be with you the way you'd like him to be. You've handled it so far, so why are you unhappy now?"

"This time he may go home and not come back. His wife is ill and no matter what, he loves her. He married her when she was sixteen. They've been together thirty years."

Her aunt slid her hand out from under Charlotte's and rocked faster.

Charlotte could feel her aunt's anguish. In some ways a person had to go through their heartaches alone, she knew that all too well. No one could suffer for you. "What are you going to do?"

There was an intake of breath and the rocking slowed as Mars, a night diamond, flashed up above them. "Nothing. Let him go. I'll stay here where my home and life are. But it'll finally be over. This last week will be hard.

"When Shawn told me, I pushed him away. I won't let him come over. I see him at work every day. It hurts, but I can't back down. Something happened when he told me he was going to return to Ireland permanently. The intensity of my reaction shook me. I wept like I wept when Charlie died. It feels like the same kind of loss. Like a death."

Her aunt looked at her. "So I'm glad you're here. Help me be strong and stay away from him so I don't make a fool of myself. Help me from going crazy. You're saving my life, Charlotte."

"We'll call it even then. I don't know what I would have done if I couldn't have come back here to you and the island. I was a mess, too."

"You would have been okay, girl, either way. We both would. We're strong women. But it's nice to have someone to be with and talk to at times like these."

Charlotte gently changed the subject. "Well, if everything's going to close down in the next week, I had better go see the Grand Hotel real quick. It's been so long since I was there. I wonder if it will look different now that I'm grown up. Has it changed much?"

"No. They've remodeled it but it's still an elegant hotel. Wealth doesn't look cheap. Come up tomorrow with me when I go into work. I have to serve at the twelve to two o'clock tourist buffet and do the high tea at three-thirty. I'll sneak you in so you don't have to pay the ten dollar entry fee and thirty-five dollars for the lunch."

"It never used to cost to get in and, wow, thirty-five for lunch now? That's steep. But you can sneak me in?"

"Sure. One of the few perks of working there. I have friends in the kitchen. They're always sending me home with leftovers. Saves on the grocery bill."

Charlotte didn't argue. If her memory served her right the Grand buffet was a bountiful feast for the rich and famous and the tourists. Free was good. Free she could afford.

"Maybe if Letty doesn't give me a job I could get one at the hotel?" Charlotte queried.

"You wouldn't want to work there. The people who stay at the Grand are snooty rich and sometimes they look down their noses at the hired help. I wouldn't want them to treat you that way."

"They treat you that way."

"I'm used to it. It's all I've ever known. I don't have a college degree and talents like you do, Charlotte. You're meant for better things."

"So it's better that I work at the Market Street Inn checking people into rooms?"

"Yeah. The regular tourists treat the workers in the village better. I see it all the time. Most of them don't mix with the high and mighty up on the Grand Hotel's main porch. It's the difference between vacation money and real money; between normal working people and the very wealthy."

"So only the very rich sleep at the Grand Hotel?"

"At six hundred to seven hundred a night, wouldn't you think so? I don't know of any working Joe or anyone down here on the lower part of the island who could afford that rate. I couldn't."

Charlotte couldn't either, not even when she had her job, and for some reason the thought of that depressed her. She'd never wanted to be rich or famous but not having any money at all hadn't been her dream either.

The rich and poor of the island made her think. "Is there that much of a money inequality here? Are the islanders that poor?"

"Some of them, yes, the ones that work in the shops and service the tourists. On the island, the biggest discrepancy is land and home ownership. Since eighty percent of the island is a state park owned by Michigan and Michigan won't sell any of it—sometimes lease, but not sell—land is at a premium. In the last thirty years people have discovered Mackinac and it's become a huge tourist draw. Land has turned into gold.

"The thing is, years ago the wealthy from across the state bought or built those fancy cottages you see on the East and West Bluff Avenues, but they only use them five or six weeks a year for their summer homes. A lot of them won't sell. Some won't even rent them no matter how infrequently they visit. The cottages are usually handed down through the families. There isn't much new construction going on, no space, and most of the islanders' kids have to move off Mackinac if they want their own homes. Most people who want to live here can't afford it.

"So housing's become very cutthroat. Even my little shack here is probably worth a bundle. If I wanted to leave the island and sell out, that is. I have people all the time trying to get me to sell. I've been offered as high as three hundred thousand dollars."

"For this?" Charlotte let out a low whistle. The house was cozy, a great water view, but not worth that much. "That's a basket load of money. It would take care of you for life. You'd never have to work again if you invested it."

"I don't want to leave. This is my home and most everyone else who lives here and loves the island feels the same way. Mac, your new friend, could make more money being a cop somewhere else, but he loves the island, too. So he stays. So we all stay."

Mac. Charlotte studied the moonlit darkness as if just thinking of him would make him appear on his red Schwinn. Her eyes searched the yard but no Mac. It would be nice if he did show up. Bess could offer him some cocoa. Charlotte could ask him if he'd heard any more ghost stories since she'd last seen him.

"It's getting late, honey." Her aunt yawned. "I have a long day at the hotel tomorrow so I'm turning in."

Charlotte was still cold but Bess had given her some gloves and a wool cap and suddenly she didn't want to go inside. She wanted a few minutes to herself. "Go ahead. I'm staying out here for a little while to admire the night. I won't stay out long."

"Suit yourself. Lock the door before you go up to bed." Bess rose and gave her niece a hug.

"I will. And Aunt Bess? Everything's going to be fine, you'll see. You're not alone any more. I'm here and we're going to have a good time. Who needs men anyway?"

"Huh, we don't. We can do fine without them. See you in the morning, Charlotte. If you want to go with me to the Grand, I leave at eleven to help set up the buffet."

"It's a date. That'll give me time to go into town and get those writing supplies and see about that job at the inn before we go."

Her aunt went inside, her footsteps slow and heavy, trudging towards her downstairs bedroom as if she were carrying troubles on her back. Charlotte hoped her being there would bring a little happiness into her aunt's life because the woman needed it. She seemed lost.

****

Charlotte remained outside for another quarter hour, listening to the night noises and reminiscing about when she'd been a girl riding across the island in the dark. She could never get enough. If she hadn't been so tired she'd have gotten on her bike for a ride. Tomorrow.

A lightless house sat on her right. Charlotte hadn't asked her aunt about Hannah McCain yet. She wondered if the old woman still lived there. Hannah had seemed old when Charlotte had been a girl but Bess hadn't said anything about Hannah being dead so she must be alive.

Hannah had never married. The island, her home, friends and garden had been enough for her. Her house, a rambling yellow frame with a long porch along the front, was like something in a fancy house magazine. Hannah's place was larger and in better condition than Bess's. She'd kept it up. It was beautiful.

Charlotte would have to go over and reintroduce herself. She and Hannah had been good friends when Charlotte had spent the summers with Bess. The old lady, a sweet but colorfully unconventional woman, used to give her books on art to read. They'd talked for hours about this and that, town gossip mainly, and had baked cookies together. Hannah had a real sweet tooth. Everyone on the island knew and loved Hannah McCain.

Charlotte couldn't wait to see her again.

She wandered down through the yard towards the shore. The moonlight guided her steps. She knew the way by heart and had no difficulty getting to the water.

Standing at the lake's edge, she looked for the ghost ships her aunt had spoken of. She never saw a one, just the empty water and the sounds it made rubbing against the rocks and shore. Perhaps if she came out there every night and kept vigil she'd see them. Wouldn't that be something?

Charlotte returned to the house and went up to bed. She fell asleep quickly and again didn't dream about Lucas, Rachel or her ill-fated wedding. Instead she dreamt about the island and Lt. Mac Berman.

He was in uniform and riding his bike through the woods up past the fort's cemeteries. There was a whole flock of Civil War phantoms following him. He wasn't scared. He smiled at her and waved, and all the ghosts waved, too. The whole bunch of them disappeared into the Grand Hotel.

She remembered thinking: *Boy, those rich hoity-toity people aren't going to like that. All those dirty ragtag ghosts traipsing through their fancy rooms making a mess and a ruckus. Tsk, tsk. Too bad, huh?*

Then she woke up and it was morning. Outside the seagulls were spreading their wings against a vivid blue sky. She could see the water lapping at the shore from her window. From downstairs came the smell of something good, maybe pancakes, and she got up smiling, threw on a robe and went downstairs.

She couldn't wait to begin the day. Get out on the island. It'd been so long and she wanted to see all of it. She wanted to see the Grand Hotel from grownup eyes to see if it looked any different.

Chapter 2

"So is Hannah still alive and kicking next door?" Charlotte was eating pancakes but her eyes were on the window that framed Hannah's house. It was early but Charlotte hadn't minded getting out of bed. She and her aunt would have time to visit.

"Oh, she's alive and as eccentric as ever. In her seventies but doesn't look or act it. She gets around pretty well. We've become real close the last few years. She calls me her adopted daughter because she doesn't have any family left." Bess slid more blueberry pancakes onto Charlotte's plate.

"In the summer she spends her days in that garden of hers. She grows tomatoes, green beans and cucumbers. The last of the tomatoes are up there in the basket on the windowsill. She keeps me in homegrown vegetables all summer and saves me a fortune. They're the best tomatoes on the island, too."

"So you haven't been alone. I'll have to go over and visit her sometime today."

"She'll be tickled to see you. She knows you're coming and has been bugging me for days about when you'd arrive."

"She remembers me?"

"Of course, she does. Fondly."

Charlotte was stuffing her mouth, enjoying the

pancakes, and thinking that she'd have to start sharing the cooking and household duties once she was settled in. It was only fair.

She hurried herself, anxious to get into town, buy what she needed, look around in the daylight, see Letty about that job and return. She didn't want to make her aunt late for work.

The women finished breakfast. Charlotte helped her aunt clean up.

Afterwards she went upstairs and put on jeans, shirt and a heavy sweatshirt. She'd tied her hair back and was going out the door when her aunt commented, "Looks like you're going to get to visit with Hannah sooner than you thought. She's in her front yard weeding. You don't dare go past her without saying hello. Bet she knows you're here and she's lying in wait for you."

Slinging her purse over her shoulder, Charlotte laughed. "Then I'll stop and chat a little with her. But I'll be back before eleven so you can sneak me into the Grand."

She stepped outside into the sunshine. It was a perfect autumn day. A crisp breeze teased at loose wisps of hair about her face and the sweet scent of dying flowers and dried leaves stirred around her.

She pushed her bike down the sidewalk, with her purse stuffed in its basket. She was in the best mood she'd been in for a long time. Being on the island and being with her aunt had freed her from the depression she'd been in for weeks. Even before the wedding had been canceled she'd been feeling uneasy and tired and not knowing why. Today for the first time in years, she had so much energy and felt as if anything were possible. A smile slipped out.

Hannah was clearing out the dead plants in her front yard when Charlotte strode up to her and put down the bike's kickstand. "Hello," she called out, loud enough to get Hannah's attention.

The old woman turned to her. "Why, hello there stranger. Long time no see."

"It's been a while." Charlotte moved closer. Her aunt was right; Hannah had barely aged at all. She appeared the same, a little smaller, with her eyes the color of faded leaves not quite as bright as when Charlotte had been a kid. Her hair, peeking out from under a wide-brimmed straw hat on her small head, was white now instead of gray-streaked. Her face reminded Charlotte of a wrinkled ferret's. She'd never worn any makeup, preferring to be as natural as God had made her. She had pruning shears in her right hand, and Charlotte noticed there was a little blood on her fingers.

Hannah's smile was instant and welcoming. Before Charlotte knew it a frail doll in her arms who smelled of dusting powder was hugging her.

"It's sure good to see you, Charlotte. Your Aunt Elizabeth needs family and friends these days with the way things are going in her life." The old woman groaned and stepped back to look at her. "She's in love with a man already taken and it's made her melancholy. I guess you know about Shawn, huh?"

"Now I do. She told me about him last night. What a mess."

Hannah cocked her head, a sad expression on

her face. "I've been there myself once or twice. Loving someone inappropriate. Shame is that Shawn's a truly nice guy. Too nice. I keep telling her to let him go and find someone else but she loves him. Says he's her true love and if she can't have him, she'll have no one. Your aunt's a stubborn lady."

Hannah wore a stylish sweater that hung on her thin frame over a long apricot flowered dress. Except for her hands, she was spotlessly clean though she'd been digging in the dirt. No matter how old the woman got she still dressed like a movie star. It was her way. She was a real classy lady.

"Glad I don't have to worry about those kind of quandaries anymore." Hannah huffed. "I'm happy with my home, my friends and my garden. Sunflowers prick your skin and roses have thorns but they give you unconditional beauty and a lovely scent. Men, they're only good for causing chaos with your heart—and leaving dirty foot tracks all over your clean floors."

Charlotte giggled. Hannah hadn't changed. She was as feisty as ever. She said she'd cared for a few men over the years but had never found anyone she loved enough to tie the knot with. So she'd had no husband, but according to Bess, she'd had a couple of sisters who'd passed away. The rest of the elderly woman's life was a mystery. Hannah was just Hannah.

"Heard about your problems, too, girl." She shook the shears at her visitor. "Good riddance to that fiancé of yours is what I say. You don't want to be with a man who doesn't love you enough to stay true. He did you a favor leaving you for that other woman. Someday, maybe not now, you'll see that right enough. So now you can move on, girl, find one who'll treat you better. There are lots of shells on the beach."

Aunt Bess must have blabbed to Hannah about the called off wedding and the rest of it. She would have if the two women were as friendly as Bess said they were. Charlotte didn't mind. Hannah never judged and, like Bess, believed there was a good reason for everything that happened in a person's life. Nothing was a coincidence.

"Come on." Hannah grabbed Charlotte's hand and led her across the yard towards her house. "I have something to show you."

Since Charlotte had been there last, Hannah had added a sun porch on to the back. Its glass windows opened out on her now dying garden. They ended up discussing how the island had changed since Charlotte used to come and spend summers there. Hannah laughed and smiled the whole time.

The old woman seemed her same old carefree self. The years had been kind to her.

Charlotte listed what she was going into town for and why. When she mentioned she was compiling ghost stories from people on the island, Hannah stated flatly, "I have a ghost story or two to tell you myself. I've been seeing spooks all my life. This island is haunted for sure, you know. In more ways than you can imagine."

"Great, then I'll be back to get those stories from you."

"Anytime. Come by for tea today at about four and I'll give you an earful."

"Sorry, Hannah, I can't make it. I'm going to have lunch at the Grand Hotel this afternoon with Aunt Bess. She's going to get me into the buffet for free and I can't pass that up."

"No, you can't." Hannah's face became dreamy and her smile was indulgent. "It's been years since I went for lunch or tea there. I love that place. Sometimes you forget how wonderful that hotel is and how scrumptious the food." Her thin shoulders rose and fell. "But the cost is too high for me. What is it nowadays?"

Charlotte told her.

"That's pure robbery!" Hannah made a face. "I wouldn't pay that much even if I had it. Years ago, as I recall, you could have that buffet for five bucks and you never had to pay to get into the hotel at all. That's terrible."

Yeah, and that was probably fifty years ago.

"That's the way it is now, Hannah. It's expensive like everything else is. You think it's costly here you should try living in a big city." Charlotte shook her head. "Now that's expensive."

"Ah, too bad about that, huh? But I wouldn't live in a dirty, noisy city. I wouldn't call that living," she groused. "Why can't things stay the same?"

"That's not life. Things change."

The old lady's eyes lit up. "Talking about writing books...did I ever tell you that one of my old boyfriends was a writer? He wrote novels. You know him, everyone does. Samuel Clements?"

Charlotte stared at her. "You mean Mark Twain?" Didn't he die around 1910? Which either made Hannah a lot older than she looked or she'd invented the relationship.

"Yes, that was him. He was a pleasant elderly gentleman. Of course he was quite old and I was quite young. It wasn't a real love affair, merely a mutual affection. We never—you know. His daughter, Ann, a friend of mine, had a summer cottage on the island. He used to spend his summers with her when he wasn't traveling all over the world. Samuel and I became friendly, though. Ah, now that's a memory.

"He was a sweet man. Someday I'll show you his books, signed by him of course, that he gave me. I still have some of his love letters, too. I've hidden them somewhere." Hannah's face screwed up as if she were trying to recall more, but couldn't. "I'll have to look for them. So many years, so many hidden treasures. These days I seem to forget where I have things, or where I put things all the time."

Oh, Hannah. She actually believed she'd known Twain. *Wait until I tell my aunt that Hannah claims to have love letters from Mark Twain. She'll get a kick out of that but she probably already knows about it.* Charlotte hid a smile behind her hand.

Hannah peered at her, looking confused. "It's hard getting old, I'll tell you that. Take advantage of your youth while you have it, Charlotte. Live. Experience things. Love. Do it now while you can." She was bobbing her head. "I'm thankful I have the memories that I have. It gives me something to reminisce on now that I'm old."

"Thanks, I'll take that advice but for now I have to be on my way."

The women moved slowly to where Charlotte's bike stood. "About having tea and the ghost stories? We have to do that real soon."

"How about tomorrow? You come for tea and I'll tell you some tales that'll curl your hair."

"You got a deal. Tomorrow at four it is. Bye for now, Hannah." She pushed up the kickstand on her bike.

"Goodbye, Charlotte, sweetheart."

The older woman continued her pruning as Charlotte rode towards town. The wind in her face and the sun on her back made her feel like a girl again. She hadn't ridden a bike in years. Now she couldn't understand why she hadn't. It gave her such a sense of freedom.

It didn't take long to buy what she needed. She stuffed the supplies into her basket and spent an hour riding around soaking in the sights like any tourist.

She passed the Butterfly House, the Carriage Stables, Fort Mackinac and the Michigan Governor's summer mansion. She rode by the shops that lined Market Street, the side avenues that spread off from it and down Lake Shore Drive. She didn't have time that morning to take the full eight-mile trip around Lake Shore Road and thought she'd do that at the end of the day. The island was at its prettiest when the sun was going down.

She went into the Market Street Inn and asked Letty, a chubby middle-aged woman with blond hair and a cherry red blouse, for a job application.

The inn, a sprawling blue-shuttered house that had been renovated into a quaint bed and breakfast, was busy. The first ferryboats from the mainland had arrived, crowded with homeless tourists looking for their rooms. As soon as Charlotte introduced herself as Bess's niece and said that Bess had sent her, Letty, all smiles, hired her on the spot. They shook hands over it.

"Just bring in that completed form tomorrow morning when you report for work at eight."

Before Charlotte left, Letty did find time to pry. "I thought you worked in advertising and had a fancy job in the big city. That's what Bess told me. Why do you want to work here? The pays not that good and it gets lonely on the island during the winter. The weather sucks, too."

Charlotte gave her an abbreviated version of her reasons and Letty accepted them. "Mackinac is a good place to heal a broken heart, sweetie. You're going to love it here. See you tomorrow."

"How should I dress?"

"Dressy casual. Nice blouse and slacks, that's all. No jeans."

They stood and chatted for a minute or two in between customers. Charlotte liked Letty from the get-go and Letty liked her. Charlotte asked questions and got the basics of the job, then left. It was ten-thirty.

She was happy as she exited the bustling establishment. She'd liked the inn immediately. It was clean and pretty, everyone seemed friendly; and she could see herself behind that desk smiling at the *fudgies*. It would be a good way to get to know the townies and gather the stories she'd need. Six hours a day would give her lots of daylight and free time to enjoy the island and work on her book. She'd start tomorrow—which left her today to have fun and see the sights again. Getting off at two also left her free to have tea with Hannah at four the next day.

She was getting on her bicycle when a husky voice behind her said, "Charlotte, my, my, we always seem to be running into each other."

She sent a quick look over her shoulder, shading her eyes from the sun, and saw the cop she couldn't seem to get rid of. Today he was dressed in blue jeans, T-shirt and a jacket.

Couldn't she go anywhere without bumping into him and shouldn't he be sleeping or something after working all night?

"Lieutenant Berman, are you following me?" she snapped, sitting on her bike, poised for flight.

"Call me Mac, remember? No, I'm not following you. I was coming down the street after picking up my mail at the post office and here you are. Just the person I wanted to see. I need to talk to you."

It was a plausible excuse. There was no door-to-door mail delivery on the island. Mail came across on the ferries or by airplane and everyone had to get it themselves from the island post office. There was a thick bundle of letters and envelopes in his hands.

Inwardly she moaned. "Hi Mac. What can I do for you?"

"It's more like what I can do for you," he offered, his eyes squinting in the sunlight. His smile, when it came, was so natural, and the way the breeze ruffled his curly hair made him look like some long ago English poet. Most police departments wouldn't normally let him wear his hair so long but on the island everything was more laid-back than a larger city. Yep, he sure was tall. She looked up.

"Do for me?"

"Last night after our conversation about you wanting to chronicle some of the island's ghostly happenings, I got to thinking."

"Yeah?" She put the kickstand down and leaned on her bike, waiting. The sun was warm on her head and shoulders. Though the air was chilly, her face was flushed. She had the random thought that she wished she would have known she'd run into Mac again so she could have at least combed her hair. It'd escaped its hair tie and half of it was hanging around her face. She tried to tuck it back into place.

"It was slow last night, usually is at the tail end of the season, so I spoke to a few of the regulars at the Mustang during my shift and collected some yarns for you. I have names and telephone numbers of the people who gave them to me if you need more details. Do you want to hear an encapsulated account of some of them? I wrote them down. Well, most of them. People sure do talk fast sometimes."

She was watching him. How sweet of him to do that for her. "Any other time, I'd say yes. Give them to me and thank you. But I'm on my way to meet Aunt Bess. We're going to the Grand Hotel. She's working today and getting me in to the buffet. I'm running late. I can't turn down free food or visiting the Grand. I haven't been there since I was a child."

"Hey, I'll join you if you'll let me. Being a police officer, I get gratis meals, too. I was going to get free food somewhere anyway. I haven't had breakfast yet. Night shift messes up my schedule. Over the meal I can give you the ghost tales I heard last night."

Her first reaction was, no, she didn't want to go to lunch with him. She wanted to be alone. Why wasn't that working for her? Her plan had been to have lunch, people watch, and explore the Grand Hotel and grounds afterwards by herself. She'd been looking forward to it.

"If I don't tell you the stories right away, I might forget some of the particulars I neglected to get down on paper. Wouldn't want that to happen now, would we?" It was a likely excuse, but it worked. He put his hands on her handlebars and smiled into her eyes. She had a hard time looking away.

The man was determined to have lunch with her.

Ah, what the heck. Lunch with Mac and three hundred people shouldn't be hard to swallow. She did want his help and she did want the stories. Her curiosity was whetted. She'd even stuffed a small notebook and a pencil in her purse so she'd be ready if she met someone with a story to tell.

"Okay. We'll have lunch together...for the book. You can give me the stories you have over the meal." She flashed him a begrudging smile. It wasn't his fault she was mad at men. Mac had been nothing but kind to her. She stole a glimpse at her wristwatch. "First I have to stop by my aunt's house and change clothes. She's waiting for me now so I need to hurry."

"Ride on then. I'll grab my metal steed, and be right behind you." He reached for his Schwinn, which was propped in front of Mighty Mac Hamburgers.

"All righty. I'll see you at Bess's." She rode away in a rush to get home and clean up. It wasn't for Mac's benefit. Oh, no. Or so she told herself. As a child, the Grand Hotel had always been a fairy tale enchanted castle to her. She was excited about seeing it again and couldn't wait. But she couldn't go into the Grand Hotel in jeans with hair uncombed. The Grand, from a bygone era of old-world hospitality and charm, where the women had worn gowns and glittering jewels and promenaded the porch with parasols while the men had worn suit coats and ties, deserved better than that. The least she could do was put on some nice slacks and a frilly top. She'd leave her white kid gloves and parasol at home.

Bess was waiting for her on the porch. "I'm supposed to be at work in twenty minutes." Beneath a heavy sweater, her aunt was dressed in her server's outfit, a navy skirt, crisp white blouse and low heels. Her hair and make-up were understated. She looked like a different woman than the one yesterday. She'll be seeing Shawn, Charlotte thought, and that's why she's fixed herself up.

"I know. I have to change real quick. I'll only be five minutes. Promise." Charlotte didn't mention the hair fixing and the make-up she intended to squeeze in as well. She'd have to hurry.

"By the way," Charlotte said as she passed her aunt, "I bumped into Mac Berman in town again and he's coming with us. He's going to lunch with me and he'll be here any second. Claims he's got some ghost stories and wouldn't take no for an answer." Charlotte dashed upstairs before Bess could say a word. Her aunt's mouth gaped open, though.

In more than five but less than ten minutes, Charlotte was on the porch, ready to go.

Mac was lounging in a porch chair discussing something with her aunt but they both got up as soon as Charlotte came out. The three got on their bikes and took the short ride to the hotel.

As she watched the crowds, the horses pulling carriages, the amiable people who sometimes waved at them as they rode by, hearing laughter, and feeling the sunlight on her face, Charlotte was struck by the change in her life in just a day.

If only her friends in Chicago could see her now. If *Lucas could see her now. Look at me. I'm on an idyllic island going to a fancy lunch at one of the most posh hotels in the world.* A handsome man was escorting her as well.

Charlotte glanced behind her and caught Mac smiling. He winked and she twisted back around to see where her tires were going. There were kids everywhere on bicycles who didn't care where they were riding. It was like bike bumper cars so the adults had to be the careful ones.

"Watch out for that horse poop, Charlotte," Mac shouted at her and though she swerved the wheel as soon as he yelled, her tires went through the pile anyway. She laughed and behind her Mac laughed, too. It was good to know the man had a sense of humor. Lucas wouldn't have laughed.

The Grand Hotel was everything Charlotte remembered it being and more. She and Mac sat at a table overlooking the Straits of Mackinac in front of a wall of windows as the clouds and the boats glided by. She felt privileged and fortunate and for the first time in a long time almost happy.

The food was plentifully exquisite; more than she'd seen in one place in her whole life and a flood of people were shoveling it on their plates. And to think some people in the world had no food to eat at all. It gave her a twinge of guilt, but it didn't last long.

"Now I know why people adore this hotel," Charlotte murmured across the table to Mac over dessert. Tiny éclairs and miniature iced cakes. As a chocoholic the desserts had pleased her immensely. Mac had a piece of lemon meringue pie.

"The waiters in Chicago never treat you this well. The food isn't this good and the view…."

"Is mesmerizing, I know." Mac was surveying the choppy waters. "I've lived here my whole life but I never get tired of the island's beauty. The life we have here is special. It's slower and simpler than most places and I like it that way. I wouldn't change a thing. I wouldn't even bring cars back on the island if I could. Even though horses scare me more than ghosts."

"I love horses," Charlotte mused as the cries of the boat horns boomed through the air outside the window.

"You ride?"

"I used to when I was a kid, but I haven't in a long time,"

Mac's eyes took in the room. "You know, this place is lovely and I don't visit it enough. I've only been up here a handful of times. I forget sometimes how lush it is with its Victorian architecture and its gardens. To be here with a pretty woman makes it even more special."

His eyes returned to her face. Through lunch, he'd disclosed tidbits about his life in between small talk and specter reports but she hadn't said much about hers. He would lean in close and their hands would touch, or his leg beneath the table would brush against hers. She knew he was aware of it but neither said a word. She listened to his stories, taking notes as she ate, but ignoring his attentions hadn't been easy. She was absolutely not going to start falling for a man she'd just met after having been jilted by another one. That would be way too needy; it would have to be a rebound.

"Our Chief," Mac was saying, "told me how he saw a carriage years ago when he was a young officer on night patrol. Not far from here, on West Bluff Road, where the ritzy summer cottages were, he saw a dark carriage pulled by four pale Percherons coming at him lickety-split through the driving rain. The rain made it hard to see except the carriage was glowing with an eerie ivory light. He thought there was a driver but he wasn't sure because he was busy scrambling to get out of the way.

"He claims the carriage rattled by him at a crazy speed...without a sound...not even the horses. There wasn't a whinny or a hoof beat. Not a hint of wheels clattering on the road. When he got up off the street where he'd fallen off his bicycle trying to get out of the carriage's way, he turned to look at it and it was gone. It had disappeared." He snapped his fingers for emphasis. "That quick."

"Ooh, a spectral carriage and horses. Frightening story. Thanks." She was scribbling as fast as she could. "I'll need to talk about it more with the Chief. Get some quotes. Make it sound more authentic."

"If he'll talk to you about it." Mac set his fork down and leaned against the back of his chair. "Sorry, but truth is, he doesn't want people thinking he sees apparitions. It would be bad for his reputation."

"Even if he does?"

"Did. Once. Many years ago. He'll probably own up to the story but he'll ask you to keep his name out of it. People here on the island are superstitious. Most of them believe if you speak about ghosts that's like you're calling them. They might show up. Then again, some people rank seeing ghosts on the same level as seeing aliens."

"It's not the same at all," Charlotte objected. "I used to think ghosts were sort of like dead memories that lived on in a place or even a person's mind, like an imprint on film, though now I'm not so sure. And aliens don't exist at all. Or anyway, I hope they don't. As far as I'm concerned if some alien spaceship landed on our planet and they'd come all that way from their home world, well, I can't see anything good coming of it. They'd want something."

"To be friends?"

"Fat chance."

"Anyway, to some people, spirits and aliens are the same. Neither one exist," Mac said. "I've known some who've seen supernatural phenomena who emphatically deny they've seen them. They don't want people to label them as crazy."

Charlotte could sympathize. Already she had three stories for her book from people who wanted to remain anonymous. Aunt Bess being one of them. She was beginning to wonder if her whole book would have to be anonymous. Maybe she should call it fiction and make up names.

Mac gave her other stories. One from a crusty codger called Buddy—no last name, just Buddy—who frequented the Mustang Lounge. Island born, he was half-Indian and peculiar. He collected knives and guns and hid them out in the woods so no one would steal them. Buddy knew everything and everyone on Mackinac and claimed he'd seen many ghosts in his life. But he believed they didn't want him to talk about them, something about they'd be angry and plague him if he did.

"Sounds to me," Charlotte commented, "like Buddy's a sandwich shy of a picnic."

"No, only a little strange. He's sensitive to his environment. He says he's a touch psychic."

"What did he see?"

"A soldier, circa early nineteenth century, in one of the rooms up at the old fort. He's seen the same spirit a couple of times. Once it was sitting in a corner in broad daylight, cleaning a gun and seemingly oblivious to him. Buddy rubbed his eyes, blinked and the ghost was gone.

"Later he saw him outside the fort on the parade grounds floating by and seemingly unaware of the humans around him. That time Buddy experienced feelings of pure terror and it scared him. Over a year later, he saw the same soldier in the dusk walking the walls with his rifle and it faded into the mist. Buddy won't go near the fort anymore."

"He was positive it was a ghost and not a trick of his eyes?"

"I suppose being able to see through it and it vanishing in front of him was a tip off."

"Suppose so."

Bess swung by their table twice, a tray of coffee and tea in her hands, but she was busy and didn't hang around long. Charlotte felt her eyes on them at different times through lunch. Nosy woman.

As the dining room emptied out they rose to their feet and groaned at all they'd eaten. "Bess is right," Charlotte announced. "I'm not going to be the least bit hungry tonight. I never should have had that last dessert."

"It wasn't only the desserts." Mac grinned. "You had extra helpings of turkey and enough bread to start a bakery. I don't know how you ate that huge salad. What are you, a rabbit?"

"Well, I don't eat in a place like this every day. It's okay to overindulge once in a while."

Mac shook his head at her. He was standing so near it gave her goose bumps. "As skinny as you are

I don't know where you put all that food."

"It went right to my legs and filled them up." She couldn't help but smile when he looked down at her legs. "You're so gullible," she told him.

She didn't know how it happened but Mac ended up tagging along with her on her rediscovery of the hotel. He wouldn't go away. Yet it was convenient having a cop everyone seemed to know accompanying her. They were allowed into places a normal tourist wouldn't have been. She got to peek into one of the best rooms. She marveled at how magnificently decorated and luxurious it was.

I'd love to spend a weekend here...if only I were filthy rich.

They wandered through the halls and rooms with Mac leading. They strolled through the lobby and its exclusive shops and up to the sixth floor. In the Cupola Bar they enjoyed a panoramic view of the island and the encircling waters, the lighthouses and Bois Blanc Island in the distance. They paused to read yellowed newspaper articles framed on the walls of menus and room prices going back to the early nineteen hundreds.

"Look at this." Mac was studying an old menu in a stairwell. "Once a breakfast at the Grand cost seventy-five cents and a deluxe room like the one you saw, with an indoor bathroom, twelve dollars a night."

"What a difference a couple of years make," she remarked sarcastically to Mac. "It's nice to know this hotel wasn't always so costly."

"Twelve dollars a night was downright extravagant in 1904." Mac had been reading over her shoulder. So close it made her nervous. She moved away as she started down the staircase. He took her hand to help her down and she let him. They came out on the second floor lobby that led to the rambling porch where the hotel's guests mingled each evening.

They'd spent so much time exploring the building that it was five o'clock—the time the hotel cleared out its tourists and welcomed the paying guests. It had a strict dress code of formal wear only for the evenings and the guests began to parade by them in flowing gowns, black jackets and ties.

"Let's go out on the porch and make believe we're two of the rich and famous," Mac joked and swept her away towards the growing crowd. Trying to keep from giggling, they made their way past the people finishing up high tea, with the tiers of fancy little sandwiches, scones, tarts and jam spreads, and promenaded out onto the open balcony.

For a few moments Charlotte actually felt like one of the very rich.

The 660-foot long porch, complete with white wicker padded chairs and tables, was out of a movie set. Waiters were stationed around handing out champagne and sherry in fluted crystal glasses. People chatted on cell phones or gazed at the grounds with the glistening lake below them.

Charlotte and Mac sauntered the length of the porch and found two chairs to sit in. Roving over the hotel, after their big meal, had worn them out. They lingered, leisurely observing the hotel's patrons.

What are they doing here? She speculated of the

people around them. Vacationing, business or pleasure? She reclined in her chair and relished the experience, part of the time studying the shifting crowd and part of the time appreciating the gorgeous vista from the porch. She and Mac laughed softly, conversed in hushed tones. They were becoming friends. She was impressed at how smart and funny he was. He knew every tiny minutia about the island, its history, and had amusing anecdotes about some of the island's inhabitants.

They remained until the shadows of the evening slipped across the veranda. The hotel's staff had set up a table of ornate china and a feast of finger foods. Soon the well-dressed guests on the porch were ambling by them, sipping aged port and nibbling on appetizers, and the two of them stuck out, rocks among the diamonds, in their informal clothes.

"It looks like they're having some kind of party," she said aside to Mac.

"No, just welcoming festivities for new guests," he whispered back. "The hotel puts on the feedbag big time every evening." He stood up and offered his hand, pulling her up. "It's our cue that it's time to leave the porch packed with the upper class, feasting, drinking and comparing financial portfolios."

"Ooh, and we're merely common folk out slumming. We should mosey on, right?"

"Right."

They walked sedately past the dressy people mingling at the food tables and took the outside entrance down the red velvet stairs and onto the spacious lawn. Charlotte glanced up at the stately white columns, the high gleaming windows, lemon yellow awnings and the endless span of the hotel with its portico of bejeweled guests chattering and laughing. There weren't many flowers left along the base of the building but the American flags snapped in the breeze along the porch's length.

"The hotel's splendid even this late in the year." Mac was also admiring the landscaping.

"It is. I imagine it's more so in the spring when the flowers begin blooming again. I'm going to have to return in April and have high tea in the parlor. That looked like fun." Her eyes drank in the scene and her heart softened further. The island was working its magic on her.

"Did you know two railroad companies built this hotel in 1887? The basic structure is built of white pine. They called it the showplace of the Great Lakes. In the beginning it was an annual summer-long escape for the wealthy from the heat and hay fever of the crowded Michigan cities."

"No, I didn't, but I know it now." A smile came out. She was having a good time with Mac and didn't want to leave. "I'd like to speak to some people who've worked here a long time and find out if any of them have seen anything strange. The tales this building could tell us if it could talk."

"Funny you should mention that. There are many eerie rumors about the Grand. I bet if you spoke to the hotel's manager you could get the gossip about the hotel and its history without any trouble. I'll give you his name and telephone number. You can call him."

"Thanks, Mac."

"Let's tour the gardens before we go. They have the neatest maze and topiaries."

It was getting late but Charlotte had no other place to be. "Lead on and I'll follow."

A horse and plum-hued carriage carrying visitors clomped by them in front of the hotel. The animal lifted its hooves smartly; the driver saluted them and the people inside waved hellos. They waved back. Perhaps the driver was Bess's Shawn. He could have been, he had dark wavy hair, but she wasn't sure.

Taking her hand again, Mac led her down steep stone stairs edged in shrubs and shade trees and out onto the well-kept lawns. They roamed around the fountains, flowerbeds and rock gardens. They peered at sheared shrubs in the shapes of horses and carriages and circled the dirt labyrinth. Charlotte didn't care much for the maze, but thought the gardens were lovely.

"You should see this place in the winter, Charlotte." Mac's eyes were taking in the dying flowers and clear blue sky. "It's so beautiful when the snow's covering everything. The hotel is closed and there's no one around. I come out on my snowmobile and ride up and down the hill behind us and down here. It's great. You'll have to come with me one day."

"All you have to do is ask me."

He looked at her. "I will. I'll even take you across the ice bridge the first time. You said you've never been across it and it can be intimidating."

"You've got a deal. I've never been on the island in the winter, never seen the ice bridge." She did a mock shiver. "It's scary, or to me it is anyway, miles of frozen water, two hundred feet deep in some spots, and the ice thick over it. It seems weird to think about traveling across it. Dangerous."

"It's not. If the weather conditions are right and the ice has been checked, it's perfectly safe."

She didn't say anything else, but she was terrified of the ice bridge. She wouldn't go ice-skating because she was scared of falling through the ice and into the water. She feared drowning; she'd had nightmares about it. No, she didn't want to ever go across the ice bridge but she wasn't about to admit that to the man walking beside her. It would make her sound like a neurotic child.

They were leaving the gardens, and the sun was lowering into the horizon when Mac caught her hand, pulled her to him and kissed her.

Catching her breath, she glared up at him. "You shouldn't have done that."

She saw the disappointment in his eyes and a tired sadness washed over her. For a heartbeat, it'd been Lucas in front of her, Lucas holding her and Lucas kissing her. The pain, forgotten for an afternoon, had returned. It wasn't as strong as it had been in the city but it was there. *It's too soon. I don't want anyone to love me right now. I have nothing to give back yet.*

Why had he kissed her? Before that everything had been fine. They'd had a fragile but growing friendship.

She could have handled that.

Mac moved away. "I'm sorry, Charlotte. I didn't mean to do that. It just happened. I couldn't help myself." He offered her an apologetic smile, reached out to touch her hair and she instinctively cringed. Her face must have shown her distress and disapproval. It was as if she'd slapped him.

No. Don't let his sad puppy-dog eyes sway you. If you let yourself care about him he could hurt you as Lucas hurt you. Stop this. Get rid of him now.

Flustered, she said the first thing that came into her mind. "Don't be sorry, Mac. It isn't you. You're a great guy. Any other time that kiss would have been the beginning of something, but I don't want you or anyone to love me right now. I don't know if I ever will. Sorry."

Here, what she did and said mattered. She had the power this time. Even though she wouldn't admit it, the shame of being dumped had left behind so much anger that it made her speak harsher than she normally would have. "Perhaps we shouldn't see each other anymore."

She'd meant to say we shouldn't see each other for a while, but her mouth had said something else. And she waited too long to fix it.

"I'm sorry. I won't bother you again."

It came out as a croak: "I meant…for right now…we'd better not see each other." A little louder, "I need time, Mac–"

But he'd already walked away from her, across the lawn and up the steps. He might not have heard the last words she'd said. He retrieved his bicycle, rode past the front of the hotel and up Grand Avenue. He didn't look back once. Too much had been done to her and she had too much pride to call out to him.

Hanging her head and feeling dreadful for hurting someone who'd been nothing but kind to her, she headed towards her aunt's house. The sun, a pale ball, was setting behind her and the cold October wind tugged at her jacket. The day had been so happy and she was sad it'd ended the way it had.

She'd make it up to him...eventually. Next time she saw him. They had only been words, after all. They didn't mean anything. She put it out of her head, pedaling strongly the whole way home, pushing her body to clear her mind.

Home. She'd come to think of Aunt Bess's house as her home already. She looked forward to going up to her room and calling a few of those telephone numbers Mac had given her for more ghost stories. When Bess returned from work, Charlotte would confide in her aunt about what she'd done to Mac. No doubt, she'd have something to say about it.

Following a late supper of soup and rolls, Charlotte told her aunt everything about her misunderstanding with Mac as they sat on the porch.

"He's a good man," Bess said. "He'll get over it. He'll stay your friend, too, if that's what you want because he doesn't hold grudges. Let him cool down. Give him time and give some to yourself, too. Tomorrow or the next day you can call him. Better yet go see him, he's easy to find, and explain why you reacted the way you did. He'll understand."

"That's good advice," Charlotte replied, hugging her aunt. "I'll call Mac and apologize tomorrow or the next day."

"You do that, honey. Now, I'm off to bed. It's been a long day."

They both went into the house.

****

The following morning Charlotte began her new job. Six hours sitting behind a desk checking people into their rooms, answering their questions about the service and gossiping with interesting people wasn't her idea of work. It was pleasantly easy and she enjoyed it. It filled her day and kept her thoughts off the past and what she'd done to Mac.

She got along well with Letty, who had a quick wit and a big heart. Her husband, Herbert, was in and out during the day on errands in between his naps. It was easy to see that Herbert loved being an inn proprietor. Loved talking and dealing with the visitors, as he and Letty called their guests.

The first couple of hours Charlotte didn't ask anyone if they'd seen a ghost in their room. After that, she figured it would be acceptable to steer the friendly banter she had with the guests to the supernatural sometimes. It could be she'd get a story she could use, though the people were mostly from off island, thus, whatever they said couldn't be put in her book. Nonetheless, it made for interesting conversations. She had it in her mind to grill Letty and Herbert about the subject as soon as she knew them well enough. Surely they would have tales to tell.

Later that day Charlotte looked out the impressive picture window and there was Mac, in uniform, riding by on his ten-speed. Before she thought about it, she smiled and rippled her fingers at him. She was relieved when he waved back, though he didn't stop and come in.

Perhaps he wasn't mad at her. Perhaps she'd read him wrong. On her break she tried calling him at the police station but the dispatcher said he was busy on a call. Did she want to leave a message? No, she told him, she'd call back. But she became busy after that and forgot.

Her first workday ended and she visited a bakery nearby to buy brownies for the night's dessert and to take to Hannah's tea. She called Mac after her shift but yet again, he wasn't reachable.

She had time before she had to be at Hannah's so she rode her bicycle around the island along the shore road, her eyes on the lookout for a certain man in uniform on a bicycle. She didn't see him.

On the docks she perched on her bike's seat and stared at Round Island Lighthouse and the Mackinac Bridge. Sunlight danced on the aquamarine water and on the sides of the ferryboats, sailboats and cabin cruisers as they sailed by. Finishing her ride about the time she had to be at Hannah's, she dropped off half the brownies at her aunt's house, took the remainder and walked over to the house next door.

When Charlotte knocked, Hannah took a long time to respond. She was about to leave when the old woman opened the door.

"You need to knock harder, child. I don't hear

as well as I once did. I thought it was some bird pecking at the door. Come on in!" Hannah gently tugged Charlotte's arm and drew her inside. "We're having tea on the sun porch at the far back there. View's better and not so sunny this time of day."

The island hadn't changed but Hannah's house had since Charlotte had last seen it. It had been remodeled, repainted and the furniture was new. In the living room was a trio of massive curio cabinets of oak that covered one wall and held Hannah's glass collection. It'd been small when Charlotte had last seen it, but was now enormous. Inset lights shone on hundreds of gleaming objects, of animals, castles and ships, behind the protective glass in the cabinets. The whole room sparkled with reflected prisms when a person passed through it.

"Your glass collection," Charlotte pronounced in awe, "is incredible."

"Well, thank you, but some nitwit keeps calling and banging on my door wanting me to sell it to him. I keep saying no. I won't sell no matter how much money they try to cram down my throat." Hannah pursed her thin lips and shook her head.

Today she was wearing a lounging outfit, loosely fitted in brown muslin a shade darker than her eyes. It set off her white hair. "It's the same with my first edition novels and my house. I won't part with any of it. I despise people who hound me, wanting something I don't want to sell."

"So do I." Charlotte thought the kitchen was appealing with new wallpaper, kitchen cabinets and counters. There were so many knick-knacks there wasn't an inch of space left anywhere. Some of the objects appeared expensive. "I love what you've done to your house, Hannah. It's lovely."

"I did the decorating myself. Not the hard stuff, just telling them what I wanted and where to put it. I'm too old to be shoving counters and cabinets around."

"If you say so. You did a fantastic job either way."

Compared to her aunt's austere and simple abode, Hannah's house was a miniature Grand Hotel bursting with miniature treasures. When Charlotte was younger, she'd wanted to live at Hannah's and now she still did.

They were on the sun porch and the windows were reflective portraits of Hannah's gardens and backyard. Outside the afternoon light was a gentle rose tint. The perfume of the last of the summer's flowers wafted through the windows and blended with the aroma of chicken salad sandwiches. Hannah had placed them in the middle of an oak table beside an elegant teapot, perfectly matched china plates on paper lace doilies, and shining silverware set out for two.

"You outdid yourself, Hannah. The table looks so pretty. You do have the magic touch."

"That's from years of practice. I've given my share of tea parties, you know."

Charlotte produced the brownies and put them beside the sandwiches. "My contribution."

"How considerate of you. You haven't forgotten I have a fondness for brownies. I always seem to burn them lately when I make them or anything else for that matter. Store bought desserts are all I get now. It's easier."

They sat down and ate sandwiches and brownies. Sipped tea. Charlotte told Hannah about her left-behind life in Chicago and Lucas and about meeting and hurting Mac's feelings. That was the way it was with Hannah. She made a person so comfortable they ended up telling her everything.

"I know Mac Berman. We go way back. I knew him when he was a kid. I see him in town all the time. He'll be back. He's probably giving you the time you asked for."

Charlotte had been thinking about Mac since their falling out the day before and wasn't sure how she actually felt. She wanted him as a friend. She liked him. Anything else, well, it was too soon and she wasn't ready to think about it. Yet after Mac had waved at her she'd thought, no, he's not mad at me and had felt a rush of relief. So in some way she did care.

As Hannah maintained, Mac was probably just giving her the time she'd asked for. That's why he hadn't returned her call. So in a few days or so she'd leave another message for him at the police station or if she saw him out somewhere, stop and talk to him. Mend their misunderstanding. It would be as if they'd never quarreled.

"What will be, will be," Hannah predicted. "Broken hearts aren't so easily gotten over. I had a man I dearly loved once leave, and at first, I thought I was doing fine. I went on with my life and pretended everything was okey dokey. It hit me months later. I became depressed, cried and threw fits. It was about a year after that before I could see through the fog and enjoy life again."

"I hope it doesn't take me that long."

"We'll see. You're not moping or crying. That's something. Now, you want to hear some of those spook stories I promised you?"

Charlotte spent the next hour listening and taking notes excitedly. She'd never known Hannah's house was haunted.

"My ghost is a fur trader, or he was, name of Wallace Stonegate. He lived here when the house was first built around 1890. Back then, though, the structure wasn't near as comfy or as spacious as it is now. It was built onto over the years.

"A bear got Wallace one day on the Mainland; tore him into shreds. He haunts his home now. But he isn't a mean, destructive or noisy apparition. Mother and father used to be scared of him but he's never hurt anyone that I know of. He's never tried to hurt me. He appears every so often sitting in a chair somewhere in the house, usually in the parlor. It must have been his favorite room. He usually has ghost dirt and grass all over him.

"Once I saw him at night in the back yard under the Lilac bush. He was a mangy-looking cuss with a wild straggly beard, ragged leather pants and muddy boots. He carries a long knife at his side. He never says a word, merely frowns at me. He looks so unhappy. I think he misses his home, is lonely or something. Or maybe he's guarding me against bears."

"Sure he isn't guarding a bag of gold doubloons he buried out in the garden or something?"

"Hmm, I never thought of that. If it were true,

it'd be something for sure. They'd be collectibles. Priceless. Perhaps I should try digging out there by that bush." She looked out the window at it.

"Then...there's the ice bridge ghosts. They say, in the winter when the ice bridge is frozen solid, that sometimes the spirits of those who've fallen into the straits and died haunt the path. You can hear them weeping on the wind from miles away even when you're on the shore."

"People have died on the ice bridge?" Her aunt had never mentioned that to Charlotte. It made her blood shiver but she wanted the story.

"Sure, quite a few over the years. In the early days, the ice hadn't frozen enough yet, or, later, their snowmobiles were too heavy or they tried to cross a weak spot on the ice. It usually happens early in the season before the freezing is complete or late when the thawing begins."

"Anyone ever see these ice bridge ghosts?"

"Some have, though most won't talk about it. The ghosts appear to the next victim before they die as they're going across the ice, or so the tale goes. So Charlotte, if you ever start over the bridge and hear weeping or see skinny white apparitions beckoning to you...get right off that ice and get yourself back home pronto." Hannah's expression was serious so Charlotte didn't dare crack a smile. At first she'd thought the old woman had been joshing her but now she wasn't so sure.

"Tell me more, Hannah."

By the time Charlotte left Hannah's house she'd scribbled five pages of notes and the two women had caught up on the last fifteen years. Hannah was an interesting woman who'd lived on the island since birth. She had the stories and was hungry for companionship.

"I'd be so lonely if not for your aunt and now you. I'm tickled you've come back, child."

"Well, so am I. I've missed you." Charlotte hugged Hannah before walking down the porch steps.

It was easy to love Hannah. From the beginning Charlotte had looked at her and seen the grandmother she'd never had. It'd been surprisingly sweet visiting with her. She looked forward to all the teas and visits and the friendship they'd have in the future.

Charlotte went home after promising Hannah she'd come again soon. She didn't know it then but tea with Hannah would become a weekly ritual, one both of them would come to look forward to. Often Bess, when she wasn't working, would join them, but most of the time it would be Charlotte and Hannah tea-klatching and gossiping about the locals, the tourists and swapping stories. Charlotte or Bess would make the snacks. The visits made Hannah and Charlotte happy.

****

So the days passed.

Charlotte worked at the inn, spent time with her aunt and Hannah, and reclaimed the island as her own and worked on her book. She felt content.

Mac didn't come to see her and for days she didn't see him anywhere either, didn't run into him though she looked. She thought of calling his job again after that first day but put the phone down each time. She hated women who chased after a man. She wasn't like that and wasn't about to start. She'd wait until she saw him somewhere, then they'd talk. Face-to-face was better than a telephone call anyway. It didn't happen. Then Mac, according to Bess, was on vacation and gone for a while. By the time he returned Charlotte couldn't bring herself to contact him. Too much time had gone by.

She'd run into him one of *these days, somewhere. She could wait.*

The end of tourist season came the final weekend of October and, almost overnight, the ferries stopped bringing boatloads of visitors. The streets and shops were no longer crowded, except for the weekends, when there'd still be leftover *fudgies* milling about searching for bargains or seeing the sights. The island became the islanders' again and many celebrated they had it to themselves. Well, most of the time anyway. It wouldn't be theirs completely until frigid weather and the snows came.

Charlotte found she liked the solitude and liked living on the island in the fall. The flowers died, the trees changed colors and there was a biting nip in the air that made her feel alive.

Sure, she had to get used to taking the ferry each week to the mainland to do their shopping. It was one of the chores she'd taken over from her aunt because she had a car there. Besides Bess was depressed and tired more often than not, since Shawn had left the island and gone home to Ireland. There were only three stores on Mackinac and given that supplies were brought in by ferry or airplane and transported across land by horse and dray wagon, food prices were steep and got worse after the tourists left. So Charlotte traveled to the mainland stores to keep costs down.

Weeks passed. Life went on and she slipped into the easy rhythm of the place, made friends, and compiled ghost sightings. Gradually the memories of her old life in Chicago dwindled until they seemed as if they'd happened to someone else, not her. She didn't miss Lucas as much as she'd thought she would. She'd become resigned to the truth that he'd stopped being the man she'd loved long before he left her. She didn't miss her advertising job at the brokerage firm or the big city, either. She missed the good money but not her previous life.

One day Mac showed up at the inn. Just like that. Charlotte looked up over the counter and he was standing there. "I was passing by and thought I'd stop in and say hello. How have you been?" He didn't seem angry or distant. He seemed like the Mac he'd always been.

Pleased he was there she caught him up on her life and tried not to let him see how his visit was affecting her. She wanted to say so much but ended up saying very little.

As they made small talk about how she was enjoying the island and how her Aunt Bess was, Charlotte met his eyes and smiled.

Go ahead; tell him you've missed him and that you're sorry. Do it. Explain why you shoved him away like you did and that you didn't mean it. But she couldn't get the words out.

"How's the ghost book coming along?" Mac

inquired. His returning smile was genuine.

"I have six chapters. Thank you for those first stories and the contacts you made for me, Mac. And for giving me the idea."

"You're welcome. When your book gets published you owe me a free autographed copy."

"If it gets published, I'll give you one." Charlotte wanted to add that she was so happy to see him. She was sorry for what she'd said to him weeks earlier, but the memories of their last parting made her hesitate and then it was too late. Mac was leaving.

"I have to be on duty in ten minutes," he said going out the door. "I'll see you around, Charlotte. Say hi to your aunt for me."

"I will." She watched him leave. She nearly stopped him to say what she'd wanted to say but she had guests she had to show to their rooms and others needing information on what there was to see on the island. She was the only one at the front desk. It would have to wait.

Chapter 3
November and December 2007

Most Saturday mornings she took the eighteen minute ferry ride to St. Ignace with her aunt's large red pull-wagon and picked up her car from the lot where she boarded it. Like most of the islanders she got a discount on the boat rides because she purchased in bulk.

She'd drive to the store, or wherever else she had to go, purchase what they needed, drive to the lot near the docks and load everything into the wagon. She'd drag it onto the ferry and to her aunt's house. It was an adventure every week. One time it stormed and she and her groceries got soaked; another time the front left wheel came off and she had to drag the wagon on two rear wheels the rest of the way home.

Winter with its snow and inclement weather came. Charlotte kept working at the inn while her aunt worked nights as a bartender at the Mustang Lounge. They'd have supper and spend the early evening together then Bess would go to the Mustang and Charlotte would work on her novel. She liked having time alone at night but missed having someone to talk to and share things with. Some nights, when Hannah didn't wander over to visit, she was even lonely.

Those were the times she thought of Mac and

didn't know why. All those stories she was gathering for her book and, in a way, she had her own ghost. Mac was like a ghost following her. She kept seeing his smile and remembering his kindnesses. She heard his voice when he was nowhere around. She'd see him on the side of the road, by a building in the fading shadows, look, but he'd never be there. Her sightings were in her mind.

Why? She didn't know. She rarely thought of Lucas anymore. Any night she expected Mac to saunter up on the porch and knock on the front door. He'd be smiling and ready to ask her out again. He didn't. They'd see each other and smile or wave but except for that one visit at the inn, Mac kept his distance.

As the weeks went by the villagers accepted her as one of their own. Wherever she went, they smiled or stopped to chat about how she liked living on Mackinac or to query about how her aunt and Hannah were doing. The island had truly become her home.

Charlotte had become protectively fond of Hannah. They visited frequently at their weekly teas when Hannah proudly displayed her treasures or when Charlotte invited her over to watch television or play cards. The old woman was lonely, too.

Hannah, with her knowledge of the island's past, provided Charlotte with interesting tidbits for her book. If some old-timer had seen a spirit, Hannah had heard of it and would tell her. Sometimes they'd exchange views on the latest murder mystery that Hannah brought home from the library. Hannah ate crime books. She could figure out who the murderer was before the clues were given. She had a knack for reading between the lines.

In November when the snow had settled over the island like a heavy blanket, Charlotte's aunt got her snowmobile out of storage, cleaned it up and showed Charlotte how to ride it. Motorized snowmobiles were allowed on Mackinac. It snowed so much that getting around was impossible without them. Most of the island's horses were shipped out to pasture on the mainland, as it was pricey to haul their feed back and forth across the straits when the ice in the water kept the ferries and boats from running. In the winter, most people trudged through the snow or used snowmobiles.

Hannah rode one and Charlotte would see her scooting about town on it, fearless in her speed and corner taking. For an old woman she could sure get around. Hers was an older model, larger and heavier than the newer streamlined ones. One day Hannah remarked offhand she had another snowmobile in her garage she'd bought a few years back but hadn't liked as much because it was too hard to steer, and Charlotte could borrow it. Hannah liked her old snowmobile.

Charlotte took her friend up on the offer. Though she'd never liked winter much she found she didn't mind careening around in the white stuff on a machine—the deeper the snow the better. She learned to bundle up in layers to stay warm and figured she'd get used to the cold eventually. Aunt Bess said she would. Everyone did if they were on the island long enough. The bad weather made it tricky to get to the mainland. It would get trickier once the ferries ceased running in January when the frozen waters became too treacherous to navigate.

"By then we pray for the ice bridge to freeze over," Aunt Bess told her. "In January, if we're lucky. It takes a week at below zero temperatures and no wind for the strait to harden. Some brave soul ventures out and spuds the thickness of the ice and if they don't fall in halfway across then it's on to the mainland. They telephone us back here to let us know it's a green light. The ice bridge is open.

"The town would have already dumped their old Christmas trees—stripped of ornaments and tinsel—out on British Landing. They'd be hammered into the ice to mark the perimeters of the bridge. It's miles long, three or four, I think. All you have to do is stay on the path close to the line of trees and avoid any slushy looking weak spots."

"People aren't afraid?" Charlotte was remembering what Hannah had said about the ice bridge ghosts. People had to know about the casualties; had to know the ice bridge wasn't always safe.

"Some people. But we've been using it for centuries and love it because it gives us the freedom to come and go anytime without paying anyone else a penny. For a month or two anyway."

The whole thing gave Charlotte the willies. Ice wasn't much of a solid to her. It cracked and it melted. She didn't like the notion of risking her life on it. But as with Mac weeks before, she didn't say anything to her aunt about that. She'd worry about crossing the ice bridge when she had to worry about it. According to Bess, some years it didn't even freeze solid. Perhaps this would be one of those.

"Has anyone ever fallen through the ice?" Charlotte questioned her aunt, knowing the answer.

"Well, no one that I can recall. Though I've heard stories about people going through."

"What happened to them?"

"They fished them out, I guess. They got cold and wet. Then they'd drag the water and retrieve their snowmobiles. So don't go fretting about it anymore."

"Strange. Hannah claims people have died on the ice bridge." Charlotte wouldn't let it go.

There was no answer at first. The two of them had been sitting on the porch on Bess's night off in mid-December. They were getting fresh air, bundled up in coats and blankets, and drinking hot chocolate. Tonight it wasn't that cold, the wind was flat and it wasn't snowing. Unless the weather was horrific, they squeezed in their porch time. It was their ritual.

Since Shawn had left for Ireland, her aunt seemed to need more of it than usual.

"Aunt Bess?"

"Over the centuries, I imagine, that's true. It's usually because of extenuating circumstances like bad weather or an early thaw. Now I recall...about eleven, twelve years ago someone went out in a blizzard and accidentally veered off the path. He went under."

"And died?"

Pause. "I think so. That was because of the storm. No one fished him out in time. It's dangerous to go out anywhere or try to do anything in a blizzard. No one's out to see you go under."

"He still died. See. The bridge is not so safe."

"Accidents happen." Bess shrugged. "As I said, it's rare. You know, sweetie, you can't worry about all the what-could-happens in life or it'll drive you cuckoo."

"You've got a point there." Yet the image of a crowd of wispy translucent beings haunting the ice wouldn't leave Charlotte's head.

Her aunt was gazing into the night. Charlotte could tell she wasn't thinking about the ice bridge. The wind had suddenly begun to howl and the water was throwing itself violently against the shore in front of them. Soon they'd have to go in. Their faces and toes couldn't take much more.

"I miss Shawn," confessed Bess, pulling the blanket around her shoulders. Charlotte couldn't see her face.

There was no moon and no lights on in the house behind them. They sat in the dark.

Since Shawn had left her aunt was inconsolable. When Charlotte had first arrived Bess and Shawn hadn't been seeing each other, but that hadn't lasted. They'd been friends for decades and soon they'd made up. Shawn had resumed coming over for supper or taking walks with Bess and Charlotte that last week. He never spent the night. Charlotte never saw him do more than touch Bess's hand or smile lovingly at her.

It was easy to see why her aunt loved him. He was a decent person. He could make her aunt— could make anyone—laugh. He was always helping people and was good to Hannah. He brought her presents, which made her smile, and then made Bess smile. Charlotte liked him a lot. To his credit he never hid the fact he was married, never hid anything. He spoke about his children and his wife with great affection. He cared about their well-being.

The first night Charlotte met Shawn at her aunt's house they invited Hannah over, picked up pizzas, and played cards. Charlotte got to know Shawn that last week and found him to be an intelligent, thoughtful man. They'd become friends by the time he left for Ireland.

That first night after Shawn had gone, she'd asked her aunt more about their relationship.

"I knew he was married from the beginning, but you don't pick who you love. You meet someone and something clicks. You end up needing him and hating yourself for it, yet it doesn't change the way you feel. You're alive when he's with you and less than alive when he's not. If being his friend was all I could have, it was what I took. I've always loved him more because of his loyalty to his family. I'd never do anything to hurt Katie or the kids. I couldn't live with myself if I did. I pray that Katie will get well. She's been sick before and recovered every time. I only want Shawn to be happy."

"You're a good woman."

"It doesn't get me anywhere."

"Peace of mind?"

"Well, that, yes. I'm lucky to have had Shawn as long as I did. He made me happy even if we were never lovers. I have the memories."

Charlotte envied them until Shawn went away and Aunt Bess fell apart. She cried at night in her room so Charlotte wouldn't hear, but Charlotte heard. Bess believed Shawn was never coming back.

Though loving someone for five years couldn't compare to loving someone for twenty and losing them, Charlotte hoped time would help heal her aunt as it was healing her.

****

Charlotte was looking forward to Christmas. She picked out gifts for her aunt and Hannah. She sent presents to her mother and father and found something that Mac would like, wrapped it, and stuck it under the tree just in case he stopped by.

At dusk on Christmas Eve Charlotte dressed up warmly, climbed on her snowmobile to join the other islanders in the middle of town around a sixteen-foot Christmas tree. The town put one up every year. She'd helped decorate it earlier in the month and wouldn't have missed the Christmas Eve celebration with the caroling and the refreshments for anything.

Aunt Bess had her shift at the Mustang Lounge and couldn't make the tree gala but they'd have their own celebration later with presents and a feast after her aunt got off work. For Bess, Christmas Eve was as important as Christmas day. They'd put up a tree and decorated the parlor. Hannah was coming over later that night to share in their Christmas Eve party. The old lady was probably peeking out the window and waiting impatiently for her to return so she could come over.

Charlotte had to spend time at the town's fete first. She'd come to cherish these holiday town gatherings because for the first time in her life she felt as if she truly belonged somewhere.

It was a frigid snowy night and the village, with the gigantic tree twinkling in the street, was like something off a Kincaid Christmas calendar. The lampposts sported large cherry ribbons and strung lights. The falling snow covering everything made the town appear mysteriously beautiful.

Charlotte, trying not to shiver too much from the cold, drank mulled cider and sang Silent Night around the tree with a group of townies she knew from her job. When she looked up she saw Mac standing a ways in front of her. He hadn't seen her yet.

He looked handsome in his uniform coat and cap, curly hair flecked with snow brushing up against his collar. He was smiling, singing, and for a moment she was so excited to see him, she almost reached out to touch him. She wanted to let him know she was there—let him know she'd had enough time to get over Lucas. She wanted to let him know how much she'd missed him as a friend, how she wanted to sit down somewhere and talk; share a meal with him while he gave her historical facts, made silly jokes and went on about ghosts. She wanted another chance now that Lucas was becoming a memory.

Seeing Mac was a timely coincidence. The day before she'd gotten his home telephone number from Hannah. She'd decided to call him that evening and invite him over Christmas Eve or

Christmas day to share in their celebration, whichever one he could make. Christmas was a good time to mend fences. She'd waited long enough for him to make another move. Now it was up to her to do it.

She'd daydreamed about opening her heart to him. *I've missed you, Mac. It's been months and I'm ready to go out with you now, see what happens.*

Smiling nervously, she moved towards him and was about to tug at his sleeve when she saw he wasn't alone. There was a woman hanging on his other arm, dressed in a fashionable sable coat, sea green scarf and shiny black boots, looking up at him. Her hair was a bright shade of gold and her skin a pale ivory with cheeks flushed from the cold. She was exceptionally pretty.

Charlotte stood there, staring, and a painful feeling of loss crept over her. It was as if she'd owned a special jewel and, not having appreciated it, someone else had taken it. She'd been a fool to wait so long to call or go see him. It was a small island and she knew where he lived. She knew where he worked. She could have gotten his home phone number from Hannah weeks ago. Her pride had deceived her into waiting until he knocked on her door again. Only he hadn't. Charlotte had blown it and now Mac had a new love.

Lurking at the edge of the crowd, she watched the happy faces. The scene of couples caroling and cuddling with one another and families laughing together suddenly made her feel lonelier than she had in months. She had no husband, lover or boyfriend. Christmas Eve wasn't a time to be alone.

A fleeting image of herself this time last year at a swanky corporate shindig with Lucas, eating fish eggs on crackers, wearing an expensive gown of glitzy silver and basking in a world that had glittered brighter than a Christmas tree...but one that had been as hollow as a glass ornament...played through her mind. For some reason it made her even sadder.

Charlotte watched the blond reach up and pull Mac's face down so she could kiss him on the lips. As miserable as she was, she was glad for him. Someone loved him and he deserved it.

She drifted away, reclaimed her snowmobile and rode the deserted streets lined in glimmering lights to her aunt's house. It'd grown colder and the snowfall heavier.

Hannah, a bundle wrapped up in a too big coat, was waiting on a porch chair. A pile of presents and aluminum foil-covered-plates were piled around her feet. The sight made Charlotte smile. Hannah had brought over a ton of food, probably store bought. Along with what Aunt Bess had baked earlier, they wouldn't go hungry. And none of them would be alone.

"You're home. About time. I've been waiting for you." Hannah's voice was hoarse.

"Sounds like you're getting a cold there, Hannah. How long have you been out here?"

"Too dang long. My bones are frozen but I couldn't stay in that house another minute. I had to get out. I got tired of listening to other people sing silly songs on the television. When I called, you said you weren't going to be gone long so I came on over. I didn't want to miss you."

"You wouldn't have. I would have come over and gotten you. But," Charlotte picked up an armful of plates and packages after she'd opened the door, "now I don't need to. Let's go in."

"Fine with me. I'm ready for the party. I got a new dress, sparkly stuff in my hair and everything. I have my best diamonds on."

Charlotte gave Hannah a hug before she let her in, tears threatening to fall. Hannah hadn't been able to wait for one of them to get home to begin her Christmas Eve and was as animated as a child. The woman's enthusiasm was catching, and Charlotte felt blessed to be her friend. It was so good to see her.

When they slipped inside and out of their coats they turned on the radio station to Christmas carols and switched on the tree lights and the front porch lights. Hannah was hungry so Charlotte served her hot apple cider, a ham sandwich and Christmas cookies. They watched holiday programs on television, ate more cookies and waited for Bess to get home from work so they could open presents.

When Bess got home, they had a fine party. She'd brought along four friends from the Mustang Lounge who had no place else to go for the evening. They played hearts, pinochle and board games, belted out Christmas carols and ate the food the women had prepared.

Remembering where and with whom she'd been the year before, Charlotte knew she liked this party much better. These were real people and she was finally living a real life. Merry Christmas.

In the wee hours of the night, Charlotte drug herself to bed, no longer feeling lonely. People cared for her and she had friends. She had a home as long as she wanted it. She had Aunt Bess and Hannah. She wished Mac could have been there with them. It was strange that she missed a man she hardly knew. She'd only spent a ferry ride, a few chance meetings and a day at the Grand Hotel with him...yet she missed him. It was strange.

As she lay in bed and ran her fingers against the frozen windowpane, she thought, *Mac was taken.* It didn't matter. There was nothing she could do. She hadn't said anything to Bess or Hannah about seeing Mac with his girlfriend, hadn't uttered a word about him until Bess asked if she'd invited him for the evening.

"No, he was busy tonight," she'd said and that had been that.

She fell asleep.

****

The snow outside on Christmas morning was shining and white when she woke. A frozen wonderland dazzled outside her window. It reminded her of Hank Ferrell's ghost yarn.

Hank had been one of their Christmas guests the evening before and had given her a story about when he'd been a child on the island one winter in nineteen-fifty, years before the flood of tourists had begun to come, and he'd seen something he'd never been able to forget.

It'd been a cruel winter that year, Hank had recalled. For some reason the ice bridge hadn't frozen and fresh supplies were hard to come by. There were those on the island who were too poor to keep buying what they needed. They scrounged or hunted what game they could find in the woods to feed their families. There were squirrels and rabbits and they filled a belly if there was nothing else. The snows came and didn't stop. The thermometer hovered around ten degrees for months.

There were many hungry people that winter.

Hank, eleven at the time, had stayed too long at a friend's house one evening and on his way home had come across two men with a boy huddled around a dying campfire in the dark. All of them were dressed like hunters in skins and furs. Hank had never seen any of them before. The men looked as skinny as twigs, had scraggly beards and hungry eyes. The boy was small and kept coughing. They were eating hunks of ice and pieces of bark and glared at the intruder when he'd stumbled into their camp.

Hank had asked if they were out hunting and one of the men had nodded.

"Dirty and tired, they didn't speak," Hank told his story. "None of them. I felt sorry for the boy. He was around my age, a little younger, so I asked him who he was and where they'd come from. He wouldn't answer. I remember wishing I hadn't eaten the candy bar I'd had in my pocket because the boy looked as if he needed it a heck of a lot more than me, but I had no food. I couldn't offer them anything.

"I had the eerie feeling that the boy knew what I

was thinking because he'd smiled and gestured for me to sit down beside him, which I did gratefully. I was exhausted and plopped down in front of their fire, with them staring at me as if I was going to be supper, and somehow I fell asleep. I wouldn't admit it but I'd been lost. Scared. The falling snow and the dark had confused me and I was waiting for the light of dawn. That's why I'd stopped. I stayed with the three of them though they creeped me out.

"Next morning I woke up. I had brush and branches piled around me like a blanket, which had kept me warm. Mayhap saved my life. All three of my companions are sitting there covered in snow and ice...frozen solid. I got up and ran for help. In the light I didn't have any trouble finding town."

"They were dead, huh?" Charlotte had asked Hank as she'd handed him another plate of ham slices and potato salad.

"I was only a kid but I could tell they were definitely dead. They weren't moving and their bodies were cold as ice cubes. First dead people I'd ever seen. I had nightmares for months."

"That's terrible. Nevertheless, as appalling as that must have been for you, how does that make this a ghost story?"

Across the table Hank had grinned at her. "Well, I'm getting to that. Because I told everybody that I'd seen them *alive*. I spoke to them and they answered, sort of. They took care of me so I wouldn't freeze."

Hank was in his late sixties, at least, and had lived on the island all his life. His wife had died two years before and his kids were grown and lived half way across the country. He was a retired ferryboat captain who liked to sit at the Mustang most nights and get drunk. Or that's what her aunt said. He had a bad leg from a boat accident, courtesy of his working days, and he loved peanuts. Bess said he'd consume every peanut in sight at the bar each night. She could never put enough out.

"The next night in bed," Hank went on, "I heard my dad telling my mom that I couldn't have been speaking to the two men and the boy—that I must have imagined it—because the police had reported that the three had been missing and the coroner claimed they'd been dead for days probably."

"Oh, so they'd been ghosts all along?"

"You got it."

Charlotte studied the drifting snow outside the window from her bed and it was as if she could almost see the three frozen hunters hunched around their dying campfire down below, the two men with beards and a frightened little boy that were frozen statues. It gave her the heebie-jeebies. Oh, but it was a good story. And Hank didn't mind if she used his name.

The book was coming along, she thought, as she got up. People were coming to her now, willingly. Her reputation was spreading. Everyone on the island knew she was writing a book on ghosts. Bess said they were beginning to call her the ghost lady, which amused Charlotte because it made her sound like a ghost. She didn't care. The book kept her mind off her empty love life. And for now, the book, Aunt Bess, her job and the island were enough.

Chapter 4

January 2008

"I'm going to ring up Mac and see about getting a search party together. Hannah's still not home and three days is too long for that old woman to be gone, especially in this weather. It's snowing like crazy out there and supposed to get worse by tonight." Bess picked up the phone.

Charlotte listened as her aunt explained to someone on the other end of the line how Hannah hadn't been home in three days and they were getting worried.

"It isn't like her, Mac, to go off without telling someone."

Charlotte's apprehension about seeing Mac face-to-face wasn't important. She lingered by the window, her eyes on the wintry world as Bess conversed on the phone. It'd been snowing for days.

Her aunt had a spare key to Hannah's house and they'd already gone over to check on her a couple of times. Hannah wasn't anywhere around.

"Yes. No. Yes," Bess was saying to Mac. "Her snowmobile's gone. I think she's on it. The snow in her driveway has no tracks in it and has had none the last two days."

Pause.

"No, I haven't a notion where she could be or

where she went. Just that she's not in her house and doesn't seem to have been for days. We've looked every day. She hasn't been home, Mac, and she always tells me when she's going to be gone for any length of time.

"Delores down at the post office says Hannah hasn't been in to pick up her mail for at least four days and her social security check has been there for three. Delores says it's not like her, not to collect her mail. She's got books and packages waiting."

Charlotte flashed her aunt a hand signal. "I think I have an idea where she might have gone," Charlotte spoke softly. "Something she said to me last weekend."

Her aunt thrust the phone into her hands. "Tell him."

"Hello, Mac?" Charlotte's voice was nervous and not only because she was worried about Hannah but because she was speaking to Mac, whom she hadn't expected to be talking to. She had no choice. They had to find Hannah. "It's me, Charlotte. I remembered something Hannah said a few days before she disappeared. We were having tea together at her house as we do every Wednesday. It's become a custom of ours."

"I know. Hannah's kept me up-to-date on your teas," Mac replied. "She thinks the world of you and always talks about you. I know exactly what you've been up to." His voice was friendly and that, along with what he'd divulged, surprised her. Mac had been keeping tabs on her through Hannah? "So, what did Hannah say?"

It was as if they'd never had a falling out. He seemed at ease talking to her and hearing his voice scattered her apprehensions of the last nine weeks. It was good talking to him again. Why had she waited so long? After all, disagreement or not, girlfriend or not, they could be friends.

"Something about having to go see someone over on St. Ignace. I gathered by the irritation in her voice it was someone she didn't want to go see. She was waiting for the ice bridge to open so she could snowmobile over. She said she was hoping it would freeze soon because she didn't want to go by plane and the ferries had discontinued running. She's afraid of planes, you know."

"I know. She's afraid of cars, too, did you know that?" A chuckle drifted over the line.

"I did. Good thing she lives on an island that doesn't have any."

"All right." He got back to the problem at hand. "About Hannah's whereabouts. The ice bridge froze five days ago and people started using it. If it weren't for this storm you'd probably know that. I mean if you haven't been out much."

"I haven't been out much. I prefer to stay inside where it's warm, unless I have to go to work."

"You sound like a mainlander. Anyway, Buddy—you know the guy who sees the soldier's ghost up at the fort—went out last weekend, drilled a hole into the ice, found it deep enough and gave the all clear to use it."

So he remembered their conversation about Buddy's ghost at the Grand Hotel. He hadn't forgotten that day after all. That made her feel better.

"A couple of us," Mac continued, "planted the evergreens Sunday to form the path and I was going to the mainland myself on it day after tomorrow. Could be Hannah went across the ice bridge to the mainland."

"She could have. But she's been gone for days. Overnight. She's too cheap to stay that long on the mainland at a hotel. You know how tight she is with her money."

"Not as tight as you think, Charlotte. Listen, I'm coming over. It's not normal for Hannah to be missing this long. I agree with you, something's wrong. Weather service says there's going to be a lull in the storm the next couple of hours, but tonight we're going to get another wallop. It's best I move on this now. I'll want to search Hannah's house. I'll need that key your aunt spoke of to get in. I'll talk to her and you as well. Tell her, and I'll see you both as soon as I can get there." He hung up.

"Mac's coming over," Charlotte informed her aunt. "He'll be here quick as he can."

"Thank goodness. I know something's happened to Hannah and I'll be relieved when the police start searching for her. How did Mac sound to you?"

Bess knew about Charlotte seeing Mac with his girlfriend on Christmas Eve. She'd finally told her.

"He sounded like Mac, friendly; obviously concerned about Hannah. He must care for her."

"He should. He's known her forever. When he was a kid he cut her grass, did odd jobs and helped her with her garden. Mac was over there a lot of the time because his father was out on the boats and his mother was a drinker. He didn't have much of a home life; so Hannah befriended and fed him. She kind of adopted him. They were close until he went off to college. They still are. He takes her out for dinner on her birthday and keeps an eye on her and the house."

"I wasn't aware of that, though Hannah said they were friends and spoke of him often." After that incident on Christmas Eve, Charlotte had wanted to grill Hannah about Mac's girlfriend but hadn't had a chance before the older woman disappeared. "You say he was at her house a lot when he was a child, but I don't remember him."

"Sure you do. Remember the scrawny kid with the crew cut? The one who used to play with that slingshot and knock Hannah's stuffed animals out of the tree limbs? The boy Hannah was forever feeding because he was hungry?"

A blurry memory surfaced of a boy crying in Hannah's garden on a summer morning. Charlotte passed by on her bicycle, and stopped to ask him what was wrong. He wouldn't tell her. He had broken eyeglasses and blood on his face. His eyes had been a rare bright blue. She'd seen the boy before but he'd run off whenever she'd tried to corner him. She'd been bigger than he'd been and pushy for a girl. She'd had nice clothes, a shiny new bike, and he'd been an unkempt ragamuffin on a scratched-up, second-hand set of wheels. He'd probably been too timid, too ashamed to talk to her.

Charlotte had often wondered what had happened to that kid.

Now she knew.

"That boy grew up to be Mac?"

"That was Mac. You remember him now?"

"Yeah, I do. But I can't believe the self-assured handsome man in uniform I know was ever that pitiful boy. He's changed."

"He has. Mac Berman is a success story. He pulled himself up from poverty and apathy and made himself into a competent man with a respected career; developed other talents, too. Hannah had something to do with it. Mac's family was poor so Hannah set up a trust fund and gifted Mac money for college. She'd promised him that if he'd make nothing less than a B through high school she'd give him the money, along with any grants he could get, to go to college. He did and she did. He made top grades in college and graduated with honors in the top five percent of his class. He majored in law enforcement and advanced criminal law and now he's going back for his master's."

Bess understood how Charlotte felt about Mac and she hoped the two would get together someday. Even after Charlotte had seen Mac with his girlfriend on Christmas Eve, Bess still believed.

Perhaps she'd only been a friend? Bess had offered. To herself Charlotte responded sharply, *Yeah, sure. Mac kisses all his friends like that. Ha.*

The Christmas Eve impromptu celebration had been two weeks past. Now it felt like a century ago. With Hannah missing, what she'd done and said seemed so poignant and so meaningful. The old woman had been in high spirits that night—the life of the party. She'd spoken of her childhood and how she'd had a good long life. She mentioned how grateful she was for Bess, Charlotte and her other friends and her home on the island. She'd drank her wine, toasted her life, and a little tipsy, she'd told amusing stories of her early life on the island and made everyone laugh. She was a born storyteller. Hannah had fallen asleep on Bess's sofa and had breakfast with them late the next morning. The three of them made a family.

After Christmas, New Year's had come and gone more quietly. Hannah, Bess, a friend of Bess's who was a chef at the Grand Hotel, Gertrude Weaver, and Charlotte had played pinochle and rummy all night at Hannah's house. No one could beat Hannah at 500 rummy when she was on a roll.

They'd watched the crystal ball descend in Times Square on the flat screen television next to the table in Hannah's lovely kitchen. They'd stuffed their faces with food and raised glasses of soda and whiskey to the New Year at twelve o'clock. No spontaneous guests, just four spinsters alone, and they had a ball. Laughing, eating and gossiping.

A little drunk, Charlotte had dialed Mac's phone number to wish him a happy New Year. She'd chickened out at the last minute when it began to ring and she'd hung up.

Reliving that night Hannah had seemed upset about something but refused to talk about it. All Charlotte could recollect was her saying something about meeting someone she didn't want to see or deal with. The old woman wouldn't say when or where, who or why. Only that she disliked the person and that person, as she'd put it, wasn't going to get what they wanted out of her. None of them were. She'd show them.

When Charlotte tried to get more information out of her, Hannah had clammed up. The old woman could be obstinate when she wanted to be. What and who had she been speaking of? Charlotte hadn't questioned Hannah further because Gertrude and her ghost story had sidetracked her.

Gertrude had worked at the Grand Hotel for twenty years. Her specialty was desserts and pastries. She was widowed, had three sons and, besides Hannah, was one of Bess's best friends. She'd seen many strange things while working late nights in the Grand's kitchen or when hurrying through the darkened corridors.

"I keep seeing this young girl," Gertrude confessed over her fanned out cards. She'd been winning half the night but she'd lost the last hand. "She's about fifteen years old or so and sometimes dressed in clothes like they used to wear in the nineteen-twenties. Rich clothes. Antique-looking jewelry. She's a pretty thing. Short dark hair with bangs, big eyes and dimples.

"I know she's a ghost and not one of the hotel's solid guests because she's got this eerie glow around her. It fades in and out, like she does. She sees me, I think, and tries to talk but she's speaking a foreign language, German, I'm sure by the harsh sound of it. I can't understand a word she says.

"Sometimes pastries are missing from the platters before they go out to the dining rooms. She likes cherry or cheese mostly. I figure she takes them. She must have a sweet tooth, though I don't know how a spirit can eat a Danish. Heaven knows. Maybe she hides them. She's a carefree ghost, though. She smiles and dances around the halls like she's come from a party. Sometimes she's dressed real fancy in a slinky dress and furs and other times she's dressed for riding. She doesn't stay around long. Once I saw her turn into mist in front of my eyes."

The thought of phantoms prancing around the halls of the Grand Hotel had made Charlotte want to run up there and see for herself. She wanted to sneak in and play ghost hunter. It was a darn shame the hotel closed for the winter. Perhaps Mac could get her in the closed down building. Then she'd remembered: Oh, she and Mac weren't friends anymore.

"Do you know who she was…when she was alive, I mean?" Charlotte had been nursing a weak white soda and whiskey. On the television, a crowd of faces had been yelling as some old rock group sang old rock songs.

"I don't rightly know. One of the old timers, Riley, a maintenance man on the grounds, reckons she's the rich German girl who died falling off her horse on one of the Grand's riding paths. That was around nineteen-twenty-three. It was a real tragedy at the time. The horse bolted and the girl lost her seat. She fell down a hill and broke her neck. Her father was an Austrian diplomat who loved coming to the Grand with his family but they said after that accident, he never revisited. Sad, huh?"

"Very sad. Can I quote you in my book? Use your name?"

"Go ahead. I've told this story a hundred times to anyone who'll listen. I know what I see and I'm not ashamed of it."

"Have you seen any other spooky things up at the hotel?"

"No, though I've felt other presences at times. Cold spots that make my soul shiver. I've heard whispers and had objects shifted around in my kitchen that I hadn't moved myself. I believe there's many lost spirits in the hotel. Other people have seen other things. I see the German girl and sometimes she follows me around. Don't know why. Maybe I remind her of someone she once knew when she was alive. I don't know.

"If you'd like I'll jot down names of a few other people who work with me who have their own stories to tell. You can call them. I'm sure they'll talk to you."

"I'd appreciate that, Gertrude." Charlotte had called them and gotten their stories as well. Now she had three more chapters for her book.

A day later, the straits became too icy for the ferryboats to travel through and the boats were docked until spring. It was a good thing Charlotte and Bess had gone to the mainland the week before and stocked up on groceries for the remainder of the winter. They'd gone together with two wagons and had loaded them to overflowing at the store. They had enough supplies to get them through until the thaw, they hoped, if it didn't come too late.

****

The week after the New Year's card game Hannah wasn't around much. She didn't call and didn't come over. Unusual enough, but Charlotte had been busy at work and on her book and ignored the nagging anxiety that something was wrong.

But when Charlotte went over for their weekly tea and Hannah hadn't answered the door, she was really worried. The next morning when Hannah still wasn't home that's when Bess thought it was time to start asking questions and start looking for her.

They hadn't seen Hannah for days. Where was she?

As Charlotte recalled the holidays, her eyes were on the snowy scene outside. If Hannah was out there somewhere she could be hurt or sick. She didn't want to dwell on that. Hannah was an old woman no matter how spunky she was. The island was eighty percent woods and there were numerous places to get lost. The snow was deep, the winds arctic and an elderly person wouldn't last long.

Charlotte was grateful when Mac got there.

"I had a time getting over here." Standing at the door he took off his goggles. The whiteness could be hard on the eyes so the islanders wore tinted goggles when riding their snowmobiles in the snow. "The wind's fierce, it nearly blew me off my machine."

"You made it, though. Where's that lull you said we were going to get?" Charlotte asked, trying not to let him see how uncomfortable his being there, real as could be and near enough to touch, made her. She'd plastered a smile on her lips.

She struggled to see the resemblance to the boy she'd once known at Hannah's house. There wasn't any. None at all. After she'd hung up the phone she'd run upstairs to take a two-minute shower, put on a more attractive sweater and a dab of make-up.

At first Charlotte wouldn't meet his eyes when he spoke. Snow was sloughing off his uniform coat and melting onto the floor. Winter had snuck in with him and cold air filled the entry hall.

"It's coming. The squall's calming down as we speak." His eyes were on her aunt. "Believe me, it was worse a few hours ago. I was out in it." He'd lost weight and looked good. With his mesmerizing blue eyes, rugged face framed with soft curling hair and competent attitude that encouraged trust he was more handsome than she remembered. Or perhaps she'd been the one to change and was seeing him through different eyes.

Charlotte handed him a cup of coffee and as he drank it he asked about Hannah. He kept smiling at her. He wasn't angry with her. Maybe he never had been.

"Let's go over and have a look at Hannah's house," he said.

The three tramped next door through the snow and let themselves in with Bess's key.

After a thorough search, Mac concluded, "The thermostat has been set on sixty and the house is chilly. She does that when she knows she's going to be gone for a while.

"No recent cooking smells, or plates in the sink or leftovers in the refrigerator. No evidence that she's been here recently. Your theory, Charlotte," Mac glanced at her, "that she might have gone across the ice bridge to visit the mainland is a distinct possibility. She uses the bridge every year, all the time. She loves it when she gets to go across for free. The thing is, that's no crime and it doesn't mean anything bad has befallen her. She might have gone shopping on the mainland and decided to layover at a friend's or some motel somewhere because of the storm.

"Hannah, you know, is quite well off. She might act tight with a dollar but she has money. She's probably out spending some of it."

"And has been gone for three days?" Charlotte was doubtful.

"She doesn't have any relatives or friends alive anymore on St. Ignace," Bess told him. "So where would she be?"

"A motel or a modest-priced bed and breakfast?" Mac didn't sound so sure.

"Hannah wouldn't stay at a motel or a B and B. She'd say it was a waste of good money when she has a perfectly fine house not far away on the island." Bess was shaking her head. "Mac, rich or not, you know how frugal she is. She would have come home if she could have."

He nodded. "I know. She does what she wants to do and goes where she wants to go. Hannah is one plucky woman. You'd never guess she's almost eighty."

"If she'd had to stay over anywhere she would have telephoned us if she were able to," Charlotte echoed what her aunt had said before. "She wouldn't have wanted us to worry like this."

"No, she wouldn't have. Still there's no indication of foul play." Mac stood by Hannah's front door, his hand on the knob. Outside the wind had died down to a soft growl.

"Something's happened to her," Bess insisted. "I feel it."

Mac let out a sigh. "All right. I'll start calling around and if there's no sign of her, I'll gather a search party and we'll start looking for her. We have miles of ground to cover, though, and with another storm nudging in, time's short."

That's when Charlotte caught sight of the scrap of paper beneath the coffee table in the living room. It must have fallen to the floor. She picked it up and read it. "It's a note from Hannah dated three days ago. She says she's gone across the ice bridge to meet someone—doesn't say who—and she'll be back by dark. At the bottom she's noted the time. Three-thirty. That's pretty late when it gets dark these days by five-thirty."

"She's not afraid of the dark," Bess said. "She would have gone anyway."

Charlotte handed the note to Mac. "She left the note in case one of us came over and wanted to know where she was. That was three days ago. Like my aunt, I have this terrible feeling something really is wrong."

Charlotte was thinking about how good Hannah had been to her since she'd come to the island; thinking about all the advice and caring, the teas and the hours they'd spent together, the books Hannah had lent her and the fascinating ghost tales and anecdotes she'd woven for her of her life. The old woman had become dear to her. She was upset that she was missing.

"Mac, I can't sit by and do nothing. I have to

help. Now. I'm going to put on my coat, get on my snowmobile and start looking while there's still light."

"You're determined to do that even with another storm coming in, aren't you?"

"Nothing will stop me."

"You going across the ice bridge?"

"Well...." No. Her fear of the ice bridge hadn't lessened and she wasn't actually sure of its location. Her fear was unreasonable and she was too embarrassed to admit it to anyone. Not even her aunt. She'd thought she'd ride around the island seeking Hannah and checking at her friends, that sort of thing, but she hadn't planned on crossing the ice. Truth was, and she knew it, if Hannah were anywhere she'd be on the route to or from the mainland. She would have used the ice bridge.

Darn it. She had to go over the ice bridge, scared or not, and she'd do it for Hannah. "I imagine I'll have to, seeing as that's the way Hannah probably went."

"But you're not going by yourself and you're not going today," Mac cautioned. "You shouldn't be alone the first time you go across to the mainland and especially not in this kind of weather. Someone should go with you. If you've never gone across, you might have a hard time finding it. And if the weather worsens, well, it's smart not to go alone."

"I have to go. Someone's got to look for her. Now."

"Then I'll accompany you. I'll show you where the ice bridge is and make sure you don't get lost. I was thinking of checking the mainland first anyway.

The uniform gets answers quicker and four eyes are better than two if you're looking for someone."

"I'll take you up on that offer. Thank you, Mac." It was the only thing she could say because she was in a hurry. All she could think about was Hannah being out in the snow somewhere, lost and alone. They had to find her, a matter of life or death, and they were wasting precious time.

Outside it was snowing again. The world was becoming grayer every minute.

"I'll stay here," Bess announced, "in case Hannah shows up or tries to call."

"Okay," Charlotte agreed.

"You might talk to someone at the grocery store in St. Ignace when you get over there," Bess suggested. "And the dollar store. A little lunch place called Freddy's. Those are some of the places Hannah frequents when she's there. She wouldn't squander a trip to the mainland, she'd use it to shop or run errands."

"We'll check them out," Mac said. "Could be someone's seen her someplace. We gotta start somewhere. While you're getting ready, Charlotte, I'll report Hannah missing and have the station put out an APB on her. That way they can start searching the woods up to and surrounding the ice bridge or visiting the places around here where she might have tarried."

Of her aunt he asked, "When we get back to your house can I use your phone, Bess?"

"Of course you can."

The three left Hannah's house, locked it up, and trudged back to Bess's. Charlotte dashed upstairs and threw on a double layer of clothing and two thick wool hats, two pairs of gloves and a facemask. She put on her new yellow parka with the fur-lined hood. She knew she looked comical, but she'd be warm.

Mac was on the phone, his face half turned away from her, when she came downstairs. He didn't know she was there so she secretly watched him. He knew what he was doing. He was confident in his job. She trusted him. She'd go anywhere with him.

Mac smiled at her when she walked into the room. It reminded her of the smile he'd given her when they'd met on the ferryboat that first morning on the island. A little more restrained. He was worried about Hannah, too.

Mac got off the phone. "Are you ready, Charlotte?" There was humor in his eyes as he took in her layers of clothing and the wool facemask in her hand.

"Ready."

"At least," he joked, "I won't lose you in the snow, not with that banana colored parka on. Whew, it's bright."

"Yeah, isn't it? Hannah gave it to me for Christmas. You like it?"

"Like I said, it's eye catching." He hid a smile. "Got a pair of goggles?"

"In my pocket."

Charlotte said goodbye to her aunt, promised to be careful, and tailed Mac out into the wintry afternoon. With her extra clothes on, it didn't feel so cold to her. That wouldn't last long. The temperature was supposed to keep dropping throughout the day.

As she sat on the seat of her snowmobile, hand shading her eyes from the snow glare, Mac came over. She'd been ready to slip on her shaded glasses but waited.

"I want you to listen to me and follow everything I tell you."

Tilting her face upward towards him, she bobbed her head. "I'm listening."

"Stay close behind me all the way, especially when we're on the ice bridge. Don't go off the path marked by the Christmas trees. You're safe if you stay five, six feet on either side of them. If you see a mushy area, go around it. If you're not sure, stop, beep your horn and I'll double back to help you. If you get into trouble of any kind, beep your horn three times in quick succession. I'll know you need immediate help."

He peered up into the sky. "Switch your lights on now. It'll be easier for us to see each other if this snow comes down any harder or when the light fades."

"Okay, Mac. Lead on." She was relieved to be doing something yet she was becoming increasingly concerned over Hannah's whereabouts every second. She wanted to get going.

Mac stomped back to his snowmobile, started it up and pulled out ahead of her. She remembered his promise that day at the Grand Hotel when they were out in the gardens to take her across the ice bridge for the first time. He was keeping that promise.

She'd thought about that day often, and how

much fun they'd had, and what could have been. But at that moment Hannah was the only thing on her mind. Where was she? Was she all right?

Charlotte and Mac headed towards British Landing where the ice bridge began. The snowplows had been busy on the roads leaving a light covering of snow so snowmobiles could run smoothly. They made as good a time as they were able.

Because of the lousy weather, there weren't many people about. Charlotte kept a lookout for any abandoned snowmobiles along the side of the road, or signs of Hannah collapsed in a heap or stumbling through the snow somewhere. She kept expecting to see her, but didn't.

The mantle of snow muffled, changed everything. The ground was glistening white. The woods were frozen crystal trees, silently motionless, for the wind had momentarily died down. The scenery reminded Charlotte of the inside of one of those fanciful snow globes.

How different Mackinac was in the winter compared to the summer. It was another world altogether. Charlotte had begun to take pleasure in it until Hannah had come up missing.

As they rode through town, billows of gray-edged smoke rose from house chimneys and darkened the skies. Most people were hibernating, warm and safe, at home before their fires and Charlotte envied them. They weren't out traipsing around in sub-zero weather in a snowstorm looking for a lost friend.

Mac led her to British Landing and out towards

Lake Huron. As they hit the edge of land and water she saw the ice bridge for the first time. The expanse of solid ice stretched into the distant horizon as if it went on forever. It was snow-covered gleaming ivory, and she couldn't tell where the island ended and the ice began.

Gloomy clouds hovered above and cried snow on the world. The uneven line of evergreen trees silhouetted against the gray was the only hint of color on the landscape. The snow and the drabness of the day muted them.

It was spooky.

Mac brought his machine to a halt as she chugged up on the right of him. "I haven't seen anyone since we left the town limits." His voice was loud enough to be heard above the rising wind and their idling engines. His face below his cap was scarlet from the cold. His lips were paler than when they'd begun their trip.

"Me, neither," she bellowed back. Her hands in her double-layered gloves were numb.

"Well, here's the bridge," Mac shouted. "Stay behind me and keep your eyes open for Hannah and any weak spots in the ice. It's supposed to be solid, though it's only been five days and we've had fluctuating temperatures the last few. It might not be safe no matter what anyone says."

Charlotte moved her head up and down, watching Mac's breath float away in mouth-sized puffs of vapor, and tried not to let him see her unease. "You take point. I'll follow."

It was eerie skimming across the ice, hearing it crunch beneath her snowmobile's treads with white stuff falling around them, the wind howling past. To know, except for the freezing of mere water, that they'd be hundreds of feet below in liquid right now with the fishes. She didn't like it.

At least it was daytime for a while longer, anyway.

She tried not to think about the churning water below the crust as they made their way towards the mainland. She stayed close to Mac and the evergreens. Her eyes scanned the ice around them for traces of Hannah, but there was nothing but smooth snow and ice. No one had traveled across except them.

Charlotte exhaled an inward sigh of relief when they reached the other side.

They drove to the grocery store two miles away from the bridge, and questioned the clerks and manager. Some knew Hannah by description or by name but no one had seen her in weeks. Charlotte had done Hannah's shopping the last couple times along with her own. It was the same story at the dollar store and the other places. No one had seen Hannah in a long time.

"Well." Mac was standing by the door inside Freddy's Bar & Grill, their last possibility. "It was a long shot since Hannah's note stated she was coming to the mainland to meet someone. It didn't say a thing about shopping or eating out."

They'd looked everywhere they could think of, prowling around St. Ignace, down the streets and alleys, hunting for Hannah's snowmobile. They'd ended up at the police station and spoke to St. Ignace's Chief of Police, Sid Willowby. He said he'd have his officers keep an eye out for anyone fitting Hannah's description. He'd contact Mac if they learned anything of interest or located her.

"Now what do we do?" Charlotte wanted to know.

"We head home. I don't know what else we can do. We don't have the time to inquire at every store or restaurant in town with nightfall and another storm coming in. It would have helped if Hannah had said where that meeting with that unknown person was going to be, or if she'd left us a telephone number, but she didn't. She could be anywhere."

They tromped out into Freddy's parking lot with snow high around their boots. The weather had worsened. The flakes were crashing down. The wind shoved them around violently. It was two in the afternoon but the clouds had deepened the day to a dusky hue.

Mac gazed into the white skies. The temperature had also plunged since they'd been in the bar. The cold froze bare skin in seconds. "I bet that blizzard's going to come in sooner than they predicted. If we don't get back we'll have to stay the night in St. Ignace."

"That wouldn't do. We have no time for that. We have to keep looking for Hannah."

"I know."

Charlotte snapped goggles on her face and thrust her hands into her gloves as the wind played a tug of war with her. "With the blizzard coming in, maybe she's made it back home. Wouldn't that be great?"

"I wouldn't count on it, but it would be great."

"So now we return to the island?"

"We go back. But we can keep looking for Hannah along the way. Stay behind me. We'll take a different route and drive on the other side of the path across the bridge. Keep your eyes open."

"I will."

They climbed on their snowmobiles and aimed them towards the island.

By the time they crossed the ice bridge Charlotte had to struggle with the wind to stay on her machine. She was sick they hadn't found Hannah, and she was frightened, tired and freezing. Her body had lost all sensation. She thought she had fingers in her gloves, but she wasn't sure.

The ice bridge was eerier returning than when they'd come, if that was possible. An early night had descended, though the snow illuminated their surroundings enough so they could see. It almost made their headlights unnecessary. The ice was lit up as if there were lights glowing beneath it. Strange noises, sounding like distant moans and cries for help, rushed by her head.

She remembered what Hannah had said about the ice bridge ghosts. In her state of mind, she could imagine misty shapes flitting around the ice behind and around them, trying to tell them something. Did they know where Hannah was? If she looked quick enough she thought she saw them with their hollow ghost eyes in their transparent ghost bodies. It seemed they were closing in on her and Mac.

Hannah believed the ice bridge ghosts appeared when someone was about to die—or had died.

She panicked as her snowmobile sped over the ice, the wind behind shoving her along, faster and faster, as if it was trying to escape something. She was practically on top of Mac as a wave of vertigo hit her. She slowed down before she rammed him.

Her machine went into a skid and barely avoided hitting one of the evergreens. She took a couple of deep breaths to push the dizziness away. Out of the corner of her eyes, she thought she saw something standing on the ice to her right, lost in the particles of drifting snow. It looked like a shadow of a woman with her arms outstretched. Then it was gone. Yet for the split heartbeat it was there, it had scared the heck out of her. It had looked like Hannah. Impossible.

Charlotte wanted to get back to her aunt's house where it was warm and safe; where there were no spectral shapes to taunt her. She'd never been out in a pre-blizzard before. She was beginning to understand what Mac had meant when he'd said that a whiteout could be disorienting. She wondered if it could also make a person see things that weren't there.

She kept her attention on Mac's silhouette when she wasn't looking for a lost snowmobile and its rider. She didn't want to see anything else. About three-fourths of the way to the other side, with land and trees in front of them, her eye caught unevenness in the snow a little ways off the secure path. Something in the air behind her, or was it in her head, whispered to *stop. Look.*

After honking the horn and blinking her lights three times, she swerved closer, but not too close, to the rough patch. She cut the engine and dug out a flashlight from the saddlebag to examine the irregularities. In the glow, she saw there were spikes in the blanket of snow covering the ice.

Had something gone through the ice there?

She was on her knees, with her face in her hands, when Mac joined her with another flashlight. He gently brought her to her feet and guided her to her snowmobile. He walked back to the rough patch. He examined it, getting as near as he dared. He directed his flashlight at the mound. Charlotte could tell by the way his shoulders slumped that he'd found something he hadn't wanted to find.

He returned to her. The wind had died down to a whisper after the roar.

"Something's gone through the ice in days past. It's been broken and refrozen."

"Hannah?" she breathed.

"Could be. It's too early to know. Sometimes something goes through and crawls out, wet, scared and cold but alive. It happens. Maybe a deer or a bear. There are bears on the mainland; did you know that? Every once in a while they wander onto the ice. Anyway, the unevenness doesn't necessarily mean something is down there and doesn't mean it's Hannah, either."

Mac put his arm around Charlotte's shoulders. "Let's go before the storm gets any worse and we get lost, too. When it passes I'll get men out here to see if there's anything down there. Come on."

He drove beside her to shore, both of them staying so tight to the evergreens they clipped a few. She wanted to reach the woods, the solid ground of the island. She wanted to get off the ice bridge and leave what she feared she'd seen on the ice—the ghosts—behind them.

****

Bess knew when she saw their faces they'd found something. She was in her robe. There was hot coffee and sandwiches waiting for them. "You found Hannah?"

"No," Mac answered first. "But we found a...disturbance in the ice on the bridge."

"Something's gone through?"

"It looks like it." Mac condensed their trip for Bess. He finished by saying that tomorrow they'd search the lake under the suspicious spot they'd found; but now he had business to take care of at the police station. He left without touching the coffee or the food.

After the door closed behind him Charlotte's thoughts were heavy. She couldn't stand to think of Hannah out there alone somewhere or to think the old woman might never come back. Her mind refused to go any further than that.

"There's something he's not telling us," her aunt said as they were eating bacon sandwiches and drinking coffee. The night blizzard was raging beyond the windows. The world outside was all snow and fury. The storm had hit full force. The house shook. Charlotte was so grateful she and Mac had made it back before the worst of the blizzard.

If Hannah wasn't below the ice she was out there somewhere, perhaps in the storm, and both realities made Charlotte feel like crying. *Poor lady. She must be so frightened. Unless she was dead.*

Charlotte pushed that thought away and told herself: *I have to stay calm and be there for my aunt. She's devastated and worried enough over Hannah being missing.*

Bess was still grieving over Shawn being gone. It'd been two months. Instead of getting better her aunt's depression was getting worse. When she wasn't working at the Mustang Lounge she'd lay around in her robe and scuffed slippers and mope or eat. She'd gained weight. Since Christmas Eve, when Charlotte had believed her aunt had made a turnaround, she'd only slipped deeper into her sadness.

Shawn hadn't written, hadn't called, and as the time went by it became apparent that he wasn't going to. Bess hadn't accepted the end of their actual friendship, not even when he'd given notice to his job that he wasn't returning in the spring. Not even when he'd gone home.

"I always thought we'd find a way for us to be together. Now that will never happen. Look at me, I'm old and chubby, who'd want me now?"

"Someone would. You just have to get out more so he can find you."

Charlotte was tired of seeing her aunt's melancholy face. She wanted to shake her, tell her to snap out of it. She wanted to help ease her pain. Charlotte didn't know how to do that other than to be there for her when she was needed.

Now this terrible thing had happened with Hannah coming up missing.

It was awful not doing anything more to find the old woman. Yet outside, the stormy night made the situation too treacherous to risk it—or Charlotte would have been out there searching.

"You're still interested in Mac," her aunt said to Charlotte as they prepared for bed. Charlotte was weary from her frozen journey and of her dark thoughts. She couldn't stop seeing that glazed opening in the ice. She couldn't stop thinking about those shadows on the frozen water. She didn't want to think about ghosts or dead people anymore, so sleep was an escape. She needed it, even if it brought nightmares. In any case, they'd be different nightmares from the one she was living.

"I do like Mac. He's a good man. We're friends again. I'm thankful. But he has someone else."

Her aunt studied her. "You haven't lost Mac until you give up. If you love the man go after him. Tell him. You don't really know if he's in love with another woman. He's not married or engaged, that I've heard of, and you don't know if he's even in love with this girl because you haven't asked. You don't know how he feels about you. You need to find out. So stop being a wimp. Fight for him."

Charlotte began to protest but knew her aunt was right. Mac had no idea how she felt now. It might make a difference and it might not. So she owed it to him, and to herself, to tell him the truth.

Her thoughts snapped back to Hannah. She couldn't wait for morning when she could continue hunting for her friend. She'd see Mac again, too. Yet how could she tell him what she felt for him in the midst of Hannah being lost? It wasn't something she had an answer for at the moment. She was too tired. Too distressed. She'd face it when the sun came up. That would be soon enough.

Hannah, where are you? What's happened to you? Please God, let her be okay.

Charlotte closed her eyes and after all the stress of the day, sleep came swiftly and with no dreams.

Chapter 5

Charlotte woke the following morning to a somber knocking at the front door. The hands of her alarm clock pointed to ten. She hadn't wanted to sleep that late. She had things to do. Twisting around in her bed, she scooted her face toward the window and looked outside into faint sunlight. The storm had ended and the snow was at least three feet deep.

Charlotte wasn't going to work that day; neither was Bess. They had to do whatever it took to find Hannah. Charlotte refused to think about the ice bridge or what she and Mac had discovered. She wanted to believe Hannah was out there somewhere alive, and not beneath the ice.

She stared down through the glass of the window as Mac stepped off the porch and peered up at her. By the seriousness of his face she knew something had changed.

She heard her aunt open the door and let him in.

With trembling fingers, Charlotte dressed and went downstairs. Her aunt was weeping at the kitchen table. Mac was consoling her.

"You found Hannah?" Charlotte didn't want the answer but she had to know.

"I'm afraid we might have. I'm sorry. Sit down. I'll tell you about it." He seemed exhausted.

Charlotte settled down beside her aunt. She

readied herself for bad news.

"At dawn this morning the rescue team began dredging the lake beneath the abnormality we found yesterday. They dragged the water. Though they didn't snag a body or a snowmobile, they're pretty sure someone went under the ice. The underwater currents are powerful and swift moving so it's possible we might not find a body until spring when the ice melts."

Mac took something out of a plastic bag he'd had in his coat pocket. He laid it on the table in front of the two women. It was a bright red mitten, wet, trimmed with black thread, and unraveling along the edges.

"Do either of you recognize this?"

Bess gasped and reached out to touch it. "It's one of Hannah's. I gave her these mittens for Christmas. They're brand new. Or they were."

Charlotte recognized the mittens, too. When Hannah had unwrapped them she'd thrust them on her small hands and had pretended they were talking eyeless puppets. She'd had everyone laughing with her puppets' lame jokes and antics.

"They found this mitten frozen into the ice on the edge of the irregularity. The rescue crew believes it belonged to the victim." Mac glanced at the mitten in the middle of the table. "If it is Hannah's, then chances are good she's the one who went into the water. I'm sorry. I loved the old woman, too, you know."

Charlotte was in shock. After they'd found the unevenness in the ice she hadn't wanted to believe that a person could be down there or that it would be Hannah.

*Not Hannah...*sweet old lady, her dear friend and like a mother to Bess all these years.

"She drowned?" Tears were trickling down Charlotte's face.

"How did she wander off the path? It isn't like Hannah to make such a mistake." Bess groaned. "She's smarter than that."

"I don't know what happened," he admitted to both women. "We might never know."

"With those undercurrents it is possible, isn't it, that we won't ever recover Hannah's body?" Charlotte asked. She'd read something once in a book about someone being swept under ice. They hadn't recovered that body either.

"It's possible."

"So how will we be sure it was Hannah?" Charlotte was assailed by an unexpected vision of a crowd of phantoms in the mist hovering on the ice and smiling forlornly at her. One of them waved with one red mitten. It was Hannah.

Mac came to his feet and stuffed the mitten into its plastic bag and then into his coat pocket. "Well, if she never comes home we'll know. The search team will continue to look for a while but I don't think they'll have much luck until the spring thaw. Then they'll be able to dredge more successfully and send down divers. Right now it's too cold and there's too much ice."

Mac turned to Bess. "We need to find out if Hannah has any living relatives. She never talked about them with me. Did she tell you anything about her family?"

"She didn't have any children," Bess said, wiping the tears from her eyes. "She had sisters but both are dead now. I don't think she has any living relatives but I'm not positive of that. She didn't speak of them anyway. She said the past was the past. You know how she was, Mac.

"But I guess we could go through her papers and her telephone numbers and try to dig up names. She's got old friends here on the island from her childhood who might be able to help."

"Those are places to start."

Charlotte was lamenting that Hannah could be dead and was furious at the useless way she'd died. After she'd put her arms around her aunt and had given her a comforting embrace, she made a pot of coffee. It gave her something to do when all she wanted was to curl up somewhere and weep. Underlying her own sorrow, she was afraid for Bess. Between Shawn's exit and Hannah's disappearance, her aunt was going to be a real mess.

Hannah's absence was going to hurt both of them so much.

Once she'd made coffee, Charlotte took out a carton of eggs and a pan.

"I'm going to make scrambled eggs, bacon and some toast," she announced in an emotionless voice. "Mac, sit back down, you look like you could use a hot meal. Will you have breakfast with us?"

She was sure he was going to say no, but he didn't. "I will. After the night and the morning I've had, a warm meal and friendly company is what I need. Thank you."

Bess was sobbing silently. Mac had his arms

around her again. "It'll be okay, Bess. If Hannah died beneath the ice she didn't suffer long. All in all, she had a long life, was happy, and was loved by a lot of people. She's in heaven now."

Mac spoke as if Hannah were really dead.

As Charlotte served the eggs and bacon, her mind replayed memories of the old woman: *Hannah out in her garden, giggling over their weekly teas, playing cards or board games with her and Bess, opening her Christmas presents like a delighted child, waving from her snowmobile out in the streets of the village.* That old woman had sure enjoyed life. She'd made people smile and had a rare joy for living. She'd taught Charlotte to be happy again; she taught her that one bad love affair in the scheme of things wasn't the end of the world.

Get off your pity pot and try again. Life is for living. Live it was Hannah's epigram for life.

Charlotte didn't want her friend to be dead. She'd miss her. No more heart-to-heart chats in Hannah's cozy kitchen while the hand-painted teapot was whistling. No more ghost stories or tall tales about past lovers. No more shoulder to cry on. No more Hannah.

Charlotte had suspected Mac was withholding information the night before so she probed, "Mac, is there something you're not telling us?"

"What do you mean?" he mumbled between bites of buttered toast, his eyes abruptly evasive and secretive.

Bess looked at him, too. "What do you think happened to Hannah? How did she go through the ice? She's been going across the ice bridge since she was a girl. How could she not know the ice was weak in that spot?"

"At first I asked myself the same thing." Mac pulled a sigh through his clenched teeth. "Hannah was sharp for her age, but who knows? She might have gotten sick. People over seventy have strokes or heart attacks all the time. That old snowmobile of hers was heavier than the newer ones. That might have helped her break through the ice.

"Yet I can't figure why she was out there in the first place with a storm and night coming. That note she left had a time on it. She didn't leave herself much daylight to get there and return."

Bess was no longer crying but her eyes were red over the rim of her coffee cup. She'd eaten just a couple bites of breakfast. "Hannah didn't care if it was the middle of the night," she said, "if she had somewhere to go, she'd go. She was fearless for her age. Healthy. She didn't have any chronic ailments that I was aware of."

None of them had eaten much. The bacon and eggs on their plates were cold.

Mac was thinking out loud. "The question I have is, what was so important that she had to go to the mainland that night? Why couldn't it have waited until the next morning?"

Charlotte and Bess shook their heads. They didn't know.

"Now that's a good question," Charlotte directed her words to Mac.

The phone rang and Bess picked it up. Charlotte bent across the table and asked Mac in a lowered voice so Bess wouldn't hear, "There's still something you're not telling us, isn't there? Come on, spill it."

His eyelids closed a moment, but he gave in. "I wasn't going to talk about it but it's going to come out eventually. For now don't say anything about this to your aunt. We don't want to upset her any more than she already is."

"Well?"

"I inspected the rough spot in the ice before they started drilling this morning. It seemed suspicious to me. There were scraps of reddish paper without writing on them embedded in the layers as they were dug out. I've seen this sort of thing before. It looked like bits of a wrapper from some sort of plastic explosive. But it's hard to tell."

Charlotte sat back. "What are you saying?"

"That Hannah's being out there and falling through the ice might not have been an accident after all. Someone might have lured her out there so she could fall through the ice that had been purposely weakened with explosives."

"Why in the world would anyone want to harm or kill a nice old lady like Hannah?" Charlotte was stunned. "Everyone loved her."

"If I knew the answer to that then maybe I'd know if a crime has been committed or not. That red stuff looked like an explosive's covering is what I'm saying, that's all. It might not be. Until it's examined at the lab, we won't be sure

"Not an accident?" she echoed. It wasn't sinking in.

"My gut instinct tells me something doesn't feel right."

"What you're saying is that someone might have killed Hannah? That's ridiculous. That would mean it was murder."

"I know. Murder's an extremely rare occurrence on Mackinac. There hasn't been a murder on the island for years, at least not since I've been in the Department anyway."

"She might have been murdered?" Charlotte was mulling the ramifications over in her head. Knowing Hannah the way she'd come to know her, she couldn't believe she'd been stupid enough to crash through the ice, but murder made even less sense. "By someone she was meeting on the mainland?"

"That's one possibility."

"Then we need to investigate and find out who she was meeting that night. And why."

"Whoa," Mac reminded her, "that's my job."

"And it's my responsibility as Hannah's friend and neighbor. If she was murdered, I want to know. I want to help find her murderer. I owe it to her, Mac. She was kind to me when I needed it the most. I want to help."

"I know you loved her, Charlotte, so did I. So did Bess. But if there was foul play in her death—and I repeat *if*—it could be dangerous sticking your nose into it. If there was a murder then there's a murderer who isn't going to look kindly on your interference."

Charlotte glared at him. "I'm not afraid."

"You should be. If someone did this on purpose and you start asking the wrong questions in the wrong places, it might make you a target."

"I can take care of myself."

Mac stared at her as if she were crazy. "Please, though, don't mention anything about my suspicion to your aunt. Not yet."

"I won't. Anyway," Charlotte finished sullenly, "at this point this conversation is unnecessary. No one's murdered anyone that we know of. As of now, if it was Hannah who went under the ice the other night so far there's no motive for it. She might be dead, and that's hard enough to swallow right now, but if so, it might have just been a tragic accident. I still can't believe someone would murder her."

Mac didn't say anything to her denials. Denial was her way of dealing with the situation. They were silent when Bess rejoined them.

"Who was on the phone?" Charlotte asked.

"Wilma down at the mercantile store. The town's grapevine is working just fine. She told me that someone went under the ice the other night on the ice bridge. It's all over the village. Jed Stern saw the rescue team down there early this morning and has spread the news to everyone he knows."

"Did you tell them we think it was Hannah?" Charlotte looked out the window at Hannah's empty house. She had a spare key, as did Bess, only Charlotte hadn't gotten around to telling her aunt about it. Hannah had given her one weeks ago. Had the old woman had a premonition of her own death? Charlotte didn't know. They'd have to get into the house and look around for clues. Until Hannah came home, they'd have to take care of the place. If she came home.

"No. I thanked Wilma for the gossip and got off the phone as soon as I could. I couldn't bring myself to talk about it yet."

It was as if saying Hannah could be dead might make it true.

Charlotte was trying to remember what else Hannah had said the week before. The old woman hadn't wanted to discuss what was bothering her but had given Charlotte the house key. "Just in case you need to get in, here, dear." Now why had Hannah done that? What had she been worried about?

Bess was crying softly as if the phone call had further distressed her. Charlotte put her arms around her. Her aunt's body was trembling.

Recently it was as if Charlotte had become the older of the two women, a wiser sister instead of a niece. Bess looked to her to keep her flagging spirits up.

"Thanks for breakfast. Sorry I wasn't hungrier." Mac rose from his chair, sending a conspiratorial look at Charlotte. *Remember, don't mention murder to your aunt. Not yet.*

"I should get back to my men on the ice bridge," he spoke to Bess. "I thought you'd like to know what we found so far, though."

"We appreciate you keeping us up to date on what's going on." Her aunt paused a second. "If Hannah's really gone, I'd like to have a memorial here at the house for her. Her birthday is next week. We could have a sort of celebration anyway to show how much we'll miss her, how much we loved her. To say that she was a special part of our lives and we'll never forget her."

"There won't be a body for a funeral, Bess." Mac was putting his coat on and his expression was weary. "Unless we find one before then."

"I know. But, if it turns out she's really gone, we can mark her passing anyway. We have to do something. Hannah was worth more than that. People will want some kind of closure. They'll want to say their goodbyes. Then if the body's found we can have a proper funeral later."

Mac nodded. "If that's what you want. Be sure to invite me for the memorial. Call me, I'll come."

Bess sent a furtive glance Charlotte's way. "You know, Mac, you're welcome here any time so don't be a stranger. Charlotte's missed you, too, though she'd be the last one to say it. Life is too short to stay mad at each other. No one knows how much time we have. Look at Hannah."

"We aren't mad at each other," Mac responded a little too quickly.

"No—we aren't." Charlotte felt her face turn red. "We've just been busy."

"I'll look forward to Hannah's memorial birthday celebration. I'll be here." Mac was watching Charlotte and when she smiled at him, he smiled back. She caught a spark of something in his eyes. Hope? Affection? He turned away too quickly for her to be sure.

"I'll walk you out, Officer," Charlotte announced before she could stop herself as Bess stayed behind in the kitchen to clean up.

At the door she stood as close to Mac as she could get and forced him to look at her. She took the plunge. "Mac, I want to tell you that I've missed our friendship. I've had time to heal. I'm ready to go on with my life. If you can forgive me for brushing you off like I did that day at the hotel...I'd like to be friends again. I never meant to hurt you. I guess all I was thinking about that day was myself."

"It's okay. You were hurting. I understood that once I thought about it," Mac said softly looking her directly in the eyes for the first time. "I never held anything you did or said against you. I've never stopped being your friend, Charlotte. I was only giving you the space you asked for. All you ever had to do was call me and I would have been here."

"I know." Studying his face, she knew it was true.

Bowing his head, he whispered, "I've missed you, too. It's good to be talking, good to know we're friends again even under the unhappy circumstances."

She almost asked about the girl she'd seen him with on Christmas Eve but she couldn't bring herself to do it. It was his business. He'd tell her if he wanted to. It seemed so unimportant now that Hannah was missing and might be dead. She still couldn't face it.

"Friends." Spontaneously she reached up and gave him a hug. He hugged her back. A peacefulness settled over her. He made her feel as if nothing bad could happen to her as long as he was with her. She hadn't been prepared for that.

"Friends." He smiled down at her. "I want you to know that you can call me anytime if you need to talk or if you're feeling sad about Hannah."

"I will."

Outside the snow had started up again, with large sparkling flakes that clung to the trees and old snow.

Charlotte was sick over the situation with Hannah but Mac being beside her calmed her. Perhaps there was a chance for them. Except it was so new, so gentle a bond, spun glass, she couldn't risk breaking it by saying the wrong thing. She had to be so careful.

"I need to get back to the rescue team. See if they've found anything else. They're expecting another foot of snow before the end of the day and there's more we can do. I'm having a friend of mine, Detective Sully Armstrong of the Grand Rapids Police Department, inspect the ice. He's flying up this morning. We'll see if he agrees with me that explosives may have been used. I'll let you know what he says."

"Thanks, Mac."

"So how's that book of yours coming?"

"You remembered. I'm flattered." She stepped away from him and leaned against the door. If she had stayed in his arms another second she might have told him how she was really beginning to feel about him. But it was too soon.

"People on the island have been gossiping about it. I overhear their conversations."

"It's going well. I've got plenty of stories, with more coming in every day."

"Could I read some of them?" he asked.

"You really want to?"

"I really want to. You know I love a good ghost story."

"How could I forget? You gave me the idea to write the book in the first place. Usually," she hesitated, "I wouldn't let anyone read what I've written. Not until after a final draft. But...for you...you can see what I have so far."

"Sometime soon?"

"Soon." She had to fight to keep from smiling.

Seeing Mac's shape merge into the curtain of snow as he drove away on his snowmobile she thought how good it was to have him around again. Sighing inwardly, she returned to the kitchen and her aunt, and the reality of Hannah being missing.

****

"Did you tell the guy that you're nuts about him?" Bess pried.

"What, and scare him off?"

"I don't think it would. I think he's been waiting for you to make a move."

"I let slip that I've missed him. We've agreed to be friends again." Getting a cup of coffee, Charlotte sat down at the table her aunt had cleared off.

Seeing Bess's teary face diluted her happiness at making up with Mac. She shouldn't be smiling when Hannah was probably...gone.

"About time you two made up." Her aunt put her face in her hands. "I can't believe Hannah could be dead. I feel so bad about it. She was such a good soul. I loved her so much."

Charlotte wished she could fix things for her aunt, but she didn't know how to do that. She couldn't make Shawn come back and she couldn't change what might have happened to Hannah. All she could do was be there for her.

"I want to go out and keep searching for Hannah," her aunt said. "Though I suspect it would be useless. She's been missing for four days. No one's seen her. That red mitten was hers. It's too coincidental not to mean something."

Charlotte was suddenly cold. She couldn't stop shivering. "Aunt Bess, let's go into the living room and make a big fire in the fireplace."

"I'd rather get drunk," her aunt muttered listlessly. When she saw the look on Charlotte's face, she added, "But I won't. Getting drunk won't bring Hannah back; it would only give me a hangover tomorrow and make me feel worse than I already do. I feel lousy enough."

"You've got a good point there. So we'll have spiked hot apple cider instead. I'll make it and you can put a little whiskey in it. Not too much, though."

They built a fire, sat in front of it, and ended up remembering Hannah. They talked about what she'd meant to them and told stories about some of the funny and generous things she'd done. "She'd love it that we're talking about her like this," Bess remarked later. "She did like being the center of attention."

The phone calls asking about Hannah and the rumors of her possible death began early and lasted throughout the day. Charlotte and Bess took turns speaking and recounting what they knew to Hannah's friends and acquaintances. Bess sniffled during most of the conversations.

It was a long day.

Outside the hours of light seeped away and by

late afternoon the snow swirled around in tiny tornadoes. The frost on the outside of the windows was so thick Charlotte had to look through the middle to see anything.

Late in the evening Mac phoned Charlotte to say a body still hadn't been found; that the search had been called off because of the foul weather. They would pick up where they left off when the snowstorm passed and the light returned. Sounding exhausted and promising to call them if anything else developed, he said goodnight. He suggested they get some rest. They were going to need it.

Charlotte and Bess retired early that night, drained from the drama, the worry and phone calls. They hoped tomorrow would bring better news, but feared it wouldn't.

Charlotte had a hard time capturing sleep because she didn't want to dream of the ghosts that haunted the ice bridge. She didn't want to see Hannah among them. Then the ghosts would own her. They'd come alive in her dreams.

She was afraid to sleep yet almost immediately she did.

Chapter 6

The next morning Charlotte awoke at dawn and dressed to go over to Hannah's. There were bound to be personal telephone notebooks somewhere over there. She was going to find them.

She left her aunt's house quietly, not wanting to wake her. Between her tears and her despair, Bess had too much spiked cider the night before. Charlotte wanted her to stay in bed as long as she could. She needed the rest.

Outside, the winds were howling. The tree limbs were grinding against each other in the storm. It was morning, the clock said so, but Charlotte couldn't see two feet ahead of her. The wind was voracious and the snow was an endless wall of white. She was beginning to understand what the islanders meant about the island having arctic winters.

She let herself in to Hannah's silent house and turned on the lights. She kept expecting Hannah to come bustling out with a plate of sandwiches or a pot of tea. She'd come home in the middle of the night and all their fears of her death were groundless. Charlotte thought she saw her around every corner. It made her sad.

An uneven pile of books sat on the kitchen table. She picked up a piece of a shattered glass horse off the floor and studied it in the palm of her hand.

Someone had been in Hannah's house. Hannah would never have left broken glass on the floor. Charlotte was sure it hadn't been there yesterday when Mac, Bess and she had been there.

She left wet footsteps behind her. Items were out of place and strewn around. Not exactly vandalism, but more like someone had been looking through or inventorying Hannah's possessions and had been clumsy about it. Objects were moved or piled up in other places rather than their original locations. Charlotte had been there enough to know where things were kept. There was a poltergeist at work or else Hannah was there, in spirit anyway. She wasn't absolutely sure but she thought some items were missing.

"Hannah?" she breathed, listening with her whole being. It was freezing in the house. "Are you here somewhere?"

No answer.

She felt silly. Maybe she'd been working too hard on that ghost book of hers. She made her way through the rest of the house, thankful there was no one else there.

She moved to the back door and looked outside for foot tracks in the snow besides hers. There were none. She went to the three other doors but there was nothing outside but smooth snow. Whoever or whatever had been in Hannah's home hadn't left a trail, but then it had been snowing all night and there wouldn't have been any to see.

She discovered the broken window in a rear guest bedroom. The pane had been smashed and the window had been opened.

That's how the intruder had gotten in.

She'd have to tell Mac. The police should know someone had broken in, had rummaged through Hannah's belongings and taken some of them. Who would do such a thing?

Someone who had known Hannah was not going to be home—or was dead. Someone who'd known Hannah's collections and rare books were worth a great deal of money. Charlotte didn't want to dwell on that so she looked for what she'd come for. She skimmed through an address book. Inside there weren't more than twenty or thirty names. Nothing helpful. Most of them had tiny descriptions of who they were to Hannah scribbled behind their names: friends, utilities or shops Hannah had done business with. Art galleries. Local restaurants Hannah liked to have deliver food. None of the names had family written behind them.

She looked for a name and telephone number that Hannah might have written on a piece of paper and stuffed in a drawer. Maybe she'd be lucky and find out whom Hannah had gone to see four nights ago. Yeah, and rocks won spelling bees. She looked around telephones, statues and any other moveable items, careful to replace them where she'd found them. She took stock of every room, peeked in drawers and cabinets. No secret messages had been left behind.

She'd about given up, thinking she was being silly and there weren't any hidden clues to what had happened to Hannah. It was all in her mind. Then she heard something fall to the carpet in the living room.

She froze. What if someone was hiding in the house? She listened but no further noises emerged, and softly murmuring a prayer, she grabbed a heavy glass bowl for protection from a cabinet and slunk into the living room. No one was there. But there were books lying on the floor below the shelves. She picked them up. They were books by Mark Twain.

Smiling at the memory of Hannah and her great love affair with the author, her eyes fell on the Twain novels in her hands: *The Adventures of Huckleberry Finn* and *The Innocents Abroad.*

How had the books ended up on the floor? They hadn't been there minutes ago when she'd let herself in the house. Odd. A wisp of chilly air caressed her cheek. Charlotte could have sworn she heard someone laugh somewhere.

Hannah?

She opened the books, Hannah's prized possessions. They were rare editions signed by the famous author. They really existed. They must be worth a fortune. There were faded letters stuffed in the back of *The Adventures of Huckleberry Finn,* considered Twain's lifelong masterpiece, which appeared to be love letters. Charlotte read one or two and smiled.

Someone had written love letters to Hannah. But not Mark Twain. Hannah must have become confused. A signature was at the bottom. Amos.

Who was Amos?

There was a letter, its paper not yellowed and tattered along the edges, that seemed recent among the stash; one that was not from Amos. After she'd finished reading it she glanced up into Mac's face.

"What are you doing here?" He was as taken aback to see her as she was to see him. Dressed in a warm wool coat, blue jeans, boots and a sock cap, his face was wind burnt. His eyes were a cop's eyes. He had his duty pistol aimed at her with his finger on the trigger.

He'd thought she was a burglar.

"Don't shoot, I'm not stealing anything!" She raised her arms mockingly and tried not to laugh the kind of laugh a person lets slip under stress or fright. The sight of a gun leveled at her had badly startled her.

"Charlotte, I almost shot you!" He lowered the gun. She could see his body quivering. "What in the world are you doing here this time of morning?"

"I was looking for the names of family Hannah might have had in an address book," she confessed after releasing a sharp sigh, "or clues to what may have happened to her. I'm not the one who made the mess. It was like this, broken window and stuff everywhere, when I arrived.

"What are *you* doing here, Mac?"

"Same reasons. I'm also keeping an eye on her property. I saw movement through the front room window so I used the key Bess gave me yesterday, and came in and found you. Sorry I scared you. I didn't mean to."

He put his gun back in the holster under his coat.

"Well." He nodded at the letters in her hand. "Did you find something?"

"Here, maybe you can figure it out." She handed him the note she'd been reading.

He read it aloud:

"Miss McCain,

Meet me at Cutter's Bar on St. Ignace at five o'clock on Sunday night the third of January if you want to take care of our problem once and for all. If you don't show up I'll have to track you down and you know what that will mean. Arlen

P.S. Take the ice bridge. It's open now and the easiest route to the meeting place."

"What do you make of that?" Her hand motioned at the paper he was holding.

"Suspicious, but vague. Who's Arlen?"

"I don't know. I never heard Hannah speak of him. I can ask my aunt, though."

"Do that. I'm familiar with Cutter's Bar on St. Ignace. I'll go talk to the owner and see if Hannah ever got there. If she did, I'll see if he recalls whom she was with. Was there an envelope for this note?"

"No, it was just the note stuffed in this book."

She gave him the book. He, as she'd done, leafed through it. There was nothing else in it. "It's a start. The note, I mean. Sunday could have been the night she disappeared. It fits the timeline."

"Could be," she countered. "Especially that part about taking the ice bridge. If you believe Hannah's death wasn't an accident then perhaps this Arlen was setting her up or something."

"I had the same thought."

Relieved to see he'd relaxed, Charlotte met Mac's gaze. She'd felt like a criminal caught in the act when he'd come in, as if she'd done something wrong by being in Hannah's home, going through her things. It hadn't been like that. She was onl^y trying to make sense of Hannah's disappearance, that's all. She'd wanted to tie up some loose ends.

His frown uneasy, Mac kept looking around. "I can't believe she's gone. It doesn't seem real."

"It doesn't. I keep waiting for her to walk in and scold us for breaking into her house." Charlotte's lips curved up weakly but Mac didn't return the smile. She could see he was disturbed over Hannah. He believed she was dead.

Mac meandered around the house. Charlotte tagged along. "I'm assessing the damage," he said. "I'll have to fix that broken window somehow so the furnace won't work itself to death and the pipes won't freeze. It's the least I can do for Hannah. She asked me to take care of the house if something ever happened to her.

"You mentioned you were looking for Hannah's address book. Did you find it yet?"

"One of them. But she had a couple squirreled away that I know of," she snapped her fingers, "and I just had an idea where another one might be."

"You have?" He'd stopped in the kitchen by the sink.

It was odd, she and Mac standing in Hannah's house without Hannah. Odd, their being together alone like this in any house at all. She knew Hannah and Mac had been close but she'd never seen the two together. She'd never seen him in Hannah's house.

"Hannah had a place where she kept extra telephone stuff." Charlotte brushed past Mac and opened a drawer next to the sink.

From deep in the narrow space, she dug out a blue notebook with the word *Addresses* embossed in gold on it. "Here's another one. It seems newer. Let's take it and the other one over to my aunt's house. We can look through them over a cup of coffee. With that broken window it's freezing in here."

It wasn't only the chilly air wafting around her body that was driving her from the house; it was Hannah's essence. It was as if Hannah was watching them. The sensation was so strong it unnerved her.

"You go over and make the coffee, Charlotte, and I'll board up that window. Hannah had plywood for just such emergencies in her garden shed. I'll put a call into the station that there's been a break-in here. Take the address books and that letter with you."

"I will." She took the note from Arlen and slid it into the newer address book. Then she retrieved the other notebook and left. She was glad to be leaving Hannah's house. At her aunt's there weren't any ghosts lurking in the dark corners, none that she knew of anyway.

She hiked back to Bess's house, made coffee, took a coffeecake out of the freezer and popped it in the oven. She kept stealing looks out of the kitchen window as she waited for Mac.

Once she thought she saw someone, a translucent figure that wavered and ebbed away under her gaze, watching her from Hannah's upstairs bedroom window. Charlotte rubbed her eyes and looked again. The window was bare.

Her aunt was bumping around in the other room. Charlotte knew the aroma of coffeecake would bring her into the kitchen soon enough.

As she waited for the cake to heat, she paged through the blue address book. There weren't many names in it. No Arlen anybody. No Amos anybody. So that was that. On the back cover written in light pencil, she could make out a faint number. No name, merely a telephone number and, by the series of digits, an off-island one.

Whose telephone number?

Mac rapped on the door as she was taking the coffeecake out of the oven. She sat across from him while he drank coffee and browsed through the blue address book.

"I'm going to call that penciled-in number on the back cover," she stated.

"It gets a little later, you can." Mac grinned at her over his cup. "But I wouldn't go calling people for at least another hour or two. It's still pretty early."

"Eight o'clock. I guess you're right. I'll wait a bit."

"Everyone knows about Hannah's disappearance," Mac informed her. "The station has been flooded with calls since yesterday."

"I know. We've been getting phone calls, too. You can't keep secrets on this island, can you?"

"No. It's a small island." Mac looked at her. "Charlotte?" He acted as if he wanted to say something else but couldn't.

"Yes?" She waited. "It's all right, Mac.

Whatever you have to say to me go ahead and say it."

He leaned back in his chair, paused, and shook his head, "Never mind. Timing's not good. It can wait."

Charlotte didn't argue. If it was about them, she didn't think she could handle it at the moment. She felt awful. All she could think about was Hannah. Mac would tell her whatever he had to tell her later.

Mac said, "I covered that broken window at Hannah's and turned the furnace up a little to keep the pipes from freezing."

"She'll appreciate that, I'm sure." Charlotte felt the sadness again. Hannah was never coming home. "Mac, when you were over at the house repairing the window, did you see or hear anyone over there?"

He gave her a strange look. "No. No one. Why?"

"Never mind." She lifted her shoulders and let them fall. "Have you heard when the storm's supposed to slack off and when you can continue hunting for Hannah?"

"Sometime tomorrow maybe. Charlotte, you should know, we might never reclaim her body. The currents could have swept it away. As I said before, it could be spring or we might never find it. I'm sorry."

"I know." Hannah's house was dark next door. The gardens were buried and dormant under several feet of snow. Spring seemed so far away. An image of Hannah's smiling face over one of her fall roses came to Charlotte. It nearly made her cry.

When Bess sauntered into the kitchen, they were discussing Hannah's birthday wake. Bess sat down and turned to Mac. "Hannah's really not coming back, is she? I mean…there's no hope at all?"

"I don't think so. I'm sorry."

"Okay then, let's plan her party," Bess surrendered, her tears had finally eased off. "I'm sure she'll be watching from wherever she is. So we better make it a good one. She would have demanded we celebrate her life, not mourn it. She confided to me on New Year's Eve that she'd lived a long good life. She'd loved and been loved and had done everything she'd wanted to do. She was happy, ready to go, and she said when she did pass away she didn't want anybody crying over her. I thought it was odd that she was talking like that, but being the beginning of a new year, I understood it.

"Now looking back, it's more like perhaps she'd had a premonition her end was coming."

"Well, she did believe in such things as premonitions and ghosts." Charlotte stared out the window into the bright day. "She might have had a feeling her time was short."

"Come to think of it," Bess mused, "she has been talking a lot these last few months about dying. I thought it was because she was about to turn eighty."

"She was going to be eighty?" Charlotte hadn't known that.

"Yeah, but she didn't look or act it. She had more gumption and energy than me. She was like a kid when it came to birthdays and holidays. She made each one special." Bess dabbed a tissue against her wet eyes. "Darn it. Saturday she's getting her birthday party."

"I'll help," Mac volunteered. "I make a mean pasta. Let me know what else you need and call me so we can organize." He wrote his home number on the back of one of his police business cards and handed it to Charlotte.

"We will." Charlotte looked at her aunt.

At the front door, as Mac was leaving, he put an arm around Charlotte's shoulder. "I miss Hannah, too," he spoke tenderly. "I'm so sorry she's gone. My childhood wouldn't have been bearable without her. She was the devoted grandmother I never had and my best friend. I'll always remember her with love. I know she's in heaven.

"Don't you worry, I'm going to do everything I can to find out what happened to her and why. I won't let you or her down. I won't give up."

"Neither will I," Charlotte whispered. She got a stern look from Mac though he didn't say anything.

He went out the door into the snow, tossing a smile back at the woman in the doorway. Through the storm door Charlotte saw him get on his snowmobile and ride away.

It was hard for her to re-enter the kitchen. Part of her had wanted to go with Mac and search for more clues to Hannah's vanishing. She almost asked him to take her along but she was positive he would have said no. It was police business now, so she hadn't tried. "Aunt Bess, you ever hear Hannah mention an Arlen somebody?"

Charlotte would have shown her the note, but she'd given it to Mac. It was evidence. He was compiling a file on Hannah's disappearance. Besides, the note would have made Bess too suspicious anyway.

"No, not that I can recollect. I don't know any Arlen myself."

"Could he be a shopkeeper or a businessman maybe?"

"There aren't any that match that name that I know. You can ask the old timers at the birthday wake who knew Hannah from way back. One of them might recall an Arlen from her past. The old woman rarely spoke of the old days to me, though. She had secrets."

"You said Hannah had no living relatives?"

"Not that I know of. That doesn't mean she didn't have any relatives left somewhere. She just never talked about them."

"Oh." Another dead end.

They waited a few more days in case Hannah showed up, and then started calling the telephone numbers in the address book to invite them to Hannah's birthday wake. They told everyone that Hannah had disappeared; that they believed she'd gone through the ice on the ice bridge—but that whether she reappeared by Saturday or not they were giving her a birthday party anyway.

Charlotte telephoned the penciled-in number from the back of Hannah's second address book. But all she got was one of those automated answering machines that made everyone's voice sound like a robot. It said that the person they were trying to reach was out or busy. Please call again or leave a short message. Charlotte didn't feel like telling a robot that Hannah was missing and might be dead so she hung up without saying anything. She'd call later. She tried two more times before Saturday but the answering machine kept picking it up so she finally left a brief message asking them to call her, Bess Conners or Lt. Mac Berman of the Mackinac Police. She said that it had to do with Hannah McCain and they needed to speak to them.

The days drug on and the storm dissipated. The search for Hannah's body in the freezing water below the ice went on but brought no results. Bess and Charlotte continued to go out looking for Hannah every day, but they didn't find her and she didn't come home.

By the Friday before Hannah's memorial birthday wake Charlotte and Bess had to accept that Hannah probably wasn't ever coming home again.

Charlotte was preparing for bed. As she had for the whole week, she couldn't keep her eyes off the windows of Hannah's house. Mac had left lights on downstairs. A shadowy figure floated from one window to another. At times she was sure it was a trick of her eyes and at other times she wasn't sure at all. Was someone over there rummaging around in Hannah's home again?

Charlotte threw her robe on, her coat and her boots. She crunched across in the snow, and let herself into the other house. She explored the first floor, and then the second and third, but encountered no one. She was shutting the door behind her when she thought she heard someone say in a soft whisper: *Don't worry about me, child, I'm doing fine.*

Charlotte spun around. No one was there. The lights in the house flickered out and then back on again. She shivered.

It had sounded like Hannah's voice but Charlotte wasn't convinced she'd actually heard it or if it had been in her mind. She returned to her aunt's house and went to bed. Of course, hearing Hannah's words had been her imagination. She'd wanted to know Hannah was at peace so badly she'd heard what she'd wanted to hear. It was as simple as that. Or so she tried to convince herself.

Chapter 7

The day of Hannah's birthday party was sunny and bright. It'd warmed up to twenty-eight degrees and the snow had ceased for a while.

Thirty-three people, all of them friends and acquaintances of Hannah's, appeared early for the party and more came and went as the day wore on. There was a birthday cake with eighty candles on it. Only the guest of honor wasn't there to blow them out.

Most people ate, laughed, and recalled stories, poignant or humorous, about the birthday girl. Charlotte and Bess found it healing to be remembering their friend and to be with others that had cared for her, too.

Hannah had loved parties and she would have loved this one. It was all about her. There were candid pictures of Hannah pasted up on a corkboard put together by Bess and Charlotte: Hannah smiling; Hannah planting roses in her garden; Hannah on Christmas Eve with big shiny bows in her hair; New Year's Eve with a highball in one hand a spread of winning cards in the other.

The gathering made Bess feel better. She'd had a difficult week, after being out each day looking for Hannah. Honoring Hannah's life seemed to give her the closure she needed. Charlotte had helped her aunt hunt for Hannah, too, but mostly for her aunt's benefit. In her heart Charlotte knew Hannah was dead. She would have been back days ago, not wanting to worry them, if she wasn't.

Mac got to the house early and helped them get ready for their guests. He brought his famous cheesy sausage pasta, extra chairs and a photo album with pictures of Hannah when she'd been younger. He had pictures of her with him when he'd been a boy. There was a photo of a grinning Charlotte, as a girl on her bike, that Mac had saved all those years.

"You remembered me, then, huh?" Charlotte couldn't get over the fact that he had.

"That first day when you said you were Bess's niece? I knew who you were right away. I was waiting for you to remember me."

"It took me a little longer," she replied, hiding the fact that she hadn't until Bess had reminded her. "But I remember you now." They compared stories of when they'd been kids. Charlotte remembered more than she thought she would. The longer she lived on the island the more her memories returned.

"I had a crush on you, Charlotte, did you know that?"

"No."

"I did. Big time. I used to chase you around town then hide if you looked my way. I didn't think I was good enough for you. I told Hannah once that when I grew up I was going to get rich and marry you."

Charlotte laughed but Mac was serious.

The party was going as well as a party for a

dead person could. People were reminiscing, eating, and visiting. They were dropping crumbs on the carpets and leaving half-empty plates of food in every open space. They were crying and giggling over humorous Hannah anecdotes and gossiping about people that weren't there.

"Have you found out who broke into Hannah's house?" Charlotte asked Mac later that day. He'd trailed her into the kitchen when she went to make more sandwiches, and wash up dishes to put them on. Paper plates wouldn't do for Hannah's celebration. For a couple minutes they were alone so Charlotte took the opportunity to get an update on the investigation.

"I'm working on it. I did a preliminary inventory there a few days ago but didn't find much, if anything missing. Televisions, computer and jewelry were all there. I lifted fingerprints, but so far no matches have come up on the criminal database.

"What gets me is when someone broke into her house not many people knew Hannah was missing or dead yet. So how did they know there'd be no one home? And if they didn't steal anything valuable, why did they break in?"

"Apparently, they were looking for something."

"That's what I thought, too. The question is what?"

"I don't know."

"Neither do I," Mac murmured. "I'm running down a couple of hunches, though. I'll let you know if any of them pan out."

"I'd appreciate that. I feel bad enough about

Hannah dying the way she did but I wouldn't feel as bad if I knew it was an accident and not something else. Murder changes a death."

"I wish I could give you that peace of mind, Charlotte, but the more I think about it, and the more time goes by, the more I'm sure something's not right. I'm sorry."

"Don't be sorry. It's your job to be suspicious."

"Yeah, but I'm just a small town cop on a little island. I'm no Monk, no Sherlock Holmes." She caught the cynicism in his voice. In the living room people were laughing, probably at some remembrance or another of Hannah. The crowd had thinned but there was still a house full.

"Thank goodness, too. Sherlock's dead. Monk's brilliant but a little weird, don't you think?"

"Just a little." Mac chuckled softly. "Did you or Bess find any of Hannah's missing relatives?" He dried the plates after Charlotte washed them.

"We've been questioning her older friends about that. Most of them said she had no one left that they were aware of. I asked if anyone knew who Arlen was. No one did. I had an interesting conversation with Hannah's lawyer, George Warren, though."

Warren was a slight wiry man in his seventies who'd retired years ago, but kept his hand in the law part-time. He was Aunt Bess's lawyer, too. "Warren told me that Hannah didn't have a valid will when she disappeared. The peculiar thing was, she'd had one for years and then last year out of the clear blue, she tore it up. She made Warren tear his copy up as well. She was supposed to have a new one made but every time Warren pressured her about it, she'd get angry. She told him she'd tend to it in her own time, that she had some loose ends to take care of first. Time ran out, it looks like, unless she'd handwritten a will and stashed it somewhere. He advised her to do that at least. It'd be better than no will at all. He also said a handwritten will, whether it had been witnessed by someone else or not, would hold up in court as long as it had her signature on it."

"Did he know," Mac asked, "if she had any living relatives?"

"If she did, she never spoke of them to him. No one was in the original will, either."

Mac hung the dishtowel on its hook. "Did Warren tell you, if she has no relatives, who did she leave her estate to in her old will?"

"I asked. It slipped out before I could stop it. Since the earlier will was null and void anyway, he said he saw no harm in telling me. Truth was, he said it didn't matter either way. In the old will she left most of her estate to charities and some old friends. Most of which were already dead."

Charlotte hadn't forgotten how the lawyer's eyes behind the gold glasses had sent a guarded look in her aunt's direction at that moment. The lawyer would have done anything for Hannah. They had been very old friends and he knew how much she'd loved Bess.

"But in her new will, he said, Hannah was going to leave everything, money in the bank and her house, to my Aunt Bess. He said Hannah called Bess her daughter of the heart. He also thought there was something keeping Hannah from putting her new will into final form and was real sorry to hear she'd disappeared before she could do that."

"She never made a new will." Mac's tone was commiserative. "Whew. That's bad news, especially for your aunt."

"I know. What happens to Hannah's estate now?"

"If Hannah doesn't have a will, not even a handwritten one, then everything will go into probate. If no one comes forward, a relative or someone with a claim, it'll go to the state."

"Oh, no. I'm relieved Hannah's lawyer never informed my aunt about the inheritance. It'd be worse if she'd expected to get it then found out she wouldn't. As much as she loved Hannah, it's going to hurt her to see the old woman's house and things pawed over at public auction by strangers.

"Unless," Charlotte went on, "Hannah did leave a handwritten will. She was a sharp cookie. I can't imagine she'd take the chance of her property going to strangers if she'd wanted Bess to have it. It only makes sense she left something somewhere that would express her last wishes."

"So she might have left a letter, a note or even a handwritten will that communicates her final wishes. It could be in that house somewhere." Mac was scrutinizing her as she prepared sandwiches and piled them on a delicately etched silver platter that Bess had received years ago as a wedding present.

"It could be and we should look for it. That inheritance would change my aunt's life. No more penny-pinching or working two grueling jobs as she has to do. Bess should have what Hannah wanted her to have. That would only be fair."

"I agree."

"Before I came in here," Mac said, "I was chatting with Gertrude Steiner, one of Hannah's oldest friends, and sometimes in the early days, rivals. She said she'd known Hannah as a young girl and her family well. Gertrude told an amusing story as she was eating your aunt's chocolate cake about something outrageous Hannah had done when she was young. Hannah had this sweet-sixteen birthday party and all her boyfriends showed up. All three of them asked her father for her hand in marriage on the same day.

"Hannah thought it was so hilarious. She made a big scene of it by rudely saying no to all three. She never wanted to get married, even back then, or at least not to any of them. Though Gertrude did say Hannah changed her mind about marriage later."

Charlotte knew who Gertrude was. She was a tiny stick woman with snow-white hair and eyes the color of sky reflected on ice, and a face wrinkled of years. She was over eighty and had known Hannah all her life. If anyone were familiar with Hannah's relationships, Gertrude would be.

"What else did you and Gertrude discuss, Mac?"

"I asked her if Hannah had any relatives still living."

"What did she say?" Charlotte had finished the sandwiches and was washing her hands. On the other side of the door Bess was calling for more food. The table was bare and the people were hungry.

"She wasn't sure. Hannah's parents, Herbert and Athena, of course, are long dead. Hannah had two sisters, Sarah and Sophie. The youngest, Sophie, who at twelve years old, got pneumonia one winter and died. Hannah took it hard. She and Sophie were close. Sophie was the most beloved of the three girls. Her dying took the heart out of the family. The other sister, Sarah, ran off young. She despised the island. She was the black sheep of the family and, according to Gertrude, as wild as a pack of cards.

"Sarah and Hannah never got along. There was a bucket of bad blood between them. It had something to do with a man, Hannah's first real sweetheart, Amos, Gertrude thought, but was never sure. She couldn't recall Amos's last name. But Sarah and Amos ran off and married instead. It'd been so long ago Gertrude couldn't completely vouch for her memory. The elopement had been an awful scandal, she did say that."

"Ah, ha, so that's who Amos was."

"Amos?"

"You know, the man who ran off with Hannah's sister and the man who wrote those love letters I showed you the other day. They were tucked in Hannah's Mark Twain books. Amos was the man who broke Hannah's heart. She said something once to me about a man in her youth who'd hurt her terribly. He turned her off on men for a long time, maybe the rest of her life. I think it was Amos—and he hurt her with her own sister, Sarah. It's pretty classic. Woman runs off with sister's boyfriend and injured sister never forgives the other. Never gets married, either."

Mac grinned mischievously. "That makes sense. Hannah never did trust men. Except me."

He lifted up the plate of sandwiches and balanced it with one hand like an experienced waiter. "Gertrude doesn't believe that Sarah ever returned to the island. Hannah supposedly never saw her sister again in all these years. Then Gertrude saw Hannah in the mercantile one day last month and they had a long conversation about the old days. If Hannah had seen her sister since their falling out, she would have said something about it to Gertrude. But she didn't say a word about that. Nothing. Just old memories."

"Another mystery in Hannah's life," Charlotte voiced, shrugging her shoulders. "She had quite a few. Did Sarah have any children?"

"That's another mystery. Sarah might have been pregnant when she ran away to St. Ignace all those years ago with Amos, Gertrude had heard. That was a big ingredient of the scandal. So there could have been one child or maybe more."

"A child or children we don't know are alive or not," Charlotte summed up. "We don't know what the last name of the father was if there was a child or children. The name Amos is all we have. So Sarah and her progeny, if she had any, will be hard to trace."

"You got it." Mac stood by the door ready to go through while Charlotte picked up another platter of food. "Gertrude suggested we look through Hannah's correspondence. Hannah might have letters from her sister Sarah stashed away somewhere if she ever received any. She kept things like that in a mauve hatbox on the top shelf of her closet.

"Right after I put this food out I'm going to go over and look for that hat box. If I find it, then when everyone leaves, we can sit down and go through it."

"You're coming back?"

"I'm coming back."

Charlotte and Mac took the food into the next room. Mac got his coat and left.

The wake lasted a while longer. The last of Hannah's friends and admirers filed out the front door as evening was closing in. Charlotte and Bess quickly cleaned up everything in silence. Afterwards they sat down at the kitchen table with cups of hot coffee.

Once or twice as they were talking, Charlotte looked out the kitchen window and saw lights on in Hannah's house. Mac was still looking around. She could have gone over and joined him but the thought of being in Hannah's house after a day of memorializing her was too much for Charlotte. She didn't want to feel or see any ghosts anywhere around her today. She didn't think she could take it.

"I'm happy we did this today for Hannah." Bess was smiling for the first time all week. "She would have really enjoyed it. I wish she could have been here."

"Who says she wasn't, at least in spirit? I'm sure she's tickled pink we honored her. Wherever she is, she knows we loved her."

"Yes, we did and I'm going to miss her so

much." There were unshed tears in Bess's eyes. "I just wish she were here and not dead. I still can't believe it. It's so awful."

The two women hugged, then Charlotte persuaded her exhausted aunt to take a nap. She'd worked the night before, had spent hours getting ready for the wake and ran around taking care of their guests all day.

Around six-thirty a knock came at the door. When Charlotte opened it, there was Mac with a large purple hatbox in his arms.

"Everyone's gone, huh?" He peeked into the empty room.

"Everyone's gone. Bess is sleeping, but come on in. There's fresh coffee and leftover chocolate cake."

"I can't turn that down."

The two of them sat in front of the fire and poked through the hatbox of stubs, notes and remnants of Hannah's life. There was no sign of a will, handwritten or otherwise, but there were paid bills and letters. They examined every item carefully.

Mac wasn't eager to leave. Charlotte liked having the company so she didn't hurry him. They were comfortable with each other and had picked up where they'd left off that fall. Friends.

Charlotte was the one who saw the slip of paper tucked in the lining at the bottom of the hatbox once they'd inspected everything else.

She pulled it out. "It's a letter."

It was an old letter in a stained envelope, much read because it was crumpled and crinkled. It looked as if someone had balled it up and thrown it away, mad at its writer, but in the end, had retrieved and saved it. The name on the back of the envelope above the address was Sarah Lukow. The date stamped on the outside of the envelope was September 1956.

"First name's right." Mac took the letter and read it. Charlotte scooted closer. "What does it say?"

"This Sarah Lukow is asking for money sounds like. Again. She writes about how hard times are and how if she can't turn to a sister, who can she turn to? She goes on to say someone called Cassie is sick and her husband, Amos, has run off again."

"Oh, so Sarah Lukow was Hannah's sister. She did marry Hannah's childhood sweetheart, Amos." Charlotte reached out and touched the letter. It was a piece of Hannah's life, a piece of history.

"That's what I get from it, too." Mac grunted, his eyes remaining on the script of the message. "By the way this letter reads, Cassie must have been Amos and Sarah's child."

"Amos was the one who wrote those love letters to Hannah." It came to Charlotte. "Oh. It makes sense now. Amos might have had a child with Sarah, but he continued to love Hannah. Those love letters were dated in the early and late fifties. Amos must have written her for years after he'd married Sarah. Then after a while no more came.

"That justifies Hannah's sour feelings about marriage. She'd lost her true love to another woman—her sister. Her sister trapped him, kept him, because she had his child."

"For a while, anyway. In the end he ran out on all three of them. What a bum." Mac flipped over the envelope. "The address on the back is 404 Easterling, St. Ignace. So Sarah didn't move too far away, only across to the mainland. I'll make some calls tomorrow. See if I can trace her from that address and track her and her daughter down.

"Yet by what Gertrude told me the sisters never reconciled."

"That Gertrude knew of," Charlotte conjectured. "But I knew Hannah as a forgiving woman who rarely held grudges. She might have gone to see her sister, wrote her, or telephoned her without telling anyone. We don't know."

Mac put the letter down on the arm of the couch and, stretching, leaned back. The night had drifted away from them.

"Do you suppose she ever sent Sarah the money?" Charlotte could hear the wind screeching along the gutters of the house and banging at the shutters. She was relieved it wasn't snowing. It was hard enough to get around town with the depth of the snow already. She and Bess would be sentenced to staying inside the house if any more fell.

"Knowing Hannah, probably yes."

"It's strange there are no more letters."

"Just this one, unless she threw the others away or there's more hidden in the house. We can keep looking."

"You know, Mac, I don't know why we need to keep searching and digging. Maybe there's nothing else to find or learn. Maybe Hannah's accident was an accident. Maybe there are no living relatives and no will. Nothing we can do will change anything. Maybe we should let it go."

She saw the cynical glint in his eyes and sighed. "I know," she groaned. "The truth is, I don't believe any of that, either. Like you, I fear there's more to all of this than what is in front of our eyes. Like you, I have a feeling Hannah's death was on purpose. I'm just tired, I guess."

Charlotte couldn't tell him she also thought Hannah's ghost might be trying to communicate with her. He'd hinted he believed in ghosts but had never said outright he did. She was afraid to tell him she was seeing things. She didn't want him to think she was crazy.

"I've been wondering where else we could look for Hannah's will or for more of Sarah's letters," Charlotte went on to say instead. "Did you go through Hannah's desk, the one made of dark wood with lots of drawers, in the left corner of the sunroom?"

"No. I didn't get to it."

"She kept bills and checkbooks there. Bess and I used to do the shopping for her sometimes. She paid in checks and took them out of the middle drawer— the tiny one. Tomorrow I'll check that desk and a few other places."

"I'm sure Hannah's lawyer, who by the way is also the executor of Hannah's estate, won't mind you going through her stuff. I have permission from him to do so. I give permission to you, too. Warren would be relieved if we found a will of any kind. He hates the thought of Bess not getting what she's due. He knows I was over there searching today. I told him."

The clock struck nine and Mac yawned. "I should go. I work the early shift tomorrow."

"Me, too. Seven a.m. comes pretty quick. It's time we call it a night." She stood up. "You look beat."

"I am. I've been on the go since Hannah disappeared. We'll continue hunting for her, one way or another, until her body is found. As far as I'm concerned, her death won't be official until it is."

"You're doing the best you can, Mac. Don't make yourself sick."

"It isn't only that I've been wearing myself out looking for her. I haven't been sleeping well. I've been having dreams; Hannah's in most of them. If she's dead it wasn't a peaceful death."

"I've been dreaming of her, too. I guess when someone you love dies that's normal."

"Perhaps." He rose and there was an odd expression on his face as if he wanted to say something else but couldn't.

If only she could read his mind.

"But," he said, "I'm not going anywhere until I see some of that ghost book of yours. I'm proud of you for actually attempting to write a book. So many people say they're going to write one, but, in the end, it's only another promise they never keep. I was pretty good at English in my college classes. In fact, I even took a few creative writing courses. I like to write, too. Songs, mostly."

"You like to write, too, huh?"

He nodded. "Oh, I'll never write a book. That's

beyond me. But I love to read them, especially spooky ones. Come on, I won't be judgmental."

She was apprehensive about showing her writing to other people but with Mac, for some reason, she found she didn't mind. She knew he'd be gentle with his criticisms if he didn't like it. Besides she'd have to get used to showing the book to other people or she'd never get it published. She had to start somewhere. She wanted him to read it. She could use the feedback.

"It's in its first draft, about half done, on my laptop upstairs. Before Hannah disappeared I had run out the first three chapters or so. You want to see them?"

"I'd like to."

"I'll go get them." Charlotte left Mac in the living room.

Returning, she gave him the folder. "I have more chapters completed than that, I just haven't edited and printed them out yet. It reads different on paper than on the computer screen. I don't know why, but it does. If you want, you can take them with you and bring them back anytime. I have them on the computer."

"Can I?" He was delighted.

"Go ahead."

"Has it been hard writing the book?" He put his coat, hat and gloves on, and then tucked the folder under his arm as he moved towards the door.

"Not really. Writing is something I'm comfortable with. I've kept a journal from the time I turned fourteen and have a trunk full of them up in the attic at my mother's house. Over the years I've written short stories for my writing classes. I did real well, too; at least my teachers always liked them."

They were at the door. It was time to say goodnight. His fingers brushed against her hair and cupped her ear and the side of her face through the long strands. She'd worn her hair up during the day for the wake but she'd released it as they'd relaxed before the fire.

Mac tilted her chin up with his fingers so he could see into her eyes.

"Your hair's grown longer since that day we spent at the Grand Hotel." His smile was as soft as his words. "I like it longer; I like it down like this."

"You remember that day?"

"Every second of it. I haven't forgotten a thing."

She'd been holding her breath and hadn't realized it until that moment. She thought he was going to kiss her on the mouth, but he didn't. Instead he bent down and brushed his lips against her cheek. The kiss made her shiver. She wanted him to put his arms around her again but he didn't. She accepted that. The day had been about losing someone they'd all cared about. It seemed disrespectful to be thinking about anything else.

He opened the door. "Goodnight, Charlotte. I'll call you soon. I promise." He went out into the wintry dark, and she was left with the silent house.

In bed, she snuggled under the blankets, staring out the window, reflecting on Mac, Hannah, and life. How quickly things could change. How quickly everything could be taken away. Hannah would have told her to cherish the moments she had and go after what her heart wanted. Life was short.

Mac said he'd call and she knew he would. She relived the moment when he'd looked at her and kissed her cheek. She relived portions of the evening when they'd seemed so close. She hadn't imagined it. He was courting her in a slow, gentle way.

Was he ever going to tell her about the girl he'd been kissing that night by the town's Christmas tree? She thought that sooner or later, being an honorable man, he'd say something. She hoped he would soon because her curiosity, her jealousy, was nagging at her. She needed an explanation.

After dwelling a little longer on Mac and the way his eyes gleamed when he smiled or the way she felt protected by his side, she found herself wondering about Hannah's new will. She wondered where Hannah might have concealed it and how much that inheritance could change her aunt's life.

If she could only find the will, if only it existed.

Before she drifted off to sleep some of the stories she'd heard that day about Hannah returned to her. They eased her heart. So many people had loved the woman. Her life had touched many others in so many ways.

Hannah, did you ever mend your relationship with your sister and are Sarah and Cassie still alive? If you left a will—where did you put it?

Oh Hannah, I'm going to miss you so much!

She'd forgotten about the penciled-in number on the backside of Hannah's second address book and the answering machine she'd left messages with but had never gotten a response from. She had completely forgotten; there was so much else on her mind.

She fell asleep.

Someone was tapping on her window. She came awake in stages and listened to the scratching, but wouldn't open her eyes, afraid of what she'd see.

After the tapping came to an end she opened her eyes. There was something written in the frost on the outside of the glass. It appeared to be a word. *M-u-r-d-e-r.*

Murder? Or it looked like it said that. She shut her eyes tightly and took a deep breath. There wasn't a word scratched in the frost. It was only her imagination. She opened her eyes again and the word was still there. Yep, it looked like Murder. Was it true? Was Mac's suspicion right that Hannah had been murdered? She didn't know. She looked away and when she looked again, the word she thought had been there was gone and in its place was another collection of letters.

W-i-l-l!

Oh, no. She was losing it. Did it mean that there was a will—Hannah's will—and she should keep looking for it?

Thanks, Hannah, she whispered, *I think,* and fell back to sleep.

The next morning she would believe she'd dreamed the messages, because there'd be nothing on the window but ice, yet she couldn't forget them.

She just wasn't sure she'd actually seen them.

Chapter 8

Mac dropped by the house briefly the next morning to see if Charlotte and Bess had recovered from Hannah's birthday wake, or that's the excuse he gave.

Charlotte thought he'd come by to see her. He'd been on duty and announced he couldn't stay long. One cup of coffee at the kitchen table with her and Bess, a few words to each of them, and he said he'd have to go. He had a ton of paperwork at the station.

"I began reading your manuscript last night, Charlotte. I got a chapter and a half done. So far I really like it. No, love it. It's spooky and mysterious and humorous at times. It makes me want to read more. I don't have one complaint. You're a good writer."

"Thank you." She was pleased, excited. He'd been the first person to read it, and he'd liked it. "If you want to read more I could run out the rest of what I've written, six more chapters, and give it to you. It'd only take ten minutes."

"I'd like that. I'll wait."

He phoned her that evening when her aunt was at work. "I wanted to let you know I'm reading your book every chance I get. That story about the ghosts Jasper Howell saw that night in the graveyard battlefield was fantastic. You know, how they chased him down the road rattling their swords and screaming because they thought he was a union deserter? You know Jasper drinks like a man lost out in the desert, don't you?"

"Does he now?"

"Yep. But he's been telling that particular tale for years so it could be true. In his mind, anyway."

"Ghost stories can be approached like that," she said thoughtfully. "Some people would say sightings are in the person's head. There's no scientific proof that ghosts are real or that the spirits in my stories are real. I have to trust the word of the tellers and that's what I'm taking down, their accounts, plain and simple. Jasper's story was a good one, though, I thought."

"It was. I can't wait to get off the phone so I can read the next chapter. By the way, have you had a chance to go through Hannah's desk yet?"

"I did this afternoon and found nothing. There were no more letters from Sarah or Amos and no will, handwritten or otherwise."

"Darn."

"That's what I said. I'll keep looking, though." She hoped he'd ask to come over and see her, but he didn't. When she hung up, she felt lonely.

She didn't see or hear from him the next day but in the late evening he called her. "Can you get off work tomorrow?"

"I am off work. Letty doesn't need me at the inn on Tuesdays and Wednesdays."

"Good. How would you like to come along to the mainland with me tomorrow and do some snooping around?"

"What do you mean by snooping?" She couldn't understand what he was talking about. She'd been padding around the house in her furry robe and fluffy slippers; working on her book and trying not to think about Hannah too much. Being alone in the house made her uneasy. Every strange noise made her look behind her. She was afraid to let her eyes wander to shadows in the corners. She kept expecting to see Hannah's ghost. It gave her the shivers.

"I mean yesterday a friend on the St. Ignace police force did a computer search on Sarah Lukow. He discovered she's been dead for years but that address on the envelope beneath her name, 404 Easterling, is still standing, sort of. The place has seen better days but someone is living there with the last name of Gofrey. Does that ring a bell?"

"No, I can't say that it does. So?"

"So I thought we'd take a day trip across the ice bridge to St. Ignace and see who lives in that house now. Could be they'll remember Sarah or Cassie. It's a lead even if it's a thin one."

Something in her stomach began to ache. In her mind she saw the twilight mist scurrying across the ice bridge and clinging to the uneven branches of the evergreens as it had that night last week. The evening sky was a dull muddy watercolor and the snow was a frigid blanket. She saw the hole that had closed and refrozen by now, gleaming in the ice with a dead woman floating face down inside it. In reality she hadn't seen it that way but that's what she now saw in her mind, along with wraithlike specters hovering in the ice fog, living on the ice.

They were waiting for her.

The weatherman on television had reported a thick fog settling over the island that would remain for days. That meant the ice bridge would be shrouded and dark, a perfect hiding place for shadows and apparitions. Was Hannah now among them?

"You want us to go across the ice bridge tomorrow?" Her eyes were glazed as she stared out the window at the gray skies. It was no longer snowing, and though it was cold it wasn't as bitter as the day they'd gone across the ice bridge looking for Hannah.

She'd never told Mac how frightening that had been for her. She'd done her best to hide her phobia for Hannah's sake because, at the time, finding the old woman had been more important. Yet the creepy feeling the ice bridge had provoked in her lingered, stronger than ever.

"That's the plan. We'll ride our snowmobiles along the Christmas tree path and over the ice like we did last week. It's the fastest and cheapest way to go."

"Mac, I don't want to go across the ice bridge again."

He was quiet for a moment. "Ever again?"

"Just for now. I have my reasons."

"You afraid of it?"

She felt like a fool but told him the truth. "I am, yes."

"I didn't know you felt this way about the bridge when you went with me before. You hid it well. Are you scared that with the higher temperatures lately it'll break up under your snowmobile?" He wasn't mocking her. His tone was sympathetic.

"No," she fibbed and gave him the other reason she disliked the ice bridge. "I can't stop seeing Hannah's body in that hole."

"You have some imagination, I'll say that." Once more there was only compassion in his voice. "Don't feel bad. Many people are afraid of the ice bridge and many refuse to go across it. Ever." He was silent a minute or two as if he were thinking. He didn't try to talk her out of it or say she was foolish for the way she felt, which made her like him more.

"Okay," was all he said. "I understand. No big deal. We'll take an airplane from the island airport, that's what we'll do. It should be easy to get passage. There's no snow in the forecast, and you won't have to pay the usual fare because I have a pilot friend, Stanley Malden, who'll fly us over for free."

"How about the fog?"

"The airplane flies above it."

She hesitated. She wasn't crazy about small airplanes, either. It was another one of her phobias. Planes tended to sometimes fall out of the sky or crash into things. But, today, she'd rather fly across than take her chances on the haunted ice. The islanders got across to the mainland all winter by air when the ferries were docked in January and none of them died, that she knew of anyway. So flying had to be safe, right? Right.

"Okay. I'll go. When we get to St. Ignace, we'll

pick up my car. The roads should be clear enough to use it, don't you think?"

"I was counting on it." She could hear the conniving in his voice.

"Is that why you asked me along? So you could borrow my car?"

"No, but that's definitely a bonus. On the map, 404 Easterling is about thirty miles from the airport. We'll need a car or snowmobiles and last time I checked Stanley didn't have room for either of those in his airplane."

"Too bad. My car on the mainland will have to do. I'd hate to walk it and my dog sled is out of commission right now because I don't have any dogs," she joked with him, keeping it light so she wouldn't have to think about that airplane ride.

"So I'll pick you up about ten in the morning? I'll bring my snowmobile. You can ride piggyback behind me to the airport. That way I'll provide transportation on this side of the water, and you can provide it on the other side. Fair deal?"

"Fair deal. See you at ten." She hung up. She was going to spend the day with Mac on an adventure. She couldn't think of a better way to use a day off.

While waiting for Mac to show up the next morning, her aunt, in her robe and with puffy eyes, shuffled into the living room and lit a fire in the fireplace.

Charlotte suspected that Bess was seeing a new man. Her aunt was staying out later than her job would have kept her. Charlotte asked about the late nights but Bess sidestepped the issue and never actually answered her.

Bess hadn't heard a word from Shawn since he'd left. She'd written him about Hannah but hadn't gotten a reply, not a letter or a telephone call. He'd kept his promise to cut all ties. Though she'd agreed, Bess was having a hard time with it.

"Ah, I see. Mac's coming by." Bess tossed in wood and lit the crumbled up paper beneath it. She turned to Charlotte with a hopeful expression. She might be unhappy herself, but she was happy for her niece.

"What makes you think that?"

"Let's see, you're dressed up on your day off, with makeup, at ten in the morning. Doesn't take a genius to figure out someone you want to impress is either coming by or you're going out to meet them. Lately you want to impress Mac so I guessed it was him. Since you're mooning around here instead of going, he's coming here."

"Smart, Sherlock."

Charlotte gave her aunt the convenient story that they were searching for Hannah's living relatives, if there were any to find. That was plausible and there was nothing about Hannah's disappearance possibly not being an accident. There was no mention about the elusive will, no sense in getting Bess's hopes up if they never found one.

"Have a good time," was all Bess said and padded off into the bathroom, probably to wash her face, comb her hair and put on a little makeup herself. She was a woman after all and a good-looking young man would soon be knocking on the door.

The Ice Bridge

Mac arrived. Bess coaxed him into having breakfast before they left.

Since Hannah had died, Bess was lonelier than ever. Charlotte gave her as much of her time as she could spare. Mac and her staying for another half-hour to eat with her aunt wouldn't kill them. She wished they could have invited Bess along, but they couldn't. They were hiding secrets. Besides, there was only room for two on the snowmobile.

"Aunt Bess, you want us to pick up anything for you on the mainland?" Charlotte asked her aunt when they were finished with breakfast and ready to leave.

"The refrigerator's packed with leftovers from the party. We're okay. Go and do what you have to do but try to have a good time as well, you both deserve it. Go out for lunch or something." There was a twinkle in the other woman's eyes that didn't fool Charlotte. Her aunt was matchmaking again.

They rode Mac's snowmobile to the airport on the center of the island and flew off in a compact Cessna plane owned by Mac's buddy, Stanley.

Down below them the island galloped by, a carpet of snow broken by starkly contrasting metal, brick and painted wooden structures rising out from it like uneven teeth. They glided over the Grand Hotel, a frozen fairyland, and the deserted streets of the village. They tipped their wings at the Chambers Riding Stables and Trinity Episcopal Church then passed over the Iroquois Hotel, Mission Point, the dock and harbor, and the ice bridge with its tree path. In the distance, they could see the magnificent five-mile long Mackinac Bridge.

The water further out in the lake had a calm flatness of bluish green light patterns that bounced off the bottom of the Cessna like a kaleidoscope. The trip was smooth and painless. It wasn't bad at all. The fog had lifted over the Straits and the view was clear.

This flying stuff isn't so bad after all, she thought. *What was I so frightened of?*

"We have an excellent pilot that's why the ride's so smooth." Mac's eyes were dancing as they watched her reactions. "Stanley's the best. He's never crashed yet."

Stanley laughed along with Mac. Charlotte didn't think it was that funny.

The Great Lakes spread out as far as she could see. They reminded her of mini oceans. The distances were so vast and the waters so deep ships had been lost on them. Charlotte thought of Bess's ghost ships. If she looked hard enough she could almost see them down there skimming across the waves towards the horizon, their sails swathed in the mists of eternity.

The flight was barely fifteen minutes long, and then they were landing at the airport in St. Ignace. She had to admit the trip was faster and warmer than the ice trek they'd taken the week before.

"I'm going to have to travel this way more often," she remarked to Mac as the airplane coasted to a complete stop. "It's quicker than the ferry or the ice bridge. Except thirty dollars a pop would be a little tough to take." She'd found out from Stanley how much it usually cost.

"Well, you could always fly free with me." Mac

slid a sideways glance at Stanley, a stocky man around fifty with busy brown eyes and a ready smile, who tipped the rim of his cap at Charlotte to show he went along with the suggestion. "Or use the ice bridge for as long as it lasts."

Charlotte lifted her eyebrows and said nothing. She knew her dread of the ice was unwarranted and childish, really. But people fell through the ice and into the freezing water...like Hannah...like those others she'd seen...and died.

It wasn't going to be her.

This thing of believing in the ice ghosts and being afraid of them, it was really silly. Yet she couldn't shake those fears, either.

They got a car ride from Stanley, who kept a company vehicle at the St. Ignace airport, to her car in the parking lot. The pilot had to return to the island airport because he had other passengers to transport. He'd wait for their telephone call to give them a lift back to Mackinac when they were done. They assured him it would be before nightfall.

Soon they were maneuvering the snowplowed streets towards a house they'd never seen. It felt weird driving her car again. It had been awhile, and she was relieved when the engine started. As she was letting it warm up Mac handed her a checkbook she recognized as Hannah's.

"I was at her house before I came over this morning. I found this in her bedroom chest-of-drawers, tucked in the rear under old birthday cards. Go ahead, look inside."

She did and was staggered at the amount of money Hannah had in the bank. "Over fifty thousand dollars." She whistled. "As frugally as she lived you'd never guess she had this much money socked away."

"I experienced the same shock."

She shook the checkbook and asked, "Are you going to give this to Mr. Warren?"

"I've already called him and let him know I've found it. He wasn't surprised. He knew she had money in the bank. He also said that her estate, with her collections, antiques and the house, was worth a lot more than what people would think.

"Warren knew different people had been trying to purchase her property for years. What her parents paid for it eighty some years ago is a drop in the bucket compared to what it'd go for now. The house and land alone would sell for well over five hundred thousand. Hannah had it appraised."

"That much? I can hardly believe it."

"Believe it. Land on the island is at an outrageous premium right now. Everyone wants to buy a piece of Mackinac, mainly because there's a huge amount of money in tourism. As large as Hannah's house is it could easily be remodeled into a bed and breakfast or some rich person could buy it for use as a summer cottage. This is not to mention Hannah's collectibles, in themselves worth thousands of dollars. There's no telling how much those signed Twain books would go for, probably hundreds of thousands.

"I was thinking," Mac went on, "what if someone wanted Hannah's land for development of some kind, wanted her collections or her priceless books—and she wouldn't sell? Now any of those things would be a viable motive to get rid of an old lady."

"You mean worth killing someone for?" Charlotte hated putting the crime into words but it was beginning to make sense. Now that she knew what was at stake.

"Probably would be." Mac's face was grave. "Because Hannah would never sell her home to anyone for any reason. She loved living on the island and would never leave. She'd never sell her treasures, either. If someone wanted money out of her or wanted her land the only way they'd get it would be to dispose of her."

"When you put it that way I almost think you're right about Hannah's death being murder. But I still can't imagine anyone killing that sweet old lady for money or land." Charlotte had wanted to tell Mac about the words scribbled in ice on her window, but in the daylight it seemed unreal, a little crazy. So she didn't speak of it.

"People kill for far less in this world, Charlotte. Usually not on our island, I must confess, but I've been racking my brain trying to make sense of the pieces I'm finding that don't fit concerning Hannah's disappearance: that letter; Hannah going out so late to meet someone and not telling anyone; her refusing to revise her will; some of the odd things she said to Bess, you and her lawyer; and those scraps of explosives I found in the ice.

"I have the gut feeling that it's not over, either. Ripples in a lake, you know."

"Is this little junket we're taking another ripple?" Charlotte put the car in gear and drove, paying attention to the road because plowed or not, it was slippery. The snow shining in her eyes made them hurt and she wished she'd brought her sunglasses. Her snowmobile goggles would look too silly.

"I don't know. I think so."

Mac was inspecting the house addresses. They were close to the house number they were looking for.

"Let's see," Charlotte was thinking out loud. "Who'd be in line for Hannah's estate if her old will was null and void?"

"Any of Hannah's or Sarah's blood heirs. Even one Hannah never knew existed until recently," Mac said thoughtfully. "We know Sarah's dead, but she had a daughter, Cassie, and that daughter might have had children of her own, which would make them Hannah's legal heirs. If they exist we need to find them."

Charlotte slowed the car down. The snowplows hadn't done a good job on the stretch they were on. The car's wheels were sliding and spinning. She had to fight the steering wheel to stay on the road. "Talking about finding people, I'd like to know who that Arlen is from that note we found along with the love letters in Hannah's Mark Twain book. The Arlen she might have or might not have met that last night."

They'd speculated about what time, give or take a couple of hours, Hannah had gone through the ice, but they weren't sure if it'd been before or after she'd gone to the mainland for her rendezvous. Mac had grilled the owner and some of the employees at

Cutter's Bar and no one could recall if Hannah had been there on that day or not. So either they'd simply forgotten if she'd been there or she might not have made it there at all. There was no way to know. Dead end.

"I'd like to know if Hannah met Arlen at Cutter's, too." Charlotte was so aware of the man sitting next to her. She'd caught him looking at her a few times. There was electricity building between them. She wondered if she touched him, would electrical sparks fly. "It would be a start. It's a shame no one there remembered."

Mac pointed at a car pulling out from a side street ahead of them. Charlotte slowed down until the other vehicle passed them.

They'd come out of a small town and into a patch of woods on Easterling Road. A rambling run-down structure, among the trees set back from the street, loomed ahead. It appeared abandoned and in need of painting. The numbers on the front were tarnished golden pieces of metal that read 404.

"There it is. Sarah's old homestead." Charlotte turned the wheel to the right and her car bounced down the rutted and snowy driveway or at least she hoped she was on the driveway. The snow was deep and it looked as if no one had shoveled it lately if at all. She parked the car next to the dirty white house.

She and her passenger sat there and gawked at the place. There was trash scattered about, some of it lumps beneath the snow. There were two dilapidated vehicles rusting away in the back yard. An old stove snuggled up against the wall of the house beside a screened in porch with half the screens ripped or broken out.

"What a dump," Mac exhaled and put his hand on the car's door handle.

"The house doesn't even look lived in to me." She met Mac's eyes. The blue in them was neon bright today. He'd forgotten to shave and had a shadow of a beard but it gave him a rugged macho look, like some movie star. She liked it. He'd become his old self again. He'd made jokes on the trip and she'd discovered he had a quirky sense of humor.

"My cop friend says it is. According to the post office, it's not a dead address. Come on, let's go have a look around."

"Isn't that trespassing?"

"Nah. I'm a police officer investigating a potential murder and for today you're my assistant. We're checking the place out, that's all. Doesn't look as if anyone's home anyway."

"Or has been for a long time," she grumbled as she tagged along after Mac into the yard. They marched through the snow up to the front of the house and Mac put his face up to one window and she looked in another, shading their eyes with their hands to see inside better.

"Looks empty." She didn't see any furniture to speak of, no sign of comfortable living or people.

"It does." Mac, a frown on his face, worked his way around to the rear of the building. She heard him yell, "Charlotte, come here. Would you look at that? The door's unlocked and a little ajar."

Oh, boy. "We're going to break and enter now?" she said when she caught up with him.

"It isn't actually breaking and entering when the door is left open. The house seems abandoned. It looks to me like the occupant has split."

"Yeah, sure. Mere technicalities. But, hey, you're the law and I'll go with what you say." They were loitering by the open door in the intense sunlight. At their backs, the bare branches of the trees were rustling in the wind while the noise of an agitated cat meowed nearby one second and far away the next.

Sound did funny things in the woods.

"Nah, we're not breaking and entering or anything. We're just making sure the house is okay. Doing our civic duty." Mac forged ahead into the silence and, with a shrug and a guilty look around, she became his shadow and followed.

The inside was worse than the outside. There was filth and litter on the floors. She kept hearing weird noises, skittering and scratching, from upstairs or downstairs in the basement. A shiver rippled through her body. She hoped—because lately she'd had enough of weird experiences—the house wasn't haunted. Sound also did funny things in an empty house.

It was chilly and murky inside. She could see her breath, but could barely see objects because only faded daylight seeped in through the dusty windows around them. Mac switched on the light and nothing happened. He tried the bulb above the sink piled high with food encrusted dishes, but still no light.

She tried to turn on the water. No water. "The utilities are off."

"They seem to be."

"What are we looking for exactly, Mac?" she asked. She didn't like being there knowing that the owner could stroll in any moment. What would they tell him or her? That they were just passing by and decided to explore their residence? That was if he or she didn't shoot them first.

"Proof someone is living here. I'm following the threads back to the blanket, that's all."

"The Sarah and Cassie blanket, huh?"

"Something like that. But we're not in luck since there's no one here." Mac halted in one of the back bedrooms and with his foot shoved at a mound of sleeping bags and blankets. Someone had been camping out. "Now, leastways."

She looked at the sleeping bags; noticed the lack of furniture in the dingy room. "I'll tell you what I think. It looks as if someone does live here but maybe he or she's run out of money. Either that or the house is vacant and someone's been squatting in it. Homeless people or a traveling vagrant?"

"I'd go with the first scenario. Someone lives here and they're broke. It explains why mail's still coming to the house. I'd say the gas and electric's been shut off for no payment. The place has been stripped. Look at the dust lines on the floor. There's been heavy furniture here that isn't here any more. Someone's selling off pieces one at a time for money, I'd wager."

"Now I know why you're a cop. You can't help but play detective."

"I wanted to be a detective, but there's not much need for them on Mackinac Island."

Until now, she thought. "Well," she told him, "you'd be a good one."

"Thanks." Mac and Charlotte meandered through the other dingy rooms, then went upstairs and looked around. There were more empty dim rooms that needed paint and loving care.

"Are we going to the basement, too?" she joked, coming down the stairs behind him into the living room. The curtains, long satiny peach panels, must have once been attractive. Now they were ragged and dirty.

"Nope. I forgot my flashlight. It'd be too dark."

"Thank goodness for small favors," she muttered under her breath. Mac hadn't heard her because he was headed for the front door. Now what was he up to?

He must have known what she was going to suggest next. "I'm checking the mailbox." Cracking the door open, he slid his hand outside to the metal box on the outside wall and brought in a pile of mail.

"Mac, I don't believe stealing someone's letters is legal."

"Don't worry. I'm only going to see what name is on the mail. I'll put them back."

"All righty. That makes me feel better. I think." Nervously she glanced out the front window, waiting for a car to drive up or for the local police to come and arrest them.

"Ah, ha," Mac exclaimed and thrust a letter under her eyes. He pulled the curtain away from the window and light spilled in so she could see the letter and the name clearly. "Arlen Gofrey," she read aloud, "404 Easterling.

"Oh, my, do you suppose it's the same Arlen who wrote that letter to Hannah?"

"I bet it is. That's not a common name and the coincidence is too great for it not to be the same Arlen." He gave her an advertisement circular like Aunt Bess got plenty of every month. "Look at the name on this one."

"Cassie Gofrey," she read the name off the sticker. She looked up at him. "Could that be Sarah's Cassie? And Arlen is Cassie's son—Sarah's grandson—and, if so, that'd make him Hannah's great nephew?"

"It would. And Hannah's legal heir." He showed her the rest of the mail. Some of it was for Cassie Gofrey and all of them were advertisements.

"You mean two people live here?" She slid her gaze around the dismal surroundings. There wasn't a couch or chairs, or television. Nothing but bits and pieces of decrepit furniture.

"Not necessarily. My guess, telling by this mail, is that Cassie is no longer with us. That like Sarah, she's dead. You know junk mail sometimes comes to an address for years even if that person no longer lives there or has passed away. "That is, if no one's notified the post office."

"You think Cassie's dead?"

"That would be my deduction."

She didn't like the picture her mind was conjuring up. It appeared someone was living here in this destitute squalor and was a distant relative of Hannah. Whoever it was may have been harassing her. And if the ice had been tampered with so

Hannah fell through, well, the combination of things just didn't look good. All her money and her estate would be up for grabs. That whole line of thought and where it led made her uneasy.

She heard a noise outside. "Let's go, Mac. We found what we came to find out and more." She spun around without seeing if he was with her or not and exited the back door. She went out into the snow-covered yard and got into her car.

Mac followed soon after, slid in and they drove away.

"I put the mail back in the mailbox and closed the doors. I left everything the way we found it. Arlen's not going to know we were there."

"You hope." She drove, trying not to let her mind linger on the selfish reasons someone would have liked to see Hannah dead. The thought that the old woman may have been murdered for her money made her ill. It couldn't be that. Hannah didn't die because she had money, did she?

"What do we do now, Mac?"

"We do what we can. I'll run a background check on Arlen Gofrey, now that we know his last name. Afterwards I'll contact Hannah's lawyer and see if he or anyone else has made inquiries yet about Hannah's estate. I might also try to have a chat with this Arlen eventually. See what I can get out of him."

"I'll go to Hannah's and keep hunting for that elusive will, more letters or notes, or for anything else that could help us. I've been thinking, whomever ransacked Hannah's house after her death might have taken her will—if it exists. It could have been Arlen Gofrey."

"That's the same conclusion I came up with. If someone else stands to gain if the will is destroyed, then your aunt is out of luck." He shook his head beside her.

When they got to the garage, Mac borrowed the attendant's phone and called Stanley to pick them up. As they were flying over the Straits of Mackinac Charlotte couldn't get Sarah and Cassie's ramshackle house out of her mind. If that building could have spoken to them, perhaps the mysteries they were searching for would be solved. Or, at least, they'd know more about that Arlen guy.

The flight back wasn't as smooth as the flight over. Stanley said they were hitting rogue crosscurrents. He reassured her, as the plane wildly bucked beneath her, that it was nothing. "We're as safe," the pilot insisted, "as babies in a cradle."

Yeah like babies in a wild rocking cradle hanging on a limb in a storm. She laughed uneasily. She felt frozen in her seat, while her heart moved with the rhythm of the airplane. Up, down. Shake, shake, shake. She was getting sick to her stomach but kept her fears to herself. The two men behaved as though the rough ride was nothing. She wasn't about to act like a scared child. She could do this. Instead, she prayed.

She was relieved when they landed on Mackinac Island. Soon they were seated once again on Mac's snowmobile, with the packed powdery stuff sliding beneath them. The fog had dissipated and the sun was out.

Her mind was tired of fretting over things she

The Ice Bridge

couldn't change. All she wanted to do was lean against Mac's broad back, her arms tight around his middle and enjoy being with him. After the weeks of being apart, it felt so good. She didn't want to think about poor Hannah being murdered for her possessions, that dreadful house in the woods or the secrets of the past, not for a while anyway.

Being with Mac was what she needed. Being alive and happy was what she needed. Hannah would approve if she enjoyed herself. In fact, Hannah would have been the first to say life is for living—so live it. It was early so she schemed how she could keep Mac from taking her home yet.

It turned out she didn't need to.

Chapter 9

Mac pulled over on the side of the road a ways outside of the airport. Over his shoulder, he asked, "What do you say, let's take a break from sleuthing and have a late lunch, my treat, at the Mustang Lounge?"

Charlotte's smile came quickly. "Sure." During the winter months the Mustang and the Pink Pony were the main hangouts of the locals. She'd eaten at the Mustang a couple of times because Bess worked there. It was famous for its cheeseburgers. She loved cheeseburgers.

They strolled into the Mustang and everyone, all six people, waved or said hello to Mac. Living upstairs and being a cop on the island, the workers and the regulars all knew him well.

The Mustang had cheap wooden tables and tattered scarlet leather chairs that had seen better days. A simple wooden bar with a mirror behind it covered the rear wall. The floor and other walls were drab, worn and as old as the town, while the aroma of a thousand fried burgers, onion rings and a strong hint of beer hung heavy in the air. But the place had a welcoming ambiance, as comfortable as a house full of friends, that wasn't lost on Charlotte. She liked going there. There were generally characters with stories loafing around wanting someone to chat with.

The Ice Bridge

After depositing themselves at a corner table Charlotte and Mac ordered lunch.

"I finished those chapters you gave me of your book," Mac surprised her by announcing.

"Why didn't you say something before?"

"I was saving it until now, so we could really talk about it. I was going to tell you over lunch how much I liked your writing. The book's good, Charlotte. Fascinating. Some of the stories actually scared me and that's not easy. You're not going to have any problems getting that manuscript published."

"Thank you for saying that. I only wish you were an editor." Charlotte was happy, though. She noticed the other bar patrons were straining to overhear their conversation. In the winter on the island gossip was a form of entertainment. "Remember it's only a first draft. I have rewriting to do."

"It sounded fine to me. I can't wait to read the rest of it."

"You'll have to. That's what I've finished so far. I need more stories before I can go on."

"Then I'll help." The owner of the Mustang was putting hamburgers in front of them and Mac petitioned, "Hey, Jack, I haven't asked you yet, you got any ghost stories you want to share with the ghost lady here?"

"Ghost stories are what you're wanting, hey?"

Mac's puppy-dog face beamed. "You got any? If you do, and they're any good, Charlotte here will put them in the book she's writing."

Jack, a middle-aged man dressed in a plaid shirt

and blue jeans, with short cropped hair, grunted at Charlotte, "Nah, not me. Never seen a spook. Don't believe in them. But Emma Jackson over there," he aimed a thumb behind him and to the left, "at that table is caretaker for a bona fide haunted cottage on the rich side of the island. Mayhap she'll tell you about it.

"Hey, Emma," Jack boomed loudly over the sounds of eating, chatter and the jukebox. "Tell Mac's friend here about your haunted cottage."

"Sure thing." The woman called Emma grinned, collected the remnants of her lunch and relocated over to their table without being asked. Flopping down beside Charlotte, she bobbed her head at them. "Hi there, Mac's friend. Hi, Mac."

She was somewhere in her sixties, with long gray hair pinned up in a neat bun. Her eyes, a pale gray like her hair, were lively in her broad face. The three of them spent a few moments chitchatting and then she said, "So, ghost lady, you want to know about my ghost, huh?"

Charlotte got her notebook out of her purse. "I sure would. I'm writing a book about ghosts on the island. So if you don't mind, tell me about it, Emma."

"Well, I work on West Bluff Road up past the Grand Hotel in one of the summer cottages. I can tell you which one but you can't put the address in your book. My employers, the Simmons, might not like it. They're a real old island family, kinda snobbish, if you know what I mean. Are you familiar with those huge mansions up there?"

"Isn't everyone? They're opulent mansions on

the island owned by wealthy people, but in the winter months most of them are empty." They were called cottages, though they weren't, and were usually three story structures, some as huge as small castles.

"You know them then."

"So your job is to take care of one of them through the winter?"

"Yep. I stay in one of the old servant's rooms and make sure the pipes don't freeze. If there are any problems I take care of them, broken windows, vermin, you know. I keep the house clean. Mostly I make sure nobody messes with it or breaks in. It's a good winter job. Easy.

"Since my husband, Fred, died I need the income. I've been working for the Simmons for five years now. They're fair people but a little strange like all rich folk. I think they're off cavorting in France somewhere right now. They won't return to the island until May."

"The ghost?" Charlotte had known women like Emma before. Once they got an audience they could talk aimlessly for hours. She'd have to keep her on track. "It must be hard living in a mansion all winter by yourself. Isn't it lonely?"

"I'm used to it. I've known the Simmons since I was young. Charles and Felicity have owned that cottage all their lives. His father owned it before them and his father before and so on and so on. It's been in the family a long time."

"The ghost?" Charlotte reminded her.

"Oh, that. The story is that around nineteen hundred or so a Phineas Simmons was married to a real looker named Victoria. They had two children but were never happy. Phineas, well off and clever as he was, was a mean one and prone to drink. He liked to beat his wife and kids. In those days, no one questioned such things as they would today.

"Rumor was Victoria hated her husband, didn't want his kids, and ran off with some young soldier from the fort. Phineas, out of grief or spite, was said to have hung himself from a rafter in the basement one night after drinking too much.

"Some believe to this day that the wife and her soldier hung him before they ran off, but no one ever proved anything. The kids were raised by an aunt on the mainland and eventually came back to the island to reclaim their home. Victoria and her soldier were never seen again.

"It's Phineas's ghost that haunts the cottage, they say. He's looking for his errant wife and her soldier-lover. He's one mad spook. Sometimes I can hear him yelling down in the basement. Scares me to no end. But when I go down there to check, there's no one around. Thank the Lord he doesn't seem to be able to hurt anyone in this century. He's all ruckus and no slap. Mainly he makes noises in the basement. You know, footsteps on the stairs, pounding on the doors—that sort of thing. You never see him. I haven't heard him in months, though. He doesn't seem to care for the real frosty weather."

Charlotte was busy scribbling when she wasn't eating her cheeseburger. "Is that the only ghost the cottage has?"

"Nope. There are others, but I don't know who

or what they are. They're like poltergeists, you know? They shift small things around in the house, open and close doors, and whisper behind m^y back. Nothing too scary. Nothing I can't handle. Old houses are full of weird sounds anyway.

"There is one, though, that you might get a kick out of. A cat ghost."

"A cat ghost?" That was a first. Sitting next to Charlotte, Mac was smirking as if he already knew the punch line.

"Yep. On stormy nights, especially, I keep hearing this cat meowing and crying in the rooms upstairs. It's real pitiful like. I'll go up and look around thinking maybe some stray cat has gotten in somehow. I never find it, though. One night last year is when I seen it was a ghost cat. I came up the third flight of stairs and there it was, this big white furry cat sitting on the windowsill. I called 'kitty, kitty,' and went up to it. I reached out to pet it—I'm a cat person, ya see—and the creature just up and dissolved into thin air before my eyes. I gave it a name. I called it Whitey.

"I hear it on rainy nights but I haven't seen it lately. Ghost cat." Emma's lips grinned. She was missing a tooth on the bottom. She paid Jack, who'd come by to refill the coffee cups, for her lunch and rose from her chair. "I have to get back to the cottage now. Night's coming on and my eyes aren't so good anymore in the dark. I bump into things. The deep snow doesn't make it any easier, either.

"But any time you two want to come up and lay in wait for Phineas, you're welcome. I can't promise he'd show, though, nor the cat. If you need any more details, Miss Graham, I'm often here for lunch or, here's my number, you can call me." Emma wrote something on a napkin and thrust it at Charlotte. Struggling into her coat, the other woman went out the door and trundled off through the snow towards West Bluff Road.

"Interesting character," Charlotte pronounced as she watched Emma stomp across the street and arduously make her way up the snow-covered road. "She reminds me of Hannah."

"She does a little. She's as eccentric in her own ways. I hear she's a book hoarder. No, really. If there's a used book sale anywhere on the island, she's there. If someone dies and there's an estate auction, she's there to sift through the dead person's belongings. She buys every book she finds. Her house is stacked from floor to ceiling with old books. She doesn't read them. She only collects them. But I don't know about her and that Whitey." Mac laughed. "A ghost cat?"

"As a cat lover myself, I don't see what's so strange about that. It's nice to think that there are cats in the afterlife. I had the sweetest cat when I was a kid called Snowball. I've been thinking of getting another cat now for a while. I just might. Most likely I'll take Emma up on her invitation and go tour the Simmons cottage one day soon.

"You hoping to catch the ghosts at home?" Now Mac was smiling.

"Nah, not so much the hanged man but I'd love to see that phantom cat. Truth is, I've always wanted to see the inside of one of those ritzy mansions up there. I've never been in one. It would be kind of neat to see how the rich islanders live. I'm nosey, I guess."

"Most of the cottages are architecturally stunning. I've been in a couple. It's amazing what unlimited money can buy, but it's more than that. Those wealthy people take excellent care of their houses. They're constantly renovating and landscaping. Because the loveliness of those homes is, along with the Grand Hotel, vital to the tourism on the island, the home owners work extra hard to make them showcases."

"I know. I'm not jealous of the owners. I'm more in awe. It takes so much back-breaking work." An image of Hannah's well-cared-for gardens drifted through her memory. Charlotte could have sworn she got a whiff of Hannah's famous roses.

"I know what you mean. One of these days I'd like to have a house and land half as beautiful."

"On the island?"

"I'd have it no other place on earth. To me, Mackinac's paradise."

"Paradise, huh?" Charlotte had begun to feel the same way. The island had become home to her. She loved it, too. "The longer I stay here the more I agree with that."

Mac gave her a look she couldn't understand and said, "I'll pay the bill. Be right back." He got up and took care of their tab with Jack at the bar.

Outside the sun was setting. In an hour, it would be dark and the world was shaded in the rainbow colors that came with an early sundown. The vista outside Jack's windows was a glittery Christmas card, a snow-covered dreamland.

Mac was at the table again. "Talking to Emma about her West Bluff cottage rung a bell for me because it's on the same road as the Grand Hotel. We have an hour or more of light, so if you're up to it how about I take you for that snow ride on the hotel grounds that I promised you months ago? With the sun going down on the snow, it's a fairyland out there. It's quite a ride down that hill on a snowmobile...exhilarating and better than a roller coaster."

There was no way she would say no. She hadn't wanted to go home yet. She'd gotten her wish. It could be fun and it would help get her mind off Hannah, murder and lost wills. She'd been spending too much time at Hannah's house, usually at night after Bess went to work, hunting for that elusive will and keeping her activities from her aunt. She was tired of being sad.

So far, Charlotte hadn't found the will, but she wasn't going to give up.

"All I have to do is go upstairs to my apartment real quick and grab a warmer coat. The temperature's already falling." Mac's gaze took in the coat Charlotte was wearing. "You don't have on your heavier parka today, but I have an extra coat you can borrow. You can layer it on top of the one you have on."

"How sweet, you remembered I freeze easily."

"Oh, I remember that blue color you turned that evening we went over the ice bridge. It made you look like a smurf." He was polite enough not to smile.

"Thanks. I realize blue is not my best color."

"Would you like to come upstairs and see my apartment or would you prefer to wait here?"

She trusted Mac so it wasn't a hard decision. "Oh, if it's okay, I'd like to see where you live. That is, if your roommate doesn't mind." She couldn't help throwing in the last remark. Maybe now she'd find out if he shared his apartment with the girl she'd seen him with on Christmas Eve.

"Oh, he won't mind. He has people up all the time."

He? Thank goodness. She couldn't believe the sense of relief she felt.

When she stepped into his place, she wasn't expecting much for a bachelor who shared an upstairs saloon apartment with another guy, but she was pleasantly surprised. It seemed Mac surprised her a lot.

His apartment was furnished in plush multihued rugs of various shapes and paintings of Mackinac on the walls. Nothing looked genuinely expensive but everything was in good taste. The colors were even coordinated. It was a truly appealing apartment.

Along one wall there were shelves filled with books of all kinds. Evidently, Mac liked to read. Everything was clean and neat and the wood surfaces gleamed with fresh polish. There was a roomy living room with a television, video recorder, stereo, comfortable couch and two fat chairs; two bedrooms and a tiny kitchen that was as neat as Bess kept hers. The apartment was much roomier than it looked from the outside.

"I made most of the furniture." Charlotte heard

the pride in Mac's voice.

"You made the furniture? You mean you took it out of a box and put it together?"

"No, I made it. From scratch. Designed each piece, cut and carved the wood with my own two hands and then put it together."

"You built the kitchen table and chairs and that entertainment center?" The pieces were made of oak and exquisitely carved.

"Every bit of it. I made my bedroom furniture, as well. Carpentry's one of my hobbies. If I wasn't a cop I'd be a cabinet maker." Mac went to a closet and dug out a couple of quilted coats.

"You would have made a good one. I adore your furniture." Charlotte ran her hands over a curve on one of the kitchen chairs. "It's so distinctive looking. I'm impressed."

Charlotte studied the entertainment center with its doors and shelves. On one shelf was an instrument case. She recognized the shape. "A fiddle?" She reached out and touched it; rubbed her hand along its surface. No dust.

"Violin actually, though it doubles as a fiddle. I've played since I was a child."

"You play violin?"

She remembered what Bess had told her so many months before, "That Mac, he's more than just an island cop, you know. He has hidden talents."

"Whenever I can. It's my other passion besides police work. I'm not a professional musician, but it makes me happy to play and sing. My voice isn't anything to write home about. Once in a while I sit in with the bands downstairs on stage for the fun of it. I mustn't be too bad because sometimes they ask me back. One even wanted me to join up but I work so many nights it isn't possible."

"Can I hear you play something?" Charlotte loved violin music. To her the violin was an instrument of the heart. It could make her cry. She favored gypsy music and the sadder the better. She had no musical talent whatsoever but she was in awe of people who did.

"You really want me to *now?*"

"I really want you to. I know the light's fading but a quick song or two won't take long. Then we'll go. Please?" She handed him the case and plunked down on the sofa, patting the spot beside her.

Outside the window in the snow, a wagon was being drug down the street by Clydesdales, the wheels creaking and groaning as the horses whinnied and snorted. The storefronts across the street were foggy with shadows as people plodded from one place to another in the dissipating light. There wasn't much day left but she wanted to hear Mac play.

The aged violin was plain and scuffed. Mac played one up-tempo song and one ballad. The slow one was a melancholy gypsy-like tune she'd heard before but didn't know its name.

"The song's called 'Golden Earrings'," Mac remarked after he was done. "Most people have heard it but can't remember the name. If you watch old movies from the nineteen-thirties and forties, you've heard it before. Most gypsy movies had it in them somewhere."

"Oh, so that's where I've heard it. I love the old movies. You play wonderfull^y, Mac. I never knew."

"Then," he said, snuggling the violin back into its case, "we're even. You're an exceptional writer and I never knew that, either, until I read your manuscript."

"We both have our hidden talents."

"I like my friends to be talented," he joked. "But right now we'd better get going if we want to ride the hills at the Grand. The light's going fast."

They bundled up in the extra coats and were off. On the way over to the Grand Hotel she couldn't get the haunting sound of Mac's violin out of her head. She wanted to hear more. It was addictive. She'd have to ask him to bring his violin along next time he came over to see her and Bess. She'd have to find out when he played with the bar band next and go hear him. Strange that Bess had never spoken of Mac's playing to her. Working nights she must have heard him often when he sat in with the bands.

On the snowmobile, her arms squeezing around Mac's chest, she heard him laugh into the wind and was content with what they had at the moment. One day at a time that's all she could see or all she wanted to see for now.

She'd stayed away from the Grand Hotel since that fall day with Mac. She avoided going back when it had still been open, roaming the grounds or bicycling past it once it had closed for the season. She didn't know why, she just had. So it was great to be there again and with Mac. It was as if they were being given a second chance and this time she wasn't going to blow it.

The Ice Bridge

Whom are you kidding, she chided her selfish self, *you know he has a girlfriend, even if he's not living with her. He has one. Where will this lead you...to another heartbreak?* She ignored the voice in her head. All she wanted was today. Today might be all she'd have. It was enough. The island and friends would be enough. Someone was laughing somewhere but she didn't see anybody.

Today the hotel and its surroundings were blanketed in sparkling lacy snow. Frozen mists roamed the grounds like whimsical winter animals. The gardens were gentle ivory hills and the once green topiary horse and buggy were now white. Shadowy trees spiked the landscape devoid of all their leaves and looked like dark skeletons sticking out of the snow.

The Grand's rambling second story porch was icy and bare and no rich people milled around on it. The lawn chairs, rocking chairs and tables were stored away. Doors were closed and locked and the blinds were pulled down over the many windows of the building as if they were sleeping eyes. Around them the sounds of the fall and the Grand's visitors were forgotten ghostly echoes.

Staring up at it as they rode by, she wondered how many more ghost stories it would give her. Gertrude Weaver, Bess's friend, claimed there were more ghosts roaming its halls than she knew of. Charlotte would have to interview other workers when it reopened in May to get them.

Mac was right; racing around the grounds of the Grand Hotel in the snowy dusk was a breathtaking experience. They laughed, shouted and waved their hands in the air, as they careened down the hill from the road in front of the hotel and into the gardens. What a wild ride. It was a good thing Mac was a competent driver or they'd have overturned after the first curve.

They spent that last hour before dark speeding around the hotel, up and down the hills and exploring the woods below until the purple twilight melted into a glowing night. The snow lit the air around them with a silky whiteness. With the shimmering Grand looming behind them and the silent woods encircling, they could have been on a distant frozen planet. It gave her an eerie feeling.

Once total darkness had fallen, the bitter cold ate through their clothes. Even with the extra padding Charlotte shivered uncontrollably. Her breath froze into ice in front of her mouth. When she couldn't feel her nose or face they called it a day and Mac took her home.

She was tired when he left her at the door. As he hugged her goodbye, she wanted to say something, ask about the other woman, ask when she'd see him again; yet she decided it was best to leave things as they were. She was afraid to know the truth. She'd rather have him as a friend than as nothing at all. He'd tell her about his girlfriend when he wanted to. Their relationship would be what it would be so she let him go without asking anything.

As Mac drove away, she waved and blew him a kiss. She'd had a good time and wished he had come in. He'd said he had someplace he had to be, and though it bothered her that he didn't say where and with whom, she hadn't pressed him.

He could have been going to see the other woman. No, she didn't want to think about that, yet it was hard not to. She was falling in love with Mac and there wasn't anything she could do to stop it. She'd tried. Staying away from him hadn't worked. Telling herself that she was still recovering from her last love affair hadn't worked. If she was going to be truthful with herself she'd fallen for him that October day when they'd explored the Grand Hotel and told ghost stories to each other. She'd only been denying it since then.

The minute she accepted that certainty she knew it was already too late. What would be—would be. She scooted through the door into the house. For a moment she'd had the awful sensation of being watched by unfriendly eyes.

You're getting paranoid. Stop it. Who'd be watching you *and why?* She locked the door and went to find her aunt. She had so much to tell her before Bess had to go to work.

Chapter 10

Her aunt's house was silent when Charlotte got inside. There was no fire blazing as usual in the hearth, no food smells from the kitchen. It was long past suppertime.

She'd seen her aunt's snowmobile out front and, seeing the clock in the living room as she passed through, she realized it was later than she'd thought. Bess should have already been on her way to work, not at home. Uneasiness came over her. Her week had been bad enough so far. She didn't need any more problems.

Charlotte found her aunt in bed, her face drained. Her eyes, as they turned to her, were anguished. It was easy to see she'd been crying.

Charlotte perched on the edge of the bed. "'What's wrong? This isn't one of your nights off." She asked softly, "So why aren't you at work?"

"I'm not going to work. I called in sick." She hung her head and with the back of her hand swiped at the fresh tears creeping down her face.

"Aunt Bess, please, what is it?"

"Nothing." Her aunt refused to look at her.

"I'm not going to leave you alone until you tell me. I mean it."

Her aunt hesitantly confessed, "You know how depressed I've been since Shawn left?"

"I know. You've tried to hide it from me, from everyone, but I know you've been hurting."

232

"I've kept it mainly to myself, yes. I didn't want to bring you down. Now with Hannah's disappearance this last week I absolutely couldn't lay anything more on you."

Bess couldn't speak of Hannah as being dead. They'd had the memorial yet it was easier for her to believe Hannah was missing. A little thing, Charlotte hadn't begrudged her of it.

"These last few weeks I'd resigned myself that it was over between Shawn and me. I was lonely so I began a romance with someone I met at the bar. The man's younger than I am, not as handsome as Shawn, but nice looking, medium height and he has a beard—and you know I like beards. Before last month, I'd never seen him before. He said he lived off of the island but was working here through the winter as a machinist down on the docks and going home on weekends. He was so charming.

"When he came on to me, I thought: Why not? He makes me feel young and pretty and I haven't felt that way in a long time. He made me feel alive again. I began to really like him. Most nights he'd be at the bar. We'd flirt and talk. Last night he asked me to go away with him for the weekend. I said yes. I was happy.

"He told me he was divorced," her voice low, "and I believed him."

Ah, now Charlotte saw where the conversation was heading. "He wasn't?"

"No. I've discovered he's married with a family. Ha, imagine that. I must attract them like spiders to sugar cane. He lied to me and made a fool of me. Some people knew, but not me. It turns out he's just another man who has wasted my time and my life when I don't have much left of either. One more man who hurt me."

"You really didn't know he was married?"

"No. Not until today, when his wife called me."

Bess had stopped weeping and anger transformed her face, but Charlotte could see the shame beneath it. "And?"

Her aunt leaned up against the headboard of her bed. Her sigh was a muffled cry. "Worse thing is she seemed like a nice woman. She was gracious, under the circumstances, but I could tell she was upset. She was wounded. Her voice was shaking. It made me feel like a monster for hurting her, though I didn't know she existed, and hadn't done it intentionally."

"Oh, Aunt Bess it wasn't your fault." Charlotte stroked her aunt's hand. "Please stop blaming yourself."

Her aunt shook her head, refusing to be consoled. "They have two kids and have been married nineteen years. She works in one of St. Ignace's gift shops. She said they've been having money troubles. She hadn't a clue that when he was staying on the island through the week he was coming to the Mustang most nights to see me. He let it slip during a fight with her that he'd been seeing another woman, gave her my name and she was frantic. So she looked up my telephone number and called me. I didn't know what to say to the poor woman. I don't know who was more shocked, she or I. I feel like such a fool!"

"What did you say to her?" Charlotte felt sorry

for her aunt, furious at the man who'd lied to her and hurt her and his wife.

"I told her I hadn't known he was married. Told her I was so sorry, and wouldn't see him again. I promised. I got off the phone real quick. I couldn't believe I'd gotten involved with another unavailable man. What's wrong with me?"

"Nothing. Bad luck is what. You're vulnerable right now and some men, the predatory ones, can sense it. He's the liar, the immoral one, not you." Charlotte put her arms around her aunt and calmed her. "It's all right. You didn't know. As I said, it's not your fault. He lied to you."

"How could this have happened to me again?" Bess sat up straighter. She dried her eyes with the tissue Charlotte had given her. "All I've ever wanted was to be loved. All I ever wanted was to be married and have children. I wanted a normal life like everyone else wants. Now, look at me, I'm almost fifty and don't have any of those things. I woke up one morning and there's gray in my hair and wrinkles on my face. My body has strange aches and pains. I'm getting older every year. Soon no one will want me. Where has the time gone?" Her head gently rocked back and forth. "What I'm most afraid of is that I've wasted my life."

"No, you haven't. You have lots of time, and life, left. This is a bump in the road. Pick yourself up. Keep going. That's what you told me after Lucas dumped me and that's what I'm telling you now; that's what Hannah would tell you if she were here."

Bess's face screwed up as if she were going to

cry again. "I miss Hannah so much." Pulling herself together she added, "She would have gone, found that creep and kicked his butt for me."

"Most likely." Charlotte gently pushed the hair away from her aunt's puffy face. "You'll see, it's going to be okay. Now you know this man's married. You can tell him off next time you see him if it'll make you feel better."

"It would. If he dares come into the Mustang again, I'm going to give him a tongue lashing and maybe more. I'm going to spread the word on him. What he really is. I'll teach him to lie to women."

"That's the way to handle it. Be glad you didn't get any more involved than you did. That you didn't go away for the weekend. You were lucky his wife contacted you."

"Yeah, lucky. Gosh," Bess groaned as she resettled on her pillow. "I'm tired. That telephone call took everything out of me."

"After you get a night's sleep everything will look better in the morning."

"I hated calling in sick. We so need the money."

Charlotte wanted to get her aunt's mind off her money shortage and the man so she assured her, "You need a night off. Would you like to come have a cup of hot cocoa and something to eat with me before you sleep? I'll tell you about my day with Mac. I had a lovely time. We had lunch at the Mustang. Afterwards we ran his snowmobile over the grounds around the Grand Hotel. He played the violin for me. I guess you know he plays the violin?"

"Of course I know. I've heard him often enough

at the bar when he sits in with the bands. He plays like an angel. I told you he had other talents. I'm pleased that you two had a good time; you deserve it. But no, I don't want hot cocoa or food. What I want to do is end this lousy night: I want to sleep and forget everything. I'm not brushing you off but you can tell me about it tomorrow. I'll be able to be happy for you then."

"Okay, you sleep. I'll be here if you need me."

Her aunt's face turned up towards her. "What would I do without you, sweetie? You're my sunshine, you know that?"

"I love you, too, Aunt Bess, and I want you to be happy, too. We're going to work on that." Charlotte produced a hopeful smile. "Now, get your rest. We'll talk more tomorrow. I don't have to work so we'll spend the day together, real quality time, okay?"

"Okay."

Charlotte switched off the light and left the bedroom. She built a fire in the living room, fixed a sandwich to eat and cocoa to drink. Sitting in front of the warm flames, she thought about what she was going to do about Bess. Losing Shawn, Hannah, and now this final calamity was too much in too short a time. Charlotte had to find a way to cheer her aunt up, and get her to believe in herself again. She wasn't sure how, but she had to find a way.

When she finished eating, she worked on her book with notes on the couch and a laptop in her lap. She wrote that story from Emma and the one from her boss, Letty, before she forgot the tiny details.

After a few hours, she couldn't keep her eyes open. The airplane flight, intruding in the house or St. Ignace, the excursion at the Grand Hotel and the crisis with Aunt Bess had worn her out. Her body wanted a soft bed. After fifteen minutes of yawning and having a hard time focusing her eyes, she gave up and went upstairs.

When her eyes wandered to the dark figure crouching in the shadows on the landing, she got a start. For a heartbeat she thought she saw someone standing there, a small womanly shape. It gestured at her or she thought it did. She could have sworn it was Hannah. She grabbed the banister, shock making her unsteady on her feet, and blinked. There was nothing in the shadows now. Only shadows.

Lying in bed, the wind crying outside her windows, she couldn't stop obsessing about Hannah and ghosts. Mostly she thought about the eerie figures she'd seen on the ice bridge, the elusive silhouettes in Hannah's house, and those words etched in the frost of her bedroom window.

If it was Hannah, what was she trying to tell her? Oh, she wished she knew.

After that night, she inspected her window often. She kept her eyes open, especially when she was at Hannah's. It was as if she were waiting for the old woman's spirit to come and tell her who killed her and why, and tell her where the will was hidden.

Yet Hannah's ghost didn't materialize; there were only tantalizingly fleeting pools of deeper darkness that was probably her frightened imagination. There weren't any more messages on the windows—nothing but thick frost on the pane.

Maybe, regardless of what Charlotte had heard or seen, the dead stayed dead. Oh, how she wanted to believe that. Writing a book about peoples' supernatural experiences, including her own, still hadn't prepared her for what was happening now.

Charlotte made her consciousness stop scampering in circles and tried to sleep. In the morning she needed to rise before her aunt and hunt some more for that missing will at Hannah's. Mac was busy looking for living relatives and more clues to her death. So it was her job to find the will, if there was one to find, and for her aunt's sake she was more determined than ever to do that.

She and Mac worked well as a team, she thought, and finally drifted off to sleep basking in her memories of the day with him. She had violin music in her head. She couldn't wait to see him again.

Chapter 11

One Saturday before the ice had frozen the ferries in at the docks, Charlotte had visited a video store on the mainland and bought some used videotapes, *The War of the Worlds* and *The Sixth Sense*. They were two movies she knew Bess hadn't seen.

In the hubbub of Hannah's disappearance and wake, Charlotte had forgotten about them. She'd tucked them away for a special day and the day was here. Watching them might get Bess's mind off her damaged pride and Hannah for a while. Charlotte laid the tapes on top of the television and then made breakfast.

As she mixed up pancakes, she mulled over what else would cheer her aunt up besides breakfast and videos. She'd had so much fun with Mac the day before on the snowmobile that she thought an outing after breakfast, combining fresh air and sunshine, would be just the thing. Besides going back and forth to work, Bess hadn't been getting out much lately.

She'd read that everyone needed fifteen minutes of sunlight a day to stay mentally healthy. Yeah, not enough sun was what was probably wrong with her aunt, she mused with a wry grin.

When the pancakes were ready to drop on the griddle, Charlotte knocked softly on Bess's door and told her breakfast was ready. She'd let her sleep late, hoping it would help. It had. The night's rest had put her aunt in a better mood. She actually smiled when she came into the kitchen and saw the pancakes on the griddle.

Charlotte unveiled her plans for the day and Bess brightened up even more. "Taking a snowmobile ride along the coast and watching movies I've been wanting to see sounds like the right medicine for the blues. I'm for it. Thanks, Charlotte. You're a good friend."

The two women enjoyed their breakfast as Charlotte summarized her adventures of the day before. Everything, that is, except her and Mac's snooping in Arlen's house. They ended up discussing life and men.

"I can't look to a man to give me happiness," her aunt admitted. "If nothing else, the last few months have shown me that. I have to find it myself. It's a shame it took me twenty years, but I know it now. I'm starting over and trying something different to find the happiness that's eluded me."

"Like what?" Charlotte stirred sugar into her coffee and put the cup to her lips. She was listening for the phone, hoping Mac would call with news about the investigation.

"I'm going on a diet first off. I'm only having one helping of pancakes. It's time I got into shape and took better care of myself, for me. Then I've been thinking of rehabbing this house and opening it as a bed and breakfast." Her aunt startled her with the announcement as Charlotte sipped her third cup of coffee. "I'm real tired of working for other people."

"Are you kidding?"

"Positively not. The way I have it worked out is I could renovate the downstairs and get three rooms out of this first level. I don't need all this space on the first floor. It's wasted. Two rooms are filled with junk and I never use that dining room.

"The second floor loft is large enough to become two modest-sized rooms. Would you mind it if I split and remodeled it to serve as both our bedrooms? Of course, you could have the lake view window. I know you love to look at the water. I'd take the other side with the window overlooking the woods behind the house. That way I'd have the lower three rooms to rent out; four rooms, if I insulate and close the back porch in. That is, if you don't mind having a smaller bedroom?"

"It's your house and my bedroom is way too big any way. Dividing it in half is fine with me."

"It's your home, too, Charlotte, as long as you're here. I don't want to do anything to make you uncomfortable. I'd only go through with this scheme if it's okay with you."

"Then go right ahead. I think it's a fabulous idea." She meant it.

Renovating the house into a bed and breakfast would solve some of her aunt's problems. It'd bring in money and place guests in her home, which would keep her from being lonely. There'd always be someone to talk to, to come home and take care of. Her aunt, as Hannah had, needed to have people around her. She needed to care for them. The best thing about the plan was that now Charlotte knew Bess was going to be okay. Charlotte hadn't seen her this excited in months. Her face was alive again.

"I'm not going anywhere." Charlotte didn't know when it had happened, when she'd resolved to stay on the island and not return to Chicago, but it had. The island had really become her home and she didn't want to ever leave it. It made her happy. For the first time in years, she felt as if she belonged somewhere.

"A bed and breakfast makes a lot of money here," her aunt stated cheerily.

"Don't I know it. I work at an inn. Letty said she makes a hefty profit renting out rooms, which enables her and Herbert to continue living on Mackinac. They like meeting the interesting people it brings into their home. Herbert loves to gab and Letty, as you do, loves to cook for them. You and a bed and breakfast here will be a match made in heaven."

"I thought," Bess continued to build on her dream, "we'd be one of those places that stay open year round. We'll make more money that way."

Charlotte stared at her. "How long have you been considering this?"

"Years, I think. But as long as I had Shawn I was too preoccupied to act on it. Then you moved in, Shawn left and Hannah vanished. Things have changed. It's been great having you in the house, cooking for you and having your companionship. Your helping with the expenses has made a difference. My bank account hasn't been this healthy in years. Now I'm not afraid to open the bills every month.

"But what made the final decision for me was last night. The predicament I'd gotten myself into made me see how lonely I've become. I need to change my life.

"For years I've desperately wanted to qui working at the hotel and the other crummy jobs I have to do every winter to survive. Without Shawr there, I've decided I can't return to the hote. anyway. I'll need another source of income. So, las night in the middle of my guilt and despair, the bec and breakfast scheme resurrected. It was like a light turned on somewhere." She thumped her fingers firmly on the table. "I'm going to do it."

"Who are you going to get to do the remodeling?"

"Me. I'm handy with a tape measure and an electric nail gun. I can drywall like a pro. Charlie taught me those skills the first years we were married. He was quite a carpenter. I have friends who'll help with the electrical and the plumbing," she said excitedly. The pain in her eyes was gone.

"I can help," Charlotte volunteered. "I'm not bad with tools. I bought a set of home improvement books years ago when I discovered Lucas didn't know what a screwdriver was for. I might hit my fingers a lot but I'll learn as we go. It sounds like fun. I can't wait to get going."

"Me, either."

They drank their coffee and talked more about the bed and breakfast idea. Charlotte wasn't about to say anything against it. Her aunt wanted, needed, to do it. It would be good for her. It'd give her a goal to work towards. After the scare of the night before it was a huge relief to see her aunt so worked up over something in a good way. She couldn't have taken much more of Bess's misery.

"Oh, by the way," her aunt said, as she rose from the table and carried her empty plate to the sink. "There was a call for you yesterday evening before you got home. I was so busy wallowing in my own wretchedness I forgot to give you the message."

"Give it to me now."

"Well, best as I can recall it was some crazy sounding man with a scratchy voice who wanted you to know that he got your messages and here's one for you: *stop snooping around where you shouldn't be sticking your nose or someone might cut it off.* Something bizarre like that. I thought it was a crank call but he asked for you by name. He knew about Hannah's death. He said something peculiar about that, too, if I heard him right. Something about old ladies like Hannah always get what's coming to them. It was a disturbing call. He was definitely a crackpot. I finally hung up on him."

"Did he say who he was?"

"He mumbled his name...what was it? Carlton...no...Arlen, that's it. He rattled the whole message off so fast and jerky like. I'd just had that call from my friend's wife, so I was rattled to begin with. I'm sorry I didn't write any of it down."

Arlen. That had to be Arlen Gofrey. What had he meant by that crack about snooping around? Did he know she and Mac had been in his house or had he meant in general?

She'd speak to Mac about the strange telephone call and see what he thought about it. The other thing that baffled her was the caller, Arlen, had said he was returning her messages...what messages? She hadn't left anyone any messages lately.

Oh. Then she remembered. She'd left a couple of messages in the last week to the penciled-in telephone number she'd found on the back of Hannah's address book. Ah, so that was Arlen's number and the phone number of Sarah and Cassie's house. That meant Hannah had been in contact with Arlen or someone in that house for something before that letter and before the arranged meeting and her disappearance.

Arlen and Hannah might have known each other at least by telephone.

There was no reason for Charlotte to feel nervous about Arlen's phone call, but she was. Something wasn't right, only she didn't know what it was. She had to think about it. She forced the whole thing out of her mind and concentrated on her aunt. Bess needed her more today than Hannah. Hannah was gone but Bess was here.

After breakfast they rode around the island on their snowmobiles, had a snowball fight out in the yard, then came in to have lunch and watch movies. As they sat in the front room before the fire and watched Bruce Willis seeing dead people, Bess talked about her bed and breakfast. She pulled out a pad of paper and began sketching the layouts of the new rooms. She spoke of how she wanted to decorate and how she intended to get the money she'd need.

"I'm going to take out a loan on my house," she said.

Bess could sure use the inheritance from

Hannah, Charlotte brooded. She could have used Hannah's house. It was three times as large as her aunt's and in better shape. Hannah's home would make an elegant and spacious bed and breakfast with very little remodeling needed. They could continue to live in Bess's house for privacy. If only.

Mac telephoned in the afternoon and Charlotte, before she could stop herself, confided in him about Bess's unsettling night. Hoping to cheer them both up, he invited them out to dinner.

"I think Bess would like that. She doesn't go to work until eight so we have plenty of time. Where are you taking us?"

"My place. I stocked the supplies in a few days ago for a pot roast feast and my famous apple pie with ice cream for dessert."

"A chef, too. Another hidden talent?"

"No. Everyone knows I like to cook and I'm good at it."

"Will you play the violin for us afterwards?"

"If you ask me nicely. I'll see you both at four or is that too soon?"

"No. When will supper be ready?"

"At four." Charlotte could hear the humor in his voice. "I have some interesting news for you I learned today. I'll tell you about it when you get here."

"Well, I have news for you, too." She was going to ask him to help remodel Bess's house for the bed and breakfast. And she wanted to get his opinion on Arlen's bizarre telephone call. "See you in less than an hour." She hung up.

Bess was ecstatic to be going out for dinner.

She'd have someone else to chat with about her plans for the bed and breakfast. They dressed up more than usual and took along a bottle of wine.

An hour later they were sitting down to their meal. Mac hadn't exaggerated; he was an excellent cook. The table had been set with care and the apartment was inviting with candles flickering everywhere. Mac was a gracious host.

"Where's your roommate, Mac?" Bess inquired.

Dressed in a silk top and her best jeans, she seemed a lot cheerier than the night before. New dreams could do that.

"Darrin's on duty tonight at the police station. We have opposite shifts, which works for both of us, because his girlfriend's here most of the time when he's off. That's too crowded for me. I like my privacy."

Charlotte tried not to let Mac see how mentioning Darrin's girlfriend affected her. *Where's Mac's girlfriend tonight? Is he still seeing her? When is he going to tell me about her?* Charlotte had wanted to ask him about the girl so often in the previous days, but something had stopped her every time.

What she didn't know couldn't hurt her.

Her aunt lifted her wineglass up for a toast. "I want to thank you, Mac, for having us over. It's nice to get out of the house and have someone else wait on me." She winked at her niece. "This is the second meal today someone else has cooked. It makes me feel special."

Charlotte laughed. She turned to Mac, a forkful of pot roast half way to her mouth. "So what's the interesting piece of information you have for me?"

Mac paused as his gaze brushed over Bess. "After our trip yesterday, when I got home last night, I rang up our friend about that matter we'd discussed earlier." Mac was talking in code but Charlotte knew what he meant, the trip was to St. Ignace and the friend was Hannah's lawyer, and nodded so he'd go on. "He informed me that there's been a claim on Hannah's estate already."

The pot roast never got to her mouth. She sent a look her aunt's way. "Who?"

"Some distant nephew named Arlen Gofrey who Warren has never heard a thing about." There was an ironic tone in his voice. They both knew too well who Arlen was.

"Now that's a coincidence, isn't it, after what we found out yesterday," Charlotte muttered, careful of how she worded things for Bess was listening closely. "Now today we learn there's an heir—"

Bess interrupted, "Is this the same Arlen who called yesterday, Charlotte?"

Mac threw Charlotte a questioning look. She shrugged. "I would imagine so."

"Arlen called you?" he directed the query at Charlotte. "What did he want?"

Charlotte repeated the telephone message as Bess had given it to her.

"That's odd," Bess said slowly, as if she'd just figured something out. "Now that I think about it, that message sounded as if this Arlen was threatening you. Now you say he's Hannah's heir...a distant nephew? Why would he call you up,

Charlotte, and talk that way to you?"

"No clue," Charlotte fibbed for them. But her eyes met Mac's. She knew they'd talk about it later when Bess wasn't around. There was no need to frighten her aunt with their suspicions.

"Charlotte," Bess pried, "what are these messages this Arlen claims he got from you?"

There was no way out of it. She had to answer A claim had been made on Hannah's estate and Arlen was breathing down their necks. It was time to start telling the truth, or part of it anyway. "I simply let this person, Arlen, know about Hannah's death, that's all. I found his telephone number in one of Hannah's address books. I didn't know who he was but thought I'd let him know of her death. I got an answering machine a couple times on his end so I left more than one message. I guess he thought I wanted something from him or was harassing him I wasn't. Or he's plain crazy. Who knows?"

"Then he was worse than rude about it. Maybe he's lying about being a relative. People come out of the woodwork when they think money's involved. The guy must be a flake. Let's stop talking about him and talk about something more pleasant." Bess dismissed the issue. Charlotte was relieved.

Bess used the bathroom after that and Mac leaned over and whispered to her, "I think it's too coincidental that our friend Arlen phoned right after we'd been in his house. I wouldn't be surprised to find out that he knew we were there."

A chill crawled across her skin. "How would he have known?"

"I don't know, but it's my speculation that he does."

"Now what?" Charlotte was watching the bathroom door for her aunt to reappear.

"We wait for his next move. Though I think he's already made it."

"Contacting Warren and attempting to claim Hannah's estate?"

"Yep."

"If there's a will giving everything to Bess, as Warren believes there is, we're going to have to find it soon," Charlotte said softly. "Or Arlen's going to get it all. After what we've learned of him, and from him, he doesn't deserve it. If he's family...where has he been all this time? Hannah needed family, especially these last years, Bess told me often enough. Yet Hannah never spoke of him. He wasn't ever around. Bess didn't know who he was. Hannah told her everything. She said she had no people left."

"I never heard of him before this, either. As far as I'm concerned, if he wasn't there for Hannah he doesn't deserve to get her estate. We should go over tomorrow and give that house the thorough once over we should have done last week. We'll hunt through every nook and cranny, basement and outside sheds. No more putting it off. If there's a will we need to find it because with Arlen closing in the way he is, time's getting short." Mac's expression was somber.

"It's not easy going through Hannah's things. Every time I go through her stuff, I feel sleazy and disrespectful. But I know we have to do it."

"We do. Let's go through the house tomorrow after you and I get off work. Around five or so?"

"Five o'clock it is."

Bess returned to the table.

Dessert and coffee were as appetizing as the meal. For a few hours, they forgot their troubles and enjoyed each other's company.

Mac thought Bess's proposal to make her house into a bed and breakfast was inspired.

"What with the island becoming more popular every year and how expensive the hotels are, bed and breakfasts are doing better than ever. Of course, I'll help all I can," Mac promised. "I've never renovated a whole house before. It'll be a challenge. Just tell me when and I'll be there."

Which pleased her aunt to no end.

After dinner, Mac played the violin. They were listening raptly to his fourth selection when the telephone started ringing behind the music. Since Mac was busy, Charlotte grabbed it and cupping her hand over her other ear, heard someone ask for Mac. She carried the phone over and gave it to him. He put the violin down.

"Mac Berman here. Jack? Yes, they're both here. You were just speaking to Charlotte. That's right, you knew I was having them for supper. What? You're kidding, er, you're not kidding?"

Charlotte could hear alarm in Mac's voice and dread washed over her. Mac was staring at Bess with sympathy in his eyes. "Sure, I'll tell them." He hung up way too quickly.

"What's wrong?" Bess demanded before he could get a word out.

"That was Jack on the phone from downstairs. He says to tell you that someone just came into the Mustang and said that your house was on fire."

"Oh, no," Bess cried and swung around to Charlotte. "We have to go!"

"Jack said that the fire department was on their way. You were lucky Smitty happened to be riding by your house, saw the flames and called it in so quickly." Smitty, who worked on the ferries when they were running, was a local that frequented the Mustang for supper most nights.

Bess was heading for the door.

"I'll get your coats." Mac dashed off to get them. When he came back he said, "I'm coming with you." No one argued. They fled out the door together and getting on their snowmobiles drove to Bess's through the darkened half-light. Night was closing in.

Charlotte was afraid to get there, afraid of what she might see.

The flames, silhouetted against the deep purple sky, licked at the first floor windows and reflected against the fire truck. Besides snowmobiles and ambulances, fire trucks were the only other vehicles allowed on the island.

Volunteer firefighters were swarming over Bess's porch and through her open front door.

"We got here in time," one of them shouted at Bess as they rode into the front yard. Charlotte took in the damage. It looked bad. The night had become frigid but the flames warmed their bodies.

The firefighter who'd yelled at Bess, ax in his hand and his face dirty from the smoke fumes, stomped over as the last of the blaze was extinguished.

Shaking, more from shock than the cold, Charlotte looked at the firefighter and recognized him as someone who worked at the mercantile. His name was Luther.

He didn't raise his voice when he said what he had to say to the three of them but they could hear him clearly enough. "Good thing we got here so fast. The fire's contained and not too much damage by my reckoning, but the fire looks questionable to me."

"What do you mean?" Mac's attention was on the smoldering boards of the house where water was running down the front and trickling into the melted snow. The outside of the house was scorched in great swatches. He didn't want to imagine what it looked like inside.

Charlotte felt awful about the fire, but one glimpse of her aunt's face, and she knew Bess felt worse. Her dreams for her bed and breakfast had just gone up in smoke and fumes.

Luther cocked his head at Mac, his eyes taking in the burnt house. "Someone might have set it. This fire behaved as if there was an accelerant added. The stench of gasoline was everywhere when we got here. So, my educated guess would be that this wasn't an accident."

Her aunt seemed confused as if she couldn't grasp what Luther was saying. All she could see was her ruined house.

Someone might have set the fire?

Charlotte got it. So did Mac. She could tell by

he way he quizzed Luther. Someone didn't like
hem. Someone was sending them a message: *you
made me angry. Now watch your step!*

The firefighters were finishing their jobs,
acking up and preparing to leave.

Bess caught Luther's arm. "You said the fire's
ut?"

"It's out."

"Can we go in?"

"Not tonight, it's too dangerous. With the fire,
moke and water damage you need to give it a night
t least to cool down. We opened all the windows
e could to let it air out but it's supposed to get
own to zero tonight, so they'll have to be closed up
gain before too long. We don't want your pipes to
reeze," Luther said to Bess. "As I said, you were
eal lucky someone spotted the fire and called it in
o fast. We got here before it got a strong hold. It's
he living room burnt up mostly. The rest of the
ouse appears to be okay. The fire didn't touch the
asic structure. It's mostly cosmetic damage; it
ould have been far worse."

Her aunt was stumbling towards the front door.
Mac was behind her. He gently took her arm and
topped her. "You shouldn't go in there yet. Not
ntil tomorrow when the fire department can give
ou the okay. There's no lights, no electricity.

"I'll tell you what. You and Charlotte are
pending the night at my place. I insist. I'll sleep on
he couch and you two can have my bedroom.
Darrin's working night shift so he won't be around
ntil morning. I have extra pajamas and new
oothbrushes. I'll take the day off tomorrow and in

the morning, we'll come back here and start the clean up."

Charlotte was touched that Mac would do so much for them. But then he was an islander Islanders stuck together.

"What do you say, Charlotte, do we stay a Mac's?" Bess turned to her, shivering from the night air and the shock of the fire.

Staying with Mac appealed to Charlotte for many reasons. They could have gone to the Market Street Inn, she was sure Letty would have found them a room, but it was late. She hated bothering her boss. Then the thought of having Mac a room away after what had happened comforted her. It wouldn't be so bad to have a cop guarding them.

Luther had said: *my educated guess would be that this wasn't an accident.* Someone had meant them harm. She was scared and they'd be safe with Mac. "We have to stay somewhere for the night. I say sure."

Bess, watching the smoke rise from her home, stunned, gave in and nodded. "All right, Mac. Thank you for the kind invitation. We'll come."

Charlotte was worried about her aunt as she put her arm around her. Bess looked as if she'd been run over by a team of horses.

"I keep telling myself it could have been worse. I could have lost my house," Bess's words were a whimper, as she let Mac lead her to her snowmobile. "I have to look at it that way or I'll go nuts. I have insurance. The house can be fixed. My bed and breakfast can still be a reality."

"Yes, it can," Mac concurred. "Come on, let's

go. It's freezing out here." The wind was whipping around them. The night was dark, moonless, but lit by the snow around them into a gray gloaming as they rode back to Mac's apartment.

Bess called off work for the night. The remainder of the evening Mac entertained and tried to cheer them up. They talked and played cards. Mac gave them more violin music, and then fed them more apple pie. He was being so considerate. It made Charlotte understand he'd become a good friend to her as well as her aunt.

They all went to bed early.

Chapter 12

The next morning they returned to Bess's house and scrutinized the living room. Everything was burnt or ruined by water. The television set was blackened, its glass broken. Half the objects in the room, including the videotapes Charlotte had bought, were lumps of melted plastic. It was a good thing they'd watched them both before the fire, as they weren't watchable now.

In the kitchen and Bess's bedroom, the walls were sooty. The air reeked with the acid smell of smoke. But, a real mercy, the upstairs was untouched.

Charlotte's computer and book notes were safe. She hadn't mentioned it the night before because Bess had felt bad enough about the fire. Charlotte hadn't wanted to add to her distress. She'd been worried about the computer but she carried a USB Reader card in her purse as backup with everything she'd written on it. No matter what, she wouldn't have lost her ghost book.

"It's going to take some work to repair all this," her aunt declared, eyeing the destruction. "I'm only grateful that we have a place to live, even if it reeks of smoke."

The last fireman had closed the windows before he'd left the night before but the smoke smell was still overpowering. "We can't open the windows again, it'll be a refrigerator. We can't live in a refrigerator. I guess all we can do is start clearing

he debris out." Tears glistened in her aunt's eyes
ut she'd been brave about the whole thing. She
adn't cried until they'd walked into the house.

After exploring the other areas of the dwelling
o be sure it was safe, Mac caught up with them in
he living room. "You know it doesn't look as
errible in the daylight. I didn't find that much
damage."

"It's terrible enough. I could have done without
he fire, that's for sure. If someone set it on purpose
hope he or she ends up paying for it in some way
r another. I hope they have bad karma for years."
3ess walked into the kitchen and slumped into a
hair. Charlotte made a pot of coffee. The utilities,
fter being checked that morning by a plumber and
n electrician friend of Mac's and found to be safe,
ad been restored.

"It's only a minor setback, Aunt Bess."
Charlotte looked at her. "Nothing some cleaning up,
crubbing and fresh paint won't put right. We'll
tart with the living room."

"Well, Bess, you wanted to remodel," Mac said
s Charlotte joined them at the table. The coffee
erked on the counter. "No time like now. You said
ou have insurance on the house."

"I sure do, thank God." Bess sat at the table
ubbing her eyes. The smoke was irritating them.

"Then when you get that money just start
efurbishing."

"Probably won't be enough to do everything I
vanted to do."

"It might. If not then get that bank loan you
vere considering."

Charlotte thought of Hannah's house sitting ownerless and perfect next to them. Bess could have used that house, that inheritance, now.

Bess and Mac discussed fixing up the house. Charlotte phoned Letty at the Market Street Inn and asked for the day off. She should have done it the night before, but after the fire all she'd wanted to do was go back to Mac's place and hide. Then sleep.

Letty, as well as half of the island, already knew about the fire. "Go ahead, Charlotte, take off as much time as you need. We didn't expect you to come in anyway once we heard the news. Tell Bess we feel for her and to hang in there. Rebuilding isn't that hard after a fire. We had one in '89. Fixed things up better than before. In the end it worked out. Take your time. Herbert's not feeling too bad this week so he'll fill in for you. Take care now. Just call me when you're ready to return to work."

Charlotte got off the telephone and poured everyone a cup of coffee. They'd had breakfast at Mac's before they'd left his apartment. No one had been too hungry.

As she placed a cup before her aunt, she asked, "You okay, Aunt Bess?"

Her aunt gave her a frail smile. "As okay as can be with the bad luck I've been having lately. This hasn't been my year. I didn't sleep well last night, but I feel better this morning. Mac's right, it's time to remodel. Time to build my bed and breakfast."

Charlotte hadn't slept well the night before either, but it hadn't only been the mysterious fire that had kept her awake. It was everything

The Ice Bridge

Someone might have murdered Hannah and now someone might be trying to scare or hurt her aunt and her. For what reason? She didn't know. All she knew was it was really scaring her.

Last night after Bess had fallen asleep she heard Mac, awake like her, moving around in the living room. She'd gone to keep him company. They'd sat and talked for a long time about the situation and what they were going to do.

"Start watching your back, Charlotte," he'd warned. "There could be someone out there trying to hurt you and your aunt."

"Wow, and I thought they were merely trying to frighten us."

"I believe it's more serious than that."

"Well, he or she didn't burn the house with the two of us in it. He or she waited until we were both out of it. That's something."

"Unless it wasn't planned that way. Perhaps you two being there or not made no difference. You both being gone might have been pure luck on your part."

The truth of that took a second to register, then Charlotte murmured, "But why would anyone try to hurt us that way? Why would anyone want us dead?"

"If I knew the answer to that question I might know what direction to send this investigation. My guess is it has something to do with Hannah's death and her estate. So keep what you know to yourself, keep your eyes open and be careful." They'd exchanged goodnights and Charlotte had gone to bed.

The night before his warning had felt overly dramatic until Charlotte had seen what Bess's house looked like after the fire. Conceivably Mac was right and someone had a grudge, real or imagined against them. They had to be cautious.

After her first cup of coffee, Bess rang up her insurance agent, Tom Garren, to whom she'd already reported the fire the night before. She let him know she was home and he could come over to assess damages and file the report.

After the insurance agent had come, taken pictures, and gone, Bess and Charlotte changed into old clothes. They went into the front room with Mac to decide what to do first. Getting out trash bags, brooms, rags and paper towels, they began piling fire-damaged items out on the front porch.

They cleared out what the fire had left behind in between phone calls of commiseration and offers from friends to help. At least the phones were still working. People had heard about the fire and began to stop by bringing gifts of food and sometimes staying to lend a hand. Soon there was a crowd of people cleaning Bess's living room.

Mac, wearing tattered jeans and a T-shirt worked hard. Every once in a while Charlotte would catch him looking at her with a strange longing on his face and her heart softened more each time.

I'm beginning to love this man but how does he feel about me? She didn't know. Loving and losing Lucas had taught her love went both ways. She wasn't begging for any man's love ever again. If he wanted her, he had to come get her. This time she was going to be loved more than she loved.

At the end of the day when their friends and neighbors left, the room was empty. Anything salvageable had been rescued and cleaned. Mac made a phone call and another friend brought his horse drawn dray wagon over and had carted the singed furniture and blackened carpets away. No charge.

Bess was sorting through a pile of wet papers at the kitchen table when Charlotte and Mac joined her for a snack. They had a refrigerator full of donated food and had fixed themselves sandwiches. The work had made them hungry.

"What have you got there?" Sandwich in hand, Charlotte was hovering around her aunt as she separated a piece of soggy paper from another and was studying it.

"Papers I'd stuffed in a drawer of that lamp table by the couch. I'd forgotten they were in there. Mostly paid bills or advertisements for things I wanted to look into, but never did. See, here's that vent-free gas log fireplace I wanted to put in my bedroom. I thought it was too expensive, but I crammed the brochure in the drawer to look at later. Like if I won the lottery or something." She let out a low snicker.

Bess stopped what she was doing and picked up a large manila envelope that was soggy and spotted with ash. "What's this? Oh, now I remember." Her aunt's expression was puzzled as she inspected the package in her hands. "Hannah gave me this to keep for her a couple of weeks ago. I don't recall why or what's in it. She didn't want me to open it, just put it in some place safe. She'd ask for it when she needed it. I'd forgotten about it."

Charlotte caught Mac's sharp look behind Bess's back and snapped her fingers in the air. "Can I see the envelope?" She held her hand out and her aunt placed the envelope in it.

Mac positioned himself by the table leaving a sandwich half-made on the counter behind him.

"Let's look inside. See what we've got." Charlotte bent the metal prongs, opened the packet and slid out the piece of paper. The water hadn't destroyed it but it was damp on the edges so she handed it carefully. She read it and her lips curved into a disbelieving smile. But underneath the smile she wanted to weep at the generosity of an old lady she'd grown to care for and who was now gone.

A woman who might have been killed for what they were now being given.

"It's Hannah's will dated about a week before she disappeared. It's handwritten, but signed." Charlotte handed the one page document to Bess. She met Mac's gaze and nodded, smiling.

"Hannah's will?" Bess echoed, confused. "Why did she give it to me?"

"Read it and you'll know why." Charlotte felt as if she'd discovered a long lost treasure. They had what they'd been looking for. Hannah's will. It'd been there all along, right under their noses. It had almost gotten burned up like so much tinder. How very lucky they'd been.

Now Bess wouldn't have to worry about money. They were going to get what Hannah had wanted them to have—all her worldly possessions. Thank you, Hannah.

The Ice Bridge

The old woman had also left part of her estate to Charlotte, who hadn't been expecting it, and tears came to her eyes. Yet reading the will had made her angry all over again that someone might have killed the old woman for what was in it. It made her msiss Hannah even more.

In the midst of her joy, Charlotte felt fresh grief. She would have, and Bess would have too, given the inheritance up just to have Hannah, alive, sitting there in the kitchen with them at that moment. It wasn't to be. Hannah was gone forever.

Meanwhile, it was gradually sinking in that her money problems, as well as Bess's, had been solved. Hannah's estate must be worth a fortune. It belonged to them now.

Mac read the document over Bess's shoulder. "Hannah left her house and everything to us?" Her aunt gasped. "I don't believe it!"

"It looks like she sure did." Mac grinned. "No one deserves it more. Bess, you were like a daughter to that woman. Hannah said you took care of her. She loved you. She was the lucky one.

"Charlotte, you were like her granddaughter. She told me that many times. The summers you spent here as a child were heaven for her. She'd been so happy the last few months with you here. She said you two women made her life so much richer. She cherished both of you so much."

"She took care of me, too," Bess acknowledged, her face reflecting conflicting emotions. "Hannah had a natural fondness for Charlotte because she reminded her of herself. She said to me the night of the Christmas party that Charlotte was like her own

blood and she loved us both more than anyone els
in the world. We must have been her daughter an
granddaughter in another life. You know how sh
believed in that reincarnation stuff.

"Come to think of it, Christmas Eve's the nigh
she gave me this envelope to keep safe for her.
was so busy with the party and my guests I neve
asked her anything about it. I crammed it in tha
drawer and forgot it until now. Good thing it didn'
burn up. We were really fortunate."

Bess had her hand to her forehead and wa
pouring over the words of the will again as if sh
couldn't believe what she was reading. She wave
the piece of paper at Mac. "Will this hold up i
court? There aren't any witnesses, merely Hannah'
written words, her signature and a date."

"It'll hold up once the handwriting is verified a
hers," Mac assured her, "and Warren can do that a
well as collaborate that you were going to be he
new heir anyway."

"I was?" Bess's eyes registered more shock. Sh
was having trouble comprehending what the wil
meant for them. Now this.

"You were." Mac explained about the first wil
that Hannah had destroyed and why they hadn'
mentioned it to Bess before. "Hannah told he
lawyer she wanted to make some changes. Mos
likely to amend the document to include Charlotte
I'd say. She didn't have a chance to get it back t
Warren, though, before her disappearance. He
money, over fifty thousand in the bank, her rar
books, collections, her house, everything, wa
always supposed to go to you, Bess. Warren hope

his new will existed but he wasn't sure. He had no clue to where it was. It's been missing until now. We've been searching frantically for it since Hannah's death."

"So that's what all the secrecy was about. I knew something odd was going on behind my back with you two, but I couldn't figure out what it was." Bess was still incredulous as she re-read the paper in her hands for the third time. "It's a miracle this didn't burn up in the fire."

"A miracle." Mac sent Charlotte a meaningful glance but what he said next was for both of them. "According to Warren, Hannah's total estate, house and all, is worth over a half a million dollars. Possibly more."

"That much? I feel as if I *have* won the lottery. Whew. My head's spinning.

"But why did Hannah give me the envelope with the will and not tell me what was in it? Why didn't she have Warren draft it up legally? Keep it in his office? If this is the only copy...it could have been ashes."

Mac was looking at Charlotte, his eyes glittering. She could tell he was happy for her and Bess. "As far as we know it is the only copy. It could be Hannah wanted you to have the will in case something happened to her. Or she had another reason and meant to tell you about her bequests but never had a chance. Maybe she was embarrassed. She never liked to talk about money and financial matters. She never liked people to know she was filthy rich.

"It doesn't matter," he tapped the paper in

Bess's hands, "at least we have her final wishes."

"But Hannah trusted Warren. She'd known him all her life. So why didn't she give him a copy or tell him that she'd given it to me?"

Mac shrugged his shoulders. "I don't have an answer for that."

Charlotte thought she knew why.

Because Hannah had been afraid someone else, such as a distant greedy relative like Arlen, would get their hands on it and destroy it. Maybe she felt the will wouldn't have been safe in her lawyer's hands because the office, left empty and unprotected every night, would be too easy to break into. Hannah must have known how ruthless some people can be when it comes to money so she'd left the will with the person she most trusted. The person it would mean the most to.

It was beginning to look like Hannah had been afraid of Arlen.

Though Charlotte knew Mac was most likely thinking the same things, he was shaking his head behind Bess at her. *Don't say anything yet.* She nodded back as discreetly as she could.

Her aunt, not easy to fool, caught the look between them. "Are you two keeping something else from me?"

Mac hid his frown, hesitated, and then seemed to make a decision. He sighed. "Charlotte, it's time we tell her what we've found out. She has the right to know if there's danger for her, which I've come to believe there is, especially since the fire. Now that we have the will and there's no longer any doubt she's going to inherit the bulk of Hannah's estate we can't take the chance of not warning her. Something else might happen."

"What in the world," Bess demanded, "are you two talking about?"

"We have to tell her," Mac repeated, seeing the uncertain look on Charlotte's face.

"Okay."

Mac gave Bess the condensed version of what they believed was going on: Hannah's suspicious death, the break-in next door, the fire, the will hidden in Bess's house for its safety because someone, besides them, was obviously searching for it. They told her all about Arlen Gofrey, who'd recently come forward to claim Hannah's estate.

It took longer for that to sink in than the fact she'd inherited most of Hannah's possessions.

When she could speak, Bess muttered, "Poor Hannah. The thought that she might have been murdered for her money and her house makes me sick. Who would do that?"

Mac spoke plainly. "There are people who'd do it for a lot less than what Hannah had. With no body yet, we can't prove there's been a murder, but I've suspected it since that explosive wrapping was found in the ice...and Hannah's red mitten."

"What do we do now?" Bess replaced the precious paper in its envelope. Her hands moved over it as if she didn't know what else to do with them. Her eyes examined smoke stains on the wall.

"You need to contact your lawyer, Bess." Mac rubbed his ash-stained fingers. There was a smudge across his forehead. "Have a face-to-face meeting as soon as possible. You need to make sure you put this handwritten copy of Hannah's will in his hands, after you copy it a few times to be safe, and have the copies witnessed and notarized.

"Warren will be relieved to see this document. By what he's said to me he knew Hannah's final requests were that you and Charlotte should get her estate, not a distant relative who never cared about her, or the state or anyone else. After Warren spoke to Arlen the other day, I gathered he didn't like him much. The man came across as untrustworthy, he said, and not really island material."

Bess was in a trance, as much from the contents of the will as knowing that Hannah might have been killed instead of dying by accident.

"Sorry," she breathed. "On top of all that about Hannah, I'm having a heck of a time accepting we could be in danger. That terrifies me. But on the other hand," she smiled, "I just realized that I don't have to get a loan. I don't have to pinch pennies and cut coupons anymore—or work at the Mustang and drag myself home in the freezing snow every night. I don't have to go back to the Grand Hotel in the spring and kowtow to people. I've got money. Security. Oh, thank you, Hannah."

Her aunt's gaze traveled around the room as if seeing her house for the first time.

"Boy, what I could do to this place now." She released a deep shuddering sigh. "Or not."

"Exactly. Aunt Bess," Charlotte said what she'd been thinking for days, "you could turn Hannah's house into the bed and breakfast, not this one. Hannah's place is much bigger and in better condition. Then you could live here."

"Or," Bess came up with another version, "I could sell this place and we could move into Hannah's third floor. There's a bathroom up there. We could put in a small kitchen. Running a business would be challenging enough, much less having two residences to take care of. You're right, Charlotte, Hannah's place would make a better bed and breakfast. We'd have more rooms to rent out.

"We could use the money from the sale of this house to subsidize any renovations we might want to make over there."

"Hannah's place wouldn't take as much work to turn into a bed and breakfast," Charlotte pointed out, "as this house would."

"No, it wouldn't. Hannah had the rooms fixed up a few years ago with fresh paint and new lighting fixtures. She had everything rewired and had private bathrooms put in most of the bedrooms. It's almost a bed and breakfast now. Strange, it was as if she knew someday it would be."

Maybe she had known, Charlotte thought. Maybe Hannah had really been a little psychic, as she'd often told her. "Well, think about it, Aunt Bess. You have time."

"I do, don't I? I'm devastated that Hannah had to die to give us this unbelievable gift. I'd change it in a second if I could have her back—but I can't—so this gift blows me away. I've never had money before. I've never had any assets other than this old house. With this bequest, for the first time in my life, I'm *free* to do whatever I want."

She looked up at her niece. "So are you, Charlotte. Why don't you stay on the island? We'll

build and run the bed and breakfast together. We'
be partners. Hannah left you her autographed firs
edition books, her glass collections and the mone
in the bank. When you're not helping run the be
and breakfast you can write. It'll be perfect."

Charlotte caught the hopeful look on Mac's fac
and knew she'd stay. Yet for the moment, she onl
said, "I'll consider it. But you should have it al
Aunt Bess. You were the one here for Hannah a
those years. I've only been here two months."

"Don't forget the summers before that. I won'
hear of keeping all of it. Hannah wanted you t
have those things and that's the way it'll be. If yo
don't want to be part owner of Hannah's Bed an
Breakfast," she smiled at the name she'd just mad
up, "I'll understand. But, please, think about it. I'
love to have you live on the island and be m
partner. It would be a good life, Charlotte."

"I'll think about it. Right now I'm tired, filthy
and way too much in shock over finding the will t
make any quick decisions. Let me sleep on it."

"I can let you do that." Bess shifted her attentio
to Mac. "Wait a minute. How can we inher
Hannah's worldly goods and she be declare
officially dead if her body hasn't been found?"

"You might have to wait until spring after the
drag the straits for the body before the estate can b
legally settled," Mac answered. "Usually the court
will go ahead and declare a person legally dea
under those circumstances." Or if they had proo
Hannah had been murdered. Mac didn't say that t
Bess.

"Spring isn't long to wait," Charlotte said to he

int. "It isn't. There are plenty of things we can do while we're waiting."

Charlotte expressed what Mac was probably worried about as well. "Arlen Gofrey's not going to e happy about this turn of events. When this will nows up and knocks out his claim, he'll be out of e inheritance and out of luck. No house. No oney. No rare books and priceless collectibles. e's going to be mad, don't you think?"

Especially if he had anything to do with annah's death.

"I'd say." Mac was eating a sandwich, and udying the scene beyond the window as if he were n the lookout for something. Night was rotating ack around. They'd worked the whole day on the ouse. "More so, if he set the fire yesterday. In that ase he's already angry and unstable." He swung round and looked at them.

"You have a suspicious mind, Lieutenant erman," Bess tsk-tsked him, shaking her head, and ent to put the will away.

"I'm a cop, what do you expect," he grumbled s she left the room. "Bess, hide that piece of paper meplace safe, you hear?"

"You better believe I will," Bess's voice echoed ack to them from the hallway.

Mac leaned over to Charlotte's ear and spoke ftly so Bess wouldn't hear. "You remember that lephone call I had at my apartment this morning efore we came back here? My friend Johnny on e St. Ignace police force gave me some more formation. The house Arlen's been squatting in no nger belongs to his family or him. His mother,

Cassie, died last year in debt. The house, which ha
two mortgages on it and delinquent back taxes, an
everything left in it, not much as we saw, is bein
auctioned off in a couple of weeks.

"Arlen will be homeless. He must be desperat
about now. So, no telling what Hannah'
handwritten document will do to him when h
learns about it."

"Do you think," Charlotte put forth, "it wa
Arlen who went through Hannah's house? That h
knew or suspected there was a will and that it migl
have been given to Bess to keep? That when h
didn't find it at Hannah's he thought it might be ;
Bess's house and tried to burn the house down t
get rid of it?"

Mac took her hand and it felt warm and stron
surrounding hers. "I had those same thoughts. If it'
true, we're dealing with a psychopath, an arsoni
and a possible killer who's now penniless and eve
more dangerous. That is, if Arlen is responsible. W
don't have any real proof of anything yet. We coul
be off track and it's not Arlen doing these things ;
all."

"How do we find out then?"

"Keep digging. I have Johnny running a trace o
Arlen Gofrey for past criminal offenses or anythin
that can tell us who this guy is we're dealing witl
So far he comes off like a troubled man who can'
or won't keep a job, a man desperate for money
That's a dangerous combination."

Charlotte swallowed, her eyes on her aunt as sh
rejoined them. Bess was still smiling about the wil
but Charlotte no longer was. She had a queas

feeling about finding it and learning they were Hannah's sole beneficiaries.

It kinda made them targets, the way she saw it. Because someone had broken into Hannah's house last week and someone had most likely set the fire yesterday...and someone might have killed Hannah. What happened if that someone wasn't done yet? What happened if that person believed Bess and her were in his or her way?

Charlotte didn't want to dwell on it. She was already paranoid enough the way it was.

Mac went home soon afterwards. Bess telephoned George Warren and made an appointment for the next day, then the two women went to bed.

Their meeting was scheduled for the morning and Charlotte couldn't wait to get that will out of their hands and into his, and hear what he had to say about the handwritten document. Mac had said it was legal, but she wanted to hear that from Warren.

Charlotte lay in bed, her thoughts racing every which way. She wondered what it would be like having money and redoing Hannah's place into a bed and breakfast. She wondered what would happen with her and Mac. She could yet feel her hand in his. She could no longer deny the feelings she was having. She was falling in love with him.

She couldn't believe she no longer had to worry about money. She couldn't believe someone wanted to hurt them, either.

She forced herself to stop brooding about everything, thought peaceful thoughts, and fell asleep with the pungent smell of smoke strong in the air around her. Her dreams were of flames and empty old houses with no furniture in them, and of Hannah. Hannah was not as she used to be, but was a wraithlike remnant of herself. She was sad, lonely, cold and wet.

Good for you, Hannah's ghost said, *you found my will.*

Now find my killer.

****

Charlotte woke in the middle of the night. She peered out the window at Hannah's house. A pale light traveled from one window to another and sputtered out somewhere on the bottom floor.

Hannah?

Charlotte should have called Mac and reported the light in the windows. Someone could be breaking into Hannah's house and stealing things. Instead, she got out of bed put on a robe and a coat over that, her boots and gloves and went over to Hannah's. It was becoming a habit.

Though she switched on the lights and went through every room, she found no one. There were no signs that anyone alive had been in the house. No wet spots on the carpets or anything out of place. She'd straightened things up last time she'd been there.

She shut off the lights and hiked back home through the crusty snow.

As she stepped up on Bess's porch she glanced over her shoulder in the darkness at Hannah's house. The light was flickering in Hannah's bedroom window again.

Chapter 13

Charlotte and Bess left the house early and rode
their snowmobiles through town to the office that
Warren rented. They'd taken the day off from their
jobs. Their bosses supposed it had to do with the
clean up after the fire, and the ladies let them
believe that.

The lawyer's office was cramped. The paper-
covered desk and their chairs crowded up the tiny
space. There were windows with a miniature view
of the town's snowy streets.

George Warren was a bird lover and the neutral
walls were crowded with likenesses of his feathered
friends. Being in his office was like being in a small
birdcage. His wife had died the year before after
forty-five years of marriage. Charlotte thought he
was lonely. It was a shame he was too old for Bess
because he seemed to be fond of her. Bess trusted
him. He was honest, informed and knew his stuff.
On top of that, his fees were reasonable.

Warren had a lot to say once he read Hannah's
will. "This will is certainly legal and valid no doubt
about it. It'll hold up in court. I'm so delighted you
found it. I know it's what Hannah wanted. After
you called me last night, Bess, I took it on myself to
contact Arlen Gofrey and apprise him of the new
situation. There was no sense in letting him
continue to think he was Hannah's uncontested
heir."

"How did he take it?" Charlotte tried not to let

her discomfort show.

"Oddly, by my reasoning, and quietly. He hardly said anything after I told him you found Hannah's will and that she left everything to you and Bess. I kept it businesslike and straightforward. I waited for him to say something but he didn't."

"Did he sound angry?" Charlotte asked.

"If he was angry he didn't let on. I admit it was a bad break for the guy but he never should have been in line for Hannah's estate to begin with. don't think he even knew Hannah. He never went to visit her or cared if she was well or ill. He only wanted her money and her possessions."

"You think he'll make a claim against her estate anyway?" Charlotte knew relatives, no matter how distant, could do that. She couldn't believe, with as much money at stake as there was, that Arlen Gofrey would give up so easily.

"I don't know. I could have told him that he could try, but I didn't. That will is airtight. I can vouch for the signature. It's Hannah's. Arlen Gofrey's a flagrant opportunist as far as I'm concerned. Whenever I've talked to him, which has only been by phone so far, I've had the feeling he was hiding something. I know people. Before the will was found he made inappropriate requests too."

Charlotte gave Warren a disbelieving look. "Like what?"

"Last week when he first telephoned me he had the audacity to ask if he could move into Hannah's house right off. He blurted out he was having money problems. I said no, he couldn't move into

e house yet. He then wanted to know if he could
ke some things out of her house to sell. I again
id no. Then he wanted to know exactly how much
oney he could get from her glass collection and
er books. He demanded to know precisely how
uch was in her bank account and what other assets
he had. I was horrified at his uncouth heartlessness.
he woman had just disappeared and was presumed
ead. They hadn't even found her body yet."

"How was he aware of what was in her house,
e glass collection and the books, anyway?" Bess
ped up. "How could he know if he didn't know
annah and he'd never been over there?"

"I asked myself the same questions." Warren
horted. The fingers of his left hand were playing
ith a tiny bird figurine on his desk, a cardinal of
xquisite red glass.

Charlotte's thoughts touched on the break-in yet
e remained silent. If Arlen had been the one
ho'd rummaged through Hannah's house then that
as how he'd known what was in it. He'd taken
ventory. Maybe he'd taken other items as well.
he was glad they'd locked Hannah's house up tight
fter that and had been keeping an eye on it.

"Terrible. This Arlen doesn't sound like a nice
an at all." Bess made a face. "Now what
appens?"

"I file this will with the court and start the legal
rocess." Warren stopped fiddling with the bird
atue to pick up his pen. He began to write
mething in a folder he'd opened.

"Can you do it this morning?" Charlotte was
ooking at the lawyer. "Right away?"

He gave her a nod. "I can if you and Bess war
me to. I'll take it to the courthouse as soon as we'r
done here. I must warn you there could be problem
getting it through the courts, without Hannah's bod
to prove she's deceased. It could take a while. We'
have to have her legally declared dead. That's th
tricky part."

"As long as the will's filed, we can wait." Bes
stood up.

Charlotte and Bess thanked Warren and sai
their goodbyes. They headed down the street i
front of the closed storefronts.

Bess was full of plans for the bed and breakfas
and was anxious to discuss them. As they walke
she talked. "I've been thinking. George is sure th
courts will honor the will so we know th
inheritance will come to us eventually. In th
meantime, we'll finish repairing my house and loo
into selling it. Being winter, it could take som
time. I'm thinking we could use the sale mone
from my house to renovate Hannah's when we ge
the green light. If we're lucky and the legal stuf
gets decided on for Hannah's estate we could hav
the place ready to open by next summer." The
Bess said a strange thing, "Unless Hannah come
back."

Charlotte stared at her aunt. Hannah wasn'
coming back, but how could she say that to Bess
She couldn't. Bess still had the tiniest of hopes tha
the old woman was alive somewhere.

"What would we do then without a house?
mean if we've sold yours?" Charlotte made light o
it. It was all she could do.

"Well, we'd have to move in with Hannah. I'm sure she'd let us. She's asked me often enough over the last couple of years, did you know that?"

"No, I didn't." It sounded like something Hannah would suggest, though.

"She once said she'd give me the whole third floor. That she was getting too old to go up all those steps. I knew it was because she thought someday she wouldn't be able to take care of that big house by herself. I think she just didn't want to be alone anymore."

"Did you ever consider moving over there?"

"I did, before you came."

They splurged and ate lunch at the Pontiac Lodge where Mac found them. He was on duty and in uniform. The night before Bess had leaked the news that they might have lunch there around twelve.

"So," Mac pressed after he'd walked in. He sat down with them at the table. "How did the visit at the lawyer's go?"

"It went well." Charlotte grinned at him as she and her aunt took turns telling what had happened. They were giddy with their good fortune. They giggled a lot. They ordered steak and invited Mac to eat with them. They were celebrating.

Mac called in to the station to report he was taking his lunch break. Then he also ordered a steak. The three of them ate their meals as they talked about the future.

Ever so often Charlotte caught Mac watching her. There was something troubling him, she could see it. He just didn't want to bring it out into the light in front of Bess. It must have something to do with the fire and Arlen. That's what it was. Mac was scared for them. He thought whoever had burned their house would try something else. That's why he was sticking so close.

But oblivious to any danger, Bess was on a roll. "Mac, when we begin working on Hannah's Bed and Breakfast, whenever that is, I'd also like you to make a few custom pieces of furniture for the rooms and partitions for the lobby. I loved the handmade furniture in your apartment. I hear you're always looking for extra work. I'll hire you to help turn Hannah's house into Hannah's Bed and Breakfast. You interested?"

"I am. Hannah's Bed and Breakfast, huh? The old woman would have been tickled with you using her name." Mac winked at Charlotte and she gave him one back. He'd finished his lunch, but hadn't had time to order dessert because his walkie-talkie had paged him. He came to his feet. "I hate to leave such good company, but lunch break is over. I have to go, ladies.

"I'll call you later, Charlotte and we'll...talk." Charlotte was sorry to see him leave. It'd been fun the three of them eating out together.

"Let's go over to Hannah's before we go home," her aunt mumbled over a piece of cherry pie. "I'd like to go through her house. See what we have to work with. It's been a long time since I was on the upper floors or in the basement. I can take stock of what we'll need to fix or change."

"Okay, we can do that." Charlotte hoped it was the first step in Bess resigning herself to Hannah

eally being gone. Bess hadn't wanted to step foot
n Hannah's house, not since that first day with
Mac. Now that she wanted to go in, it must mean
he was ready to start accepting Hannah's death.

They paid for their lunch and snowmobiled over
o Hannah's house. They walked through it and
ried to imagine it as a bed and breakfast. Bess
otted down notes and took measurements. They
emembered happy times with Hannah and laughed
oftly over some of them.

For Charlotte, being there wasn't as spooky as
he last time. It was daylight and Hannah's essence
vas nowhere around. She couldn't help thinking
hat Hannah's spirit must be calmer now. They had
eads to what had possibly happened to her that
ight on the ice; they had a suspect and Hannah's
vill had been found. Hannah was getting what
he'd wanted.

"The old lady's in heaven, that's what I think."
Bess stood in the living room, cradling one of
Hannah's favorite glass horses. The light in the
oom glinted off the slick surface and made pretty
olors on the walls. She caressed its smooth surface
vith her hands, her teary eyes taking in the rest of
he collection. "She sure was a collector, wasn't
he?"

Charlotte murmured, "Amen to that. She had
reat taste, too."

"It's growing dark outside already," Bess
nnounced after they'd spent time going through the
ouse. "How fast the day's gone. Let's go home,
nake some coffee and do some more cleaning in
he front room. If I'm going to sell that house we

need to get it into shape."

"Let's do it."

They were crossing the yard between the two houses, dodging the evening shadows when Charlotte heard a loud series of pops. Bess, with shrill cry, collapsed into the snow.

A tiny fast moving object whizzed past Charlotte's head. She dropped down beside her aunt, snuggling as low to the ground in the snow as she could get. Her heart was pounding so loudly in her chest she couldn't hear anything else.

Those were bullets! Someone's shooting at us. Stay down. Stay perfectly still and let the shooter believe he's hit us...and pray the bullets stop and the person trying to kill us leaves.

On the ground Bess moaned, "I've...been...hit. I'm hurt." Her hands clutched at the front of her coat. She passed out. Lying in the snow beside her, moving slowly so their attacker wouldn't see, Charlotte opened her aunt's coat. There was a lot of blood over Bess's sweater.

The popping noises began again. Snow sprayed around them. Charlotte grabbed her aunt's upper arms and began dragging her towards their house. There was no sense in playing possum if the bullets kept coming.

Horrified and trembling, Charlotte kept her head down and moved as swiftly as she could. There was no thinking about it. She didn't slow down until she had Bess inside the house with the door locked behind them. Shaking, she slid down to the floor afraid she was going to throw up. She couldn't do that now.

She had to take care of her aunt first.

Finding the emergency numbers kept by the lephone, Charlotte called the medical center and ld them her aunt had been shot. She asked for an nbulance immediately. Then she phoned Mac. linutes later, as the ambulance was arriving, Mac as at the door.

"Someone shot Bess," Charlotte cried, tears reaming down her face. "I cut open her sweater ith a scissors. There's a bullet wound. It's bad. I d to drag her back to the house. Whoever shot her ied to shoot me, too." She was so distressed her ords ran into each other.

"Slow down," Mac spoke soothingly, his arms ɔing around her. "Tell me what happened."

Charlotte obliged him as the attendants loaded ess into the ambulance. Her aunt was unconscious id barely breathing.

Charlotte had never been so scared in her life. ess couldn't die, too. She just couldn't.

Mac watched the men load Bess into the nbulance. Charlotte had never seen him angry but ɛ was angry at whoever had done this. He helped ɛr get in beside her aunt and promised he'd see ɩem at the hospital. He closed the door.

With the siren blaring and Bess unconscious ɛside her on a stretcher, the ride to the new ɩedical center on Market Street was a nightmare ɔr Charlotte. Bess had lost so much blood. She ɔoked dead. Charlotte was terrified she was.

The Medical Center wasn't a big city hospital, ut it was equipped with some of the latest ɛchnology. It had a full time doctor on staff. Bess

had a chance. Charlotte and Mac waited while th
doctor and nurses worked on her aunt.

"Mac, you think Arlen Gofrey had something
do with this?" Arlen was like a ghost, too, she'
been thinking. No one had met the guy, no or
knew him, but he'd woven his way into ever
aspect of their lives and had changed them foreve
She was beginning to hate him.

"I wouldn't be surprised. I was going to call yc
or stop by tonight to let you know that Georg
Warren's office was ransacked this afternoo
Warren called the police station about two o'cloc
He said he'd gone out for lunch and when h
returned the place was a shambles. Nothing seeme
to be missing that he could tell, but he was sti
checking. He'd let us know."

"Hannah's handwritten will?" Charlotte's breat
was trapped a moment in her throat as she waite
for the answer.

"Safe. Warren delivered it in person to th
courthouse immediately after Bess and you left th
morning. He filed it with the proper departmen
after he'd made copies. He wanted the will to b
safe and then he went to lunch. Afterwards h
discovered the office had been broken into and th
copies of the will he'd made and left on his des
were gone. Tomorrow he's going to call th
courthouse. He has a friend there who'll mak
notarized copies from the original."

"Thank God the original will was already safe.'

"Smart move." Mac's eyes were on the door t
the operating room. Every time someone cam
through his nervousness showed. "If Arlen is ou

guy he must not have thought the lawyer would get rid of the will so soon. That was a mistake on his part. He's not so bright after all.

"After we're sure Bess is out of danger I'm going to that house on St. Ignace and see if I can roust him out. If he's the one that set the fire, burglarized Warren's office and shot at you two this evening, he's probably holed up back there waiting to hear on the news what the outcome was."

"He's waiting to hear if he succeeded in killing us or not, you mean?"

"You got it, and he might try again to get at both of you when he hears you're alive, if someone doesn't stop him first. I have to find him and question him now. I can't sit around and wait for the next dangerous incident to happen."

"You'll need my car." Charlotte dug the keys out of her purse and handed them to Mac. "You know where it is. Just don't run it off into a ditch."

He gave her a sarcastic look. "I'll take as good a care of your car as if it were mine."

She couldn't find it in herself to say anything clever back. Every time she thought about how close she'd come to being shot and how close Bess was to dying, a sinking coldness came over her—and a simmering anger. If Arlen had done this, she wanted to kill him. She'd never felt that sort of hatred before. It made her stomach ache.

Yet she was unhurt and alive. Though Bess, the doctor had warned them when they'd brought her in, might not make it. She'd lost a great deal of blood.

Charlotte knew she should call her mother and

father and let them know Bess was in the hospital, but until she was sure her aunt was going to make it or not, she'd wait a little longer. She didn't want to upset them if she didn't have to.

"Mac?"

"Yes?"

"Be careful. If Arlen's doing all these things then he is dangerous. Nuts too, maybe. Does he think no one will put two and two together and get four? How can he justify burning down houses and shooting guns at people? He'll get caught eventually. What's he thinking?"

"He's not. He's desperate. *If* it's Arlen." Mac's voice was frustrated. "We don't have any real evidence it is, merely suspicions and hunches. We could be wrong and it's not him at all."

Then who was trying to kill us? The thought that someone was sent shivers through her.

"Your hunches are enough for me, Lieutenant Mac Berman. Though I wish you'd have another officer ride along with you for back up." *I don't want anything to happen to you, too,* she wanted to say, but didn't. *It'd sound too much like I need you. I love you.* She couldn't tell him that yet. Not when she didn't know how he felt.

"There's only one other cop on duty tonight on the island. He's breaking up a bar fight at the moment. I asked for back up when I called the shooting in. But, if it'll make you feel better, I'll phone my friend on the St. Ignace police force and ask him to go along with me. That way I won't be alone if Arlen is at his house. Would that ease your mind?"

The Ice Bridge

"It would." She wiped tears from her cheeks. uddenly she was in his arms, her exhausted body radled against his. It was so good to have him hold er. She wished she could linger in his embrace all ight and never leave. No one would try to hurt her s long as she was in Mac's strong arms.

No one.

"Charlotte," he warned her, his lips against her air, "don't go anywhere unless I'm with you. Vhomever did this might try again. Once we know ess is okay, I'll make sure you get home safely efore I leave for St. Ignace. I want you to stay ere. Lock the doors and keep away from the indows. I'll get the officer on duty tonight, after e's done with the disturbance at the bar, to keep an ye on your aunt's house when I'm gone. Don't you o out again. You understand?"

She rubbed her head against his chest. Her ords were subdued. "I don't believe our assailant, hoever it is, is lurking anywhere around here aiting to get me. He's long gone. I would be. No ne is stupid enough to hang around after trying to ill someone."

"Not so. Some killers like to revisit the scene of eir crime. They get off on it."

She looked up into Mac's face, then out the indow. "It's hard to believe anyone would want to ang around outside tonight for any reason. There's o moon and the temperature is below zero. It's as old out as a freezer. I heard on the news earlier that nother snowstorm is coming in. The winds have icked up, and see, it's beginning to snow. No one's oing to be out tonight unless they're crazy. I should be safe."

"Thanks for calling me crazy."

"Sorry. Can't you wait and go after Arle
tomorrow, Mac?"

Outside the snowflakes were thick and the win
was screeching. In the short time they'd been in th
waiting room the weather had changed for th
worst.

"No, I can't. You're not out of harm's way
Charlotte," he said. "Not as long as the shooter'
out there somewhere. He'll try again. I know it. H
wanted to kill both of you. You're both in Hannah'
will. I need to find out if it's Arlen or eliminate hir
as a suspect. I need to do something."

Charlotte didn't have a response but knew Ma
was right. Slumping down into a chair, she let Ma
hold her hand as time drug by. They didn't sa
much. They waited, watched the clock and th
doors to the surgery suite.

Charlotte was about to go looking for Dr. Garre
when he came out from behind the doors. His fac
was as weary as his voice. "Your aunt is stable. W
removed the two bullets. They were of a sma
caliber or she wouldn't be with us now. One wa
dangerously close to her spine. She is a real luck
woman; she should be dead. But it'll be touch an
go through the rest of the night. The next twenty
four hours will determine if she makes it or not. A
we can do is wait. She needs time."

"Can I see her?"

"Not now. She won't know you're ther
anyway. Go home for the night, Miss Graham, an
let us do our jobs. There's nothing else you can d

ow. Let your aunt rest and begin to heal. We'll now more by tomorrow." The doctor's face was professionally empathetic, as he reached out and indly patted her shoulder. "Don't worry, we're all oing the best we can for her. Go home and get ome rest yourself. You've had quite a shock."

"Thank you, Doctor." Charlotte shook his hand, lieved that her aunt hadn't died; that she had a nance to recover. It was all she'd wanted to hear. It as all that mattered.

"What happened?" The doctor was curious nough to ask. "Two bullet wounds? Kind of nusual for Mackinac, isn't it?"

Mac stepped in. "Someone shot at Mrs. Conners nd Miss Graham outside their home earlier tonight. m looking into it." The doctor knew Mac was a olice officer. He'd brought accident victims in efore but never any with gunshot wounds. This as a first.

The doctor's lips tightened into a thin line. When I accepted this job I was told there wasn't ny real crime on the island. That's why I moved ere. I thought my family would be safe. What's oing on?"

"There isn't much crime normally on the island, can attest to that." Mac was honest. "This is more private vendetta than a random act of violence, oc. The shooter had a motive. Greed."

"I don't see as that's any better than a random t." The doctor, a slight man, sighed aloud. He bbed his fingers above the bridge of his nose. His asses shifted but didn't slide off his face. The telligent eyes behind them were a vivid hazel.

"It isn't an excuse, it's merely an explanation
Mac was defensive. He didn't like anyone thinkir
badly of his island. "Believe me, Doc, Mackinac
safe. We're going to catch this guy, I promise."

"I hope you do. Quickly." The doctor sa
goodnight and disappeared behind the doors agai
He said he had a young boy with appendicitis
see.

"You heard what the doctor said, Charlott
your aunt is stable. You can't do anything mo
tonight. Come on, I'm escorting you home." H
took her arm and led her to the door, pausing lor
enough for them to get their coats and put them on

She rode behind him on his snowmobile in h
fat yellow parka, holding him tightly for protectic
from the wind and because otherwise she wou
have fallen off.

Bone tired from events of the last few day
she'd been through so much beginning wi
Hannah's disappearance. It was one bad thing aft
another. She wanted to go to bed, sleep and forg
the world. Tomorrow she'd face her problems ar
be able to deal with them, but not anymore tonight.

Poor Mac. She felt sorry for him having t
travel to the mainland and track down a suspect i
the frigid dark, after working all day and waitir
around in a hospital most of the night. She fe
guilty that she was going home to a warm bed ar
he wasn't.

He ushered her into the house and for a momen
after the door closed behind them, he held her in h
arms again. She could hear his heart beating ar
warmed herself with his nearness. When he kisse

her, it was a soft kiss of promise. Looking into his eyes, she thought she recognized love.

Again, bad timing. Their home had been torched. Someone was trying to kill them. Were she and Mac ever going to have their chance? She pulled away but he wouldn't let her go.

"I know you're tired and distraught, Charlotte, and I have someplace to go. I won't keep you long. But when all this is over we have to have that serious talk I mentioned before, you and me."

"About what?" She played innocent but knew what he was referring to. Her head was stuffed with cotton. Her mind was moving in slow motion. Bess's blood was all over her clothes.

"About us. I want you to know that...." he hesitated and the words rushed out as if he were afraid he'd lose his courage to say them, "...I love you. There I've said it. We can sort the rest of it out later, when this is over and you and your aunt are safe."

She didn't know how to reply. Telling her he loved her was the last thing she'd expected him to say. Yet it was what she'd been hoping to hear, just not at that moment; not that night after all that had happened. Not with Bess in the hospital fighting for her life. It was too much to take in.

"It's okay, don't say anything now. I understand. I wanted you to know, that's all."

She gave him an encouraging smile. "I know. And yes, we need to talk. Tomorrow. Once we know my aunt is out of danger." She was now wide-awake. It must be the trauma of being shot at and seeing her aunt almost bleed to death in her arms, or the shock of knowing Mac loved her. But she knew the moment she laid her head down sleep would come.

Mac seemed to be waiting for her to say something else, but she didn't, so he continued, "Before I leave, I'm going to search through the house. I want to make sure you're alone. Wait here."

"It's clear," he stated when he came back. "No one else is here."

"Thank goodness." She'd been slumped on the bottom step of the stairs and got up. She swayed. Mac caught her.

"Get some sleep, Charlotte. You look as if you're ready to deflate. Lock the door behind me," he instructed her sternly. "I'll phone tomorrow morning to let you know if I found Arlen. The doctor said he'd telephone you or me if Bess gets worse so I'm going by the police station and borrowing a cell phone. I gave the number to the hospital and I'm giving it to you in case you need to reach me. If you try and can't, it could be that I'm out of range or in a dead spot. The ice bridge is notorious for that. So try again and again until you get me. Understand?"

She nodded.

Producing one of his business cards from the station, he wrote a number on the back of it. He laid it on the table by the telephone near the front door.

"Get some sleep," he told her. "Call me if you need me. For anything."

"I will." She glanced at the card on the table with the number on it. "Thanks, Mac," she

urmured. "You've been so good to Bess and I.
'e're so much trouble."

"No you're not. And you don't have to thank
e, Charlotte. I'm here because I want to be. Being
ith and helping you two has been the best thing in
y life lately. You've spiced it up all right."

Then in a softer voice, he added, "I was lonely.
ow I'm not."

What had he meant by that? He had a girlfriend
ıt he was lonely?

Laying another kiss on her lips, he was gone and
ıddenly her arms and the house were empty.

She couldn't daydream about Mac, though,
:cause she kept seeing Bess lying in the snow,
eeding, with that glint of fearful panic in her eyes
; her blood seeped away. Charlotte said a prayer
ır Bess in the hospital and for Mac out in the storm
ınting the bad guy.

Locking the front door behind him, she climbed
ı to her bedroom and fell asleep as soon as her
:ad hit the pillow. She was too drained to even
ke her stained clothes off.

The next thing she knew she was waking up to
e shrill ringing of the telephone on the nightstand.
he clock showed three in the morning as she
·abbed the phone.

Chapter 14

"Hello, hello?" Half asleep, she garbled th
words into the receiver. Her sense of realit
distorted, as it usually did when she awakened fro
a deep sleep by outside influences. Was this real o
was she dreaming? Real. But she didn't know
she'd been asleep a minute or hours.

The hospital. Bess. Charlotte came to realit
with a rush.

"Hello," a voice vibrated across the wire. "Mi:
Graham?"

"Yes!"

"This is nurse Seaton down at the Medic;
Center. Dr. Garret asked me to give you a call an
let you know that your aunt, Elizabeth Conners, ha
taken a turn for the worse. I'm sorry. She came t
for a brief spell and asked for you. You need t
come down here right now. It could be a matter c
only minutes. The doctor would have called but h
has to stay with her."

The dim room around Charlotte faded int
darkness for a second. She felt dizzy. When
passed, she exhaled, "I'll be right there. Thank yo
nurse." She'd wanted to ask for more details but th
fear of her aunt dying before she could get there ha
frozen the words in her throat.

She hung up and sprang out of bed. She hurrie
down the stairs, nearly tripping on the bottom on
Her brain wasn't working yet. All she could thin

out was that Bess was dying. She couldn't grasp

Get your coat. Hat. Gloves. Purse. Hurry. Not uch time. Oh, Bess! She should have telephoned r mother and father and told them of Bess being ot. Now it was too late. *Hurry.*

Mac had warned her not to leave the house or go ywhere by herself. Yet her aunt needed her.

Call Mac on his cell phone, that's what she'd . Where's the card he gave her with the number it?

It wasn't on the phone table where he'd left it. e searched everywhere for it, a sick feeling reading inside her. She looked under the phone, der the white lace doily, on the floor. It wasn't ywhere. Had she put it somewhere else and rgotten? No. She hadn't. Maybe. She couldn't call.

It could be a matter of only minutes, the nurse d said. She got off her knees, threw on her coat d other winter garb, and dashed for the door. She uldn't waste time searching for that card. She had go. She'd just be careful and make sure no one as following her.

Besides, no one would be outside now. It was ter three in the morning, cold as dry ice and owing like crazy.

There was no sign of the officer Mac had said ould be guarding the house. It could be he'd taken break or because of the brutal weather had gone me. She didn't blame him. No one would be out this mess, except people going to see the dying.

It was so cold the snowmobile's engine didn't

want to turn over and when she was about to beg
walking, it finally caught and started. Sh
maneuvered the machine down the driveway int
the snow-packed street. The headlights glowed in
weak arc before her through the falling snow.

A year ago if someone had told her she'd be c
Mackinac driving a snowmobile around in the we
hours of a winter night—in a blizzard, no less—sh
would have thought they were insane. She loathe
the cold and hated driving at night on snow and ice

Bumping down the road, it felt as if it'd bee
winter forever. It was no wonder people didn't sta
on the island past October. The frigid air singed he
throat. She couldn't see ten feet in front of her.

She pushed the snowmobile as fast as it woul
go with the weather conditions and aimed it for th
Medical Center. Praying to God the whole way, sh
promised Him anything, if Bess wouldn't die befor
she got there—or that she wouldn't die at all. That
was a terrible mistake.

She'd passed the closed Mission Point Hot
when the other snowmobile came out of nowhere.
rammed her. Her body flew off the machine. Sh
landed in the center of the street as her ride rockete
off the shoulder of the road and smashed into a tre
The snowmobile's lights radiated into the dar
spaces of the forest as the motor continued t
whine.

She sat up in the road, rubbing her arm whic
was hurting, and focused her eyes on the rider o
the other snowmobile. He'd veered away at the las
second, ripping along the side of her machine an
skidding around her after she'd tumbled off.

The Ice Bridge

"What the heck did you do that for!" she yelled over the wind, shaking her fist at him. *I don't have time for this,* she thought furiously. *I have to get to the hospital.*

She hobbled towards her snowmobile. She was sore, but nothing felt broken so she kept moving. Please let the snowmobile still run. Damn that guy! What had he been thinking...or drinking? She was reporting him to the police. That's what she was going to do. Tomorrow. First thing. Now she had to go. She'd almost gotten to her machine when she looked down the road.

The other snowmobile was spinning around and returning.

Fear sunk its teeth deep into her and gave her a good hard shake. This hadn't been an accident. The guy had crashed into her on purpose. *Oh, oh.*

A vision of Bess and her running between the houses as someone shot at them and her aunt's house on fire replayed in her mind. There wasn't enough time to get to her snowmobile. The person who'd smashed into her was coming right at her.

She ran in the opposite direction, stumbling off the road and trying to hide but there was nowhere to take cover in her yellow parka. She was a big lemon yellow target.

The other snowmobile came up alongside, the motor died and someone was throwing himself at her. She collapsed in the snow, fighting her attacker with gloved and frozen fists. It was like hitting someone with balls of cotton.

She should have listened to Mac and stayed in the house. But Bess was dying and she had to get to her. What else could she have done?

She yelled but knew no one would hear her with the howling wind. Her mugger wasn't much bigger than she was but he was stronger. She could have been wrong, but she thought he was a man by the way he moved.

Then something hard hit her on the side of the head and everything dazzled into black.

****

When she awoke, her head throbbed so much she nearly cried out. She was crowded in a sitting position on her own snowmobile with someone behind her.

Her hands were tied together. There was something over her mouth. She tried to reach up and pull the thing off but a hand came out of nowhere and slapped her gloved fingers away.

A whisper in her ear: "Don't do that, Charlotte. I'll have to knock you out again."

The voice sounded familiar but she couldn't place it, not then anyway. Her eyes stung as she looked around. She had no idea how long she'd been out, but they were somewhere on Lake Shore Road, she guessed. They seemed to be out of town. There were trees, shoreline and water on the right.

They were heading towards the ice bridge. In a horrifying moment, she knew who had her and what he was going to do with her. He was the same person who'd started the fire, broke into the lawyer's office and tried to shoot Bess and her.

It was the same person who might have killed Hannah.

She was going to disappear as Hannah had. She

as going to be dropped into a hole in the ice that
ossed the Mackinac Straits and her body would be
st forever in the swift currents.

He was going to kill her, too.

Charlotte struggled, knowing her life depended
1 escaping from the man behind her. She tried to
rike him in the face with the back of her head and
at hard thing hit her again. She passed out.

When she came to, she felt a chill beneath her.
1e was being dragged across the ice. Somehow,
e tape had worked its way off her mouth, but the
an didn't notice. The winds were placid and every
tle sound was magnified. She could almost hear
e snow falling. Looking up she saw the spiky
atlines of an evergreen, then another and
10ther—a path of evergreens.

She was on the ice bridge.

Smarter this time, she waited until he stopped
illing her wherever he was taking her. She kept
om moving and pretended to be unconscious until
1e heard him plod away. The wind had returned.
1e heard it sighing. She opened her eyes a little.
fter they adjusted to the faint light from the snow
1d ice, they followed a figure as it hunched over,
)ing something to the ice. The man was dressed in
dark long coat and a wool facemask that showed
1ly his eyes and mouth. In the eeriness, with the
ind growling around them like a hungry animal,
1d the gleaming darkness, he could have been a
10st person. He could have been one of the ice
ridge ghosts.

But he wasn't. He was all too real.

She heard a drill. There was no power out there

so it had to be a cordless. He was making holes i
the ice. The drill rattled away loudly in the silenc
and sounded like someone hammering nails into he
coffin. Now he was kneeling down, busy wit
something, sticking something down into the ic
He was putting something together. She wa
enthralled by his performance. She couldn't sto
watching.

He was going to blow a hole in the ice and stu
her into it. There was no help coming. If it'd bee
daylight she could have counted on people soon
or later using the ice bridge. She could have gotte
help. But it was after three in the morning and n
one was coming. If she wanted to save her life sh
was the only one there to do it.

Terror gave her strength and as soon as his bac
was towards her, she came to her knees and then he
feet and willed her body to run towards shore.
was so far away but she pushed herself and ran a
she'd never run before. The ice was slippery, bu
she couldn't afford to fall. Her legs were rubbe
Her head ached. The shore and trees for her to hid
among were slowly coming nearer through th
curtain of falling snow.

She really thought she'd make it.

Behind her there was a hush and then a muffle
explosion. She heard someone running behind he
screaming words she couldn't understand becaus
of the horror pounding in her head. She ran fast
but it wasn't fast enough. She was tackled an
brought down crashing to the ice like one of thos
poor cows at the rodeo.

She fought but it didn't do any good. He wa

o strong.

"You're not going to get away! Not this time. op fighting!" he shouted at her. "You're gonna ve a little accident, Charlotte. You're gonna sappear forever so I can get what's coming to me. hat belongs to me. I need it, not you or your aunt. eed it!"

She took a chance. It couldn't hurt to try. "Arlen ofrey? It's you, isn't it?"

The man gave no answer, but in the distance ere was a low roar of a snowmobile.

"It is, isn't it? Let me go, Arlen. Don't do this. s true my aunt and I inherited Hannah's estate; at's what you're after, isn't it? But we can work mething out, I promise!" She lied. She'd say ything to get free, to stay alive.

"It's too late," his voice was more snarl than ıman. "I can't go back now. I've done too much. ou and your aunt have to die, too. It's the only ay, so I can get what I'm supposed to get. Be what n supposed to be. Rich."

"No, killing us isn't the only way." Charlotte ıd a rough time keeping her voice from cracking. e'd said: *You and your aunt have to die, too. Too. e had killed Hannah! Oh, no.*

"You don't have to kill me, Arlen. Please, ıu—"

"Shut up! Shut. Up!"

Arlen ceased talking to her after that no matter hat she asked, pleaded, or said as he yanked her wards her watery grave.

She screamed and kicked, but he continued to ag her. They'd gotten a distance away from where

he'd left the snowmobile and as he towed her pa
the machine she began a fresh round of shriek
trying to grab him or scratch at his face.

She could see the hole out of the corner of h
eye. The water sloshed against the jagged edge
waiting for her.

"Please, don't do this," she begged as he lifte
and slammed her down on the snowmobile's sea
She started to wiggle off. He took something fro
his pocket, a metal bar, and raised it as if he we
going to hit her again. Slapping at him, she shove
the bar aside.

They fought for the weapon and she was losin
when Arlen abruptly released her arms. Surprise
Charlotte slid to the ground and stared up.

Someone was fighting with her kidnappe
Another snowmobile, lights and engine on, rumble
beside hers. *"Police! Get away from her, Arlen! It
over."*

It was Mac.

With night around them, the men wrestled in th
snow. While Charlotte scooted towards them, sh
was careful to stay away from the opening in th
ice. She had to help Mac. Something heavy clunke
to the ground. Her fingers searched around fc
whatever Arlen had used to hit her.

She found the metal bar, picked it up an
slammed it at the man fighting with Mac. With
loud grunt, Arlen fell to the ice and began moaning

Mac drew his gun, brought Arlen to his kne
and handcuffed him.

Then he was helping her up, holding her an
asking if she were all right. He was talking loudly

her ear so he'd be heard over the idling snowmobile and the wind that had picked up. The main brunt of the storm was finally coming in.

"I'm okay," she yelled as abruptly the wind died down. "I've got a heck of a headache, but other than that and being scared to death, I'm fine. *Thank God you* showed up when you did, Mac." She was so happy to see him she was crying, tears freezing on her cheeks in two ice trails, but she got the words out between sobs. "How did you know I was in danger?"

"I didn't, but I think I had help," he muttered under his breath, then spoke louder. "I've been on the mainland trying to find Gofrey. He wasn't at the house so I sent Johnny back to the St. Ignace police station and I returned to the ice bridge. I had a hunch Arlen had doubled around to finish what he'd started earlier tonight. When I reached the crossing I thought I saw someone further out on the ice gesturing at me to hurry it up. It was the oddest thing.

"It was a small figure, a woman, on foot. I couldn't make out a face. I couldn't tell who it was. It wasn't easy to see with the snow blowing. I followed but couldn't catch up with her. She was always ahead of me, running on the ice. How she kept from slipping is a mystery. She led me to you and then disappeared. I don't know where she went." He looked around. Except for Arlen, they were alone.

"Then I heard your screams and the explosion and got to you as quickly as I could."

An eerie silence had settled around them like a

shroud.

"It was probably Hannah," Charlotte said. "She's one of the ice bridge ghosts. You know…the people who have died over the years crossing the ice bridge. She was trying to help us. Me.

"You and Hannah saved my life."

Mac looked at her but he didn't reject her statement. "Okay, let's get you to the hospital now. I think that bump on your head is worse than you think."

"No, I don't need to go to the hospital, Mac. I'm fine. I'm just a little dizzy. The bumps don't even hurt now, not too much anyway.

"It was Hannah, I'm telling you." Charlotte's eyes scanned the ice looking for her old friend. "She's gone now." She released a disappointed moan.

"She's dead, Charlotte."

"I know that."

Mac propped her up with one arm. He used the other to hold the gun on his prisoner. "Are you well enough to drive your snowmobile?" he asked her.

"I'll try."

"I'm going to put the prisoner in front of me on my machine. Take him to the station. Throw him into a cell where he can't hurt anyone anymore."

"Your prisoner is Arlen Gofrey."

"I gathered that." Mac stared at the man, whom he'd unmasked after he'd subdued him. They didn't know what Gofrey looked like but he was sure it was Sarah's grandson and Cassie's son, Arlen.

Mac shone a flashlight in the other man's face. "You are Arlen Gofrey, aren't you?"

No reply. Her attacker hung his head and played upid. In the harsh spotlight, he was ordinary oking with short hair and a mousy face. When he d raise his head, he defiantly glared at them with ean, demented eyes.

"Are you Arlen Gofrey? We're going to find out yway, so help yourself some by telling us the th. You Arlen Gofrey?"

Finally the man answered, "That's me."

"Arlen Gofrey, besides this kidnapping and sault tonight did you break into George Warren's ffice today, set a fire at Elizabeth Conners' place o days ago; shoot at her and Charlotte Graham tside their house this evening and…did you kill annah McCain?"

"Aren't you supposed to read me my rights or mething? I want a lawyer," Charlotte's assailant apped, looking away and hunching down into mself. "I got the right to one, so I want one. I n't say another word until I get one."

Mac stopped trying to get Arlen to talk and oke to Charlotte, "Follow me to the station. I'll ed you to tell your story and press kidnapping, sault and attempted murder charges against this an-who-wants-a-lawyer here."

"I can do that."

Then she remembered Bess at the hospital.

"Oh, Mac, I need to get to the hospital. Dr. arret's nurse phoned me before this happened and ld me that Bess was dying. She could be dead by w. The hospital was where I was going when I as abducted." She clutched Mac's arm, terrified it as already too late.

Arlen let out a nasty chuckle and Charlot[
knew. She turned towards him and hissed, "Th
was you on the phone earlier, wasn't it? You call[
pretending to be a nurse and said that my aunt w[
dying to lure me out so you could grab me, didn
you?" Now she understood why his voice h[
struck her as familiar. He'd been the voice on th
phone, not a nurse at all.

A second impious chuckle slipped from his lip[
"It worked pretty good, didn't it?"

She couldn't help herself and kicked him. M[
had to drag her off or she would have kicked Arl[
again. "Leave him be, Charlotte. He's going to p[
for what he's done." Mac pulled his cell phone o[
of his coat pocket and using the phone's menu h[
the button for the hospital. He was relieved wh[
the call went through. He talked quickly and th[
hung up.

"Charlotte, your aunt's fine. The worst is ove[
The real nurse on duty says she's sleepir[
peacefully. You can see her after ten o'clo[
tomorrow morning."

Aunt Bess was all right. She wasn't dyin[
"Thank God," Charlotte blurted out. "I was s[
worried." The relief was so great she felt dizz[
again.

"Now let's get Arlen here to the station." M[
yanked the other man up from the ice and shov[
him toward the snowmobiles. Charlotte tagge[
along. As they passed the opening in the ice th[
was supposed to have been her grave, she couldn[
look at it.

Mac heaved his prisoner onto the snowmobil[

figured out how you caused Hannah's accident. I
ard the explosion as I was crossing the ice. You
red holes and planted explosives. Then you
ited until Hannah McCain drove over the spot
u'd booby-trapped and set it off from a distance
transmitter signal. Am I right?"

Arlen said nothing.

"Did you learn that on the Internet?" Mac hadn't
en a computer in Arlen's house but he could have
ed someone else's or gone to a library.

Arlen remained silent.

"Did you murder the old woman for her
oney?"

Arlen said nothing. He'd meant it when he said
was waiting to speak to a lawyer. He didn't seem
rry for anything he'd done.

Slouched on her snowmobile, Charlotte tailed
ac and Arlen back across the ice and down Lake
ore road towards town. Fatigue and delayed fear
ught up with her about half way to the police
tion. She could hardly keep her seat. The wind
d quieted but it was snowing and if anything,
rder than before. She had a difficult time keeping
r machine on the road.

She wanted to go home and burrow under the
arm covers of her bed and sleep for a week. That's
w long her psyche needed to recover from the
ening's nightmare.

But she had to make sure Arlen was behind bars
st so Bess and she would be safe.

Knowing her aunt was going to pull through
ade her weariness and the knocks on the head
em unimportant. But she practically fell asleep at

309

Mac's desk as she waited for him to book Arle
She barely got through her account of what h
happened. Mac had to keep waking her and said h
reaction was probably a form of post-trauma
stress.

He tried again to get her to go to the hospital f
a checkup but she firmly resisted. "I only want to ,
home and get some sleep. I'm okay."

Taking pity on her, he accompanied her hor
before conducting Arlen's interrogation. "I
question Arlen more after I make sure you're safe
home." Charlotte didn't say a word against it.

Inside the house, Mac embraced her brief
before he left. "I thought I was going to lose y
and seeing you fighting on the ice for your life wi
Arlen made me see how much I've come to lo
you."

Charlotte was half-asleep, someone had tried
kill her and she wasn't thinking straight so she d
what she'd promised she wouldn't do. "How c
you love me when you're seeing someone else?"

"Seeing someone else? What are you talki
about?" Confusion flooded his face. He grabbed h
arms when she tried to twist away.

Now she had to tell him. Make it quick. So he
go and she could go to sleep. Her limbs were
heavy, her mind so slow. She had to force the wor
out. "Christmas Eve I saw you kissing some wom
with blond hair at the tree lighting. You two look
like a couple. I was right behind you. I'd be
hoping to find you there. I was going to speak
you, invite you to Christmas at the house, then I sa
you with her and I left."

Mac's expression relaxed. A smile slowly formed. "That was Abigail. A sweet woman I met on the mainland in September and dated a few times. That's all. Yes, I was with her that night but it was the last time. I haven't seen her since. She was more serious about me than I was about her. I knew I'd hurt her if I kept seeing her so I stopped. It never went very far. I told her I loved someone else. She said she understood and was actually glad for me."

It was as if a burden left Charlotte. She actually felt happy, happier than she'd been in a long time.

"Charlotte, don't you know I couldn't get you out of my mind? I've been in love with you since the first time I met you on the ferry coming over here. No...I believe I've loved you since we were kids and you were so nice to me. I've always known it but never thought I had a chance until you returned to the island last summer.

"That day at the Grand Hotel I thought you were saying you didn't want to ever see me. That you were shoving me away as if what I wanted meant nothing. I was hurt and ran away, which was so immature of me. When I had time to think about it I realized you needed time to heal. Lucas had really done a number on you. So I decided to wait. No matter how long it took.

Charlotte was paying attention now and her voice quivered when she said; "I've been waiting to hear what you just told me or something like it for a long time, Mac. Now I can tell you how I really feel. I love you, too, and not only for all the kindnesses you've shown my aunt and me, but for you and who you are. Once you stopped coming over, I started missing you. I thought it was already too late but I'd fallen in love with you. I think I've loved you since that day at the Grand Hotel, but I was still recovering from my broken engagement. My wounded pride got in the way. Then I thought you had a girlfriend. I've been waiting for you to tell me about her."

"I don't have a girlfriend, Charlotte. I have no one but you. I love you and from now on I want to be with you, no one else. I want you to know that."

"I know it now. You saved my life tonight." Charlotte smiled radiantly at him, lifted her lips up and offered them, offered her arms and her heart. The feeling she had for him was so different than what she'd had for Lucas. This was the real thing. Finally. They shared a kiss and she knew she'd come home. She knew this was the man she'd been meant for. She'd never be alone again. She had Mac and he had her.

As tired as she was, she knew that everything in her world was looking up. They'd caught Hannah's murderer. Bess was going to be okay. They had an inheritance that would change their lives for the better.

And Mac loved her.

They held each other and kissed again. They talked briefly about what the future might hold, as she yawned and tried to keep her eyes open.

"I'll see you in the morning at the hospital," Mac whispered and said goodnight.

Then he was gone. She trudged up to bed.

When she awoke the snow had stopped and the

n was out, large, glowing and a harbinger of hope.
eep reclaimed her. She didn't revive again until
ac was rapping loudly at the front door. It was
ne-thirty. She peeked out the window. Mac lifted
large bakery bag up as a greeting. She waved, put
a robe and slippers and went down to meet him.

"I just came from the hospital. Bess is awake,"
intoned cheerfully as she opened the door. "She
ked for you and I said you'd be up there before
o long. I thought I'd escort you over there before I
o to work."

"Thank you, Mac. It was sweet of you to bring
stries. Come on into the kitchen. Sit down. I'll
ake coffee." She was anxious to see her aunt, but
owing Bess was doing better eased her mind and
ve her time.

"Did you tell Bess about last night?" Charlotte
ked. "About capturing Arlen?"

"No, not yet. She was too groggy. She's under
e effects of strong pain medication. Doc says
e'll be more alert in a few hours. When you see
r you can tell her everything if she's able to
derstand."

"I will. She'll be comforted to know her
sailant's been caught and locked up. But I think
l wait a day or two to tell her about Hannah being
urdered for her estate and all."

"That would probably be best. I questioned
rlen for hours last night and, in the end, he
nfessed to everything. He broke into Hannah's
use, broke into Warren's office, he set the fire,
ot at you two and hit Bess…and he murdered
annah. For her money, possessions and her house.

He already had a buyer for most of it. He was
deep in debt, he thought murder was his only w
out."

"Didn't he have a job?"

"No. Seems he has some mental instabili
problems. Surprise, surprise. His mother spoil
him into believing he deserved a lot more than I
wanted to work for. He has difficulty keeping I
temper and dealing with people, especially authori
figures. He's either quit or been fired from eve
job, mostly low-level service jobs, he's ever ha
He didn't make it through high school. He's n
good at much of anything except blowing up thing
which by the way he did learn how to do on tl
Internet at an acquaintance's house.

"Arlen's mother supported and cared for hi
until she died last year. As we saw when we visite
he'd hocked and sold everything he could in h
house. He'd run out of money and knew he w
going to be forcibly evicted from the only hon
he'd ever known.

"Then he found some old letters from Hannah
his grandmother in with his mother's old papers; d
some more poking around and discovered he w
Hannah's great nephew, her only surviving blo
relative; her heir.

"Someone told him that Hannah was filthy ri
and that her house alone was worth a bundle. It w
old family money. Something I hadn't even knov
about, but now looking back, it makes sense.
always wondered where Hannah's money can
from."

"She inherited it from her parents?"

"Apparently. She invested it wisely, though, er the years and it grew. Arlen contacted her and ed to coerce money out of her by saying he was stitute and needed cash. He said that being her ly blood relative, he deserved it; after all it was nily money and he was family. She had to give it him. She must have said no. Then he harassed d threatened her when she refused to help him. ou can imagine how Hannah reacted to that."

Charlotte took in a deep breath and let it out. 1ost likely she told him to get lost. She would ve hated that he was so weak he couldn't take re of himself. She would have despised that he ly wanted her for her money. She wouldn't have ood for being blackmailed into giving him ything, no matter what he threatened."

"That's when he got the idea to kill her and get e whole shebang," Mac continued. "Only it isn't as easy as he thought it'd be. He learned mehow there was a will—maybe Hannah told m herself, I don't know—and that he wasn't in it. he had to locate it and get rid of it. He thought it is in her house and that he'd find it, but he didn't.

"When you and Bess found it and filed it, Arlen, ulless rat that he is, determined the only way out r him was to kill both of you. Arlen confessed that planned to dispose of you last night, then sneak to the hospital and suffocate Bess. Both of his oblems would be solved. He'd inherit everything Hannah's. There'd be no one left to contest it.

"He's a sick man all right. You could almost el sorry for him."

"I don't. He murdered Hannah," she said coldly.

"I don't either, really. He killed a defensele old woman, tried to hurt the woman I love and n friend, Bess. Now he's going to be locked up in cell somewhere for a long time where he can't hu anyone else. He won't need a job there. I'm on grateful that his plans didn't succeed."

"Not any more than I am." Charlotte reach out to touch his arm. He bent over to kiss her.

"You better hurry it up, girl," Mac urged he "Your aunt wants to see you."

Within a half-hour, Charlotte was dressed ar they were riding through the snow towards tl medical center.

****

Life went on.

Bess eventually came home from the hospit Charlotte quit the inn to help her aunt recuperate home.

Warren reported that their petition for Hannah estate was coming along nicely. Once the sprin thaw came and the authorities could resume tl search for Hannah's body and her snowmobi everything could be finalized. The water whe Hannah had gone through the ice was only about hundred feet deep so they should be able to fir something by March or April.

Arlen Gofrey had been charged and w awaiting trial on the charges of arson, kidnappir and attempted murder. Charlotte would have to there to give her testimony of what happened tl night he assaulted her. She'd have to relive it, Bess would have to relive her shooting, but at lea Arlen would be locked away so he couldn't hu them anymore. First-degree murder charges against him for Hannah's killing would have to wait until the court declared Hannah officially dead.

Bess put her house up for sale and they began planning Hannah's Bed and Breakfast.

The ghost book was nearing completion. Charlotte had tacked on a chapter about Hannah and the ice bridge from that snowy night. With his permission, she'd put Mac's name to it, though he still didn't believe it had been Hannah's ghost that had helped them but some trick of his tired eyes. But Charlotte was sure, in some way, it had been. Even if it had only been in Mac's mind the results had been the same. Her life had been saved.

She hadn't seen any strange lights in Hannah's house since. Though whenever Charlotte was over there she often felt the old woman's presence as if she were watching over her—along with Hannah's fur trader, Wallace Stonegate. Maybe they were a couple. All old houses had ghosts of one kind or another.

"We could use that little tidbit in the bed and breakfast's brochure," Charlotte had conveyed to her aunt, amused. "Two ghosts free when you rent a room at Hannah's Bed and Breakfast."

"Don't laugh. I'll use it. Anything to make our business unique will help fill the rooms."

One night two weeks after Bess had come home from the hospital Charlotte opened the door and, as so many nights before, there was Mac. He'd begun coming by for one thing or another. They'd grown closer each day.

"I came for supper," he announced.

"Again? Weren't you here last night, too?"

"I was, but I brought supper from the Mustang, remember? You ate two burgers and all my onion rings." The sun shone on his contented face.

"All right. I guess it's our turn to cook. Come on in. We're having pork chops."

"I like pork chops." He was still standing on the porch.

"Good."

"Food isn't the only reason I came by. After supper we're going to talk about where this romance is going." He pulled her into his arms in the sunlight and kissed her.

After the kiss, she said, "Well, we have a lot to discuss then." She supposed he wanted to ask her to marry him. She'd seen it coming for weeks. She was finally ready. She loved him and wanted to be with him. This time it was right. No tiny nagging doubts like she used to have with Lucas. She was truly happy and wanted to begin their life together on the island. Maybe that meant marriage.

"Come in, Mac."

Chapter 15

Five months later

"It's going to be lovely, Bess," Charlotte was [s]ying as they sat in Hannah's kitchen having [br]eakfast. Around their plates and coffee cups the [tab]le was cluttered with the final plans for Hannah's [Be]d and Breakfast. It hadn't taken as much work as [th]ey'd thought. Hannah had kept the repairs up-to-[da]te and the way the house was laid out had been [pe]rfect to begin with.

They'd been living in Hannah's house for weeks [si]nce Bess had sold hers. The fire damage in Bess's [pl]ace repaired, the house and furniture had sold [ea]sily. Her aunt received more money for it and its [co]ntents than she'd dreamed possible. Property [va]lues on Mackinac, as Mac had always said, were [ex]tremely high.

She'd never understood how huge Hannah's [ho]use was until they moved in. She and Bess took [th]e two loft rooms on the third floor, and they both [ha]d plenty of space and their own tiny, but [ad]equate, bathrooms.

All total the house had four regular bedrooms on [th]e first floor and when they were done would have [si]x on the second. Some of the rooms were small, [bu]t comfortable, and they'd transformed large [cl]osets into private bathrooms. It'd been their main [re]modeling job, along with the welcoming lobby on [th]e first level. The view from the windows of the [gr]ounds, the beach and the water were spectacular.

When the straits had thawed, the rescue tea
had continued searching for Hannah's body b
hadn't found it. They found her snowmobil
though, and her purse with identification in it ar
that was enough to have Hannah declared legal
dead. Her will was honored. Charlotte and Bess ha
taken over ownership of all that had been Hannah'

It was strange living in Hannah's hous
Charlotte kept expecting to turn a corner or open
door and see Hannah grinning that impish smile
hers. She never did. They missed her and Charlot
imagined they always would.

They liked their new neighbors, a family wi
three children, who'd bought Bess's house. Tl
father owned a small souvenir shop in town and b
wife worked at the Medical Center. She was tl
nurse who'd taken care of Bess when she'd been
the hospital. She'd had her eye on Bess's place for
long time. They promised they'd take good care
it and Charlotte was sure they would.

The sound of hammering echoed a few roon
over and Bess was humming cheerfully, off key a
usual, to herself. Mac was building a reservatic
desk in the new lobby. She'd called him f
breakfast three times but he was too engrossed
what he was doing to spare a few minutes fi
anything as mundane as food. On his days off fro
work he was there most of the time helping the
prepare for the grand opening a few weeks away,
late June.

Charlotte had no doubt they'd be ready. They
been working nonstop, planning, tearing out wal
and painting for weeks. Mac had proven invaluab

th his carpentry skills and optimistic attitude.
ss was a different woman now that she had her
am and didn't have to worry about money.

"Mac ought to just move in with us," her aunt
d one day. "He's here all the time. He hardly
es back to his apartment anymore." She'd
overed completely from the gunshot wounds and
d gotten stronger every month until now no one
uld have known she'd been at death's door.

The greatest change was that she was her old
lf. She was now the Bess Charlotte had grown up
owing and loving. Her aunt had lost weight and
ught herself a new wardrobe. She wore jewelry
d make-up again. She laughed more and looked
years younger than when Charlotte had arrived
the island last October. She was grateful that she
ver had to go back to the Grand Hotel and service
e buffet tables or work another night at the
ustang Lounge. Now the customers she'd wait on
uld be in her own establishment. Instead of a
aitress she was a respectable business owner.

Charlotte knew Bess still missed Shawn but
e'd put her heartache behind and was eagerly
oking forward to the future as they all were.
ey'd celebrated Bess's fiftieth birthday two
eks before with an intimate party. Charlotte had
ven her a cell phone as a present. Bess told her
ece that night that it'd been the best birthday
e'd had in years.

"I did ask Mac to move in," Charlotte retorted,
nd he's thinking about it." Her aunt was right;
ac was there whenever he wasn't working
yway. They'd kept him busy hammering and

sawing. Charlotte took up the rest of his time. S
and Mac spent every extra minute they had togeth
walking, riding bicycles, talking or kissing.

They were happy.

"Are you two going to get married soon?" Be
posed the question she asked at least twice a wee
She'd seen them together and expected they we
heading that way.

Charlotte wasn't sure she wanted to share h
secret but seeing her aunt's expectant face s
couldn't help it. "He's asked and I said yes a
we're thinking about a simple wedding here
Hannah's Bed and Breakfast some evening in t
garden, if that's okay with you, around say ea
August?"

Bess clapped her hands together and thre
herself at Charlotte for a hug. "I knew it! I'm
thrilled for you two. He's a great guy and lucky
have you, Charlotte."

"So he tells me, but I'm the fortunate one. I
real love this time. I've found the other part of r
heart." Her voice was a whisper. "I never thoug
I'd love again after Lucas but everything's differe
with Mac. He doesn't care what I do for a livir
how I look or how much money I have. He lov
me for myself, not someone he wants me to b
He's not the kind to let a woman down or walk o
on her. This is a love I feel will last a lifetime. We
grow old together."

She'd never been so sure of anyone or anythi
in her whole life as she was of Mac Berman. S
trusted, admired and loved him.

The banging noise had died away and M

strolled into the room, stretching as he walked. His face and clothes were covered in blue paint splotches. He enjoyed rehabbing Hannah's house. They all did because they didn't have to do it alone.

The money from the sale of Bess's house and Hannah's bank account had enabled them to hire other people. Some days they'd had a full crew working. It had helped them repair Bess's house and finish the bed and breakfast in record time.

Charlotte cuddled Mac and gave him a kiss. "Sit down and eat, honey. It's cold but I'll reheat it in the microwave if you'd like."

"Nah, don't bother. It'll be gone in a minute. I'm starved." Mac sat down and shoved in the food as he talked. "Whew. The lobby is about done, ahead of schedule. I'll work on that cabinet you wanted for it tomorrow." He was also designing a large table for the main dining room so they could feed everyone breakfast continental style once the bed and breakfast opened.

Charlotte brought him a plate of toast and placed it with a flourish in front of him. Mac grabbed her arm and pulled her into his lap for another kiss.

"Breakfast was delicious as usual. You're starting to be some chef."

"I'm learning. I've got to be able to help feed all those *fudgies* when they stay with us." Bess would be doing the cooking and baking for their visitors, as she called them. Charlotte wanted to help, so as practice she'd been cooking for Mac, Bess and the workmen.

Giving him another kiss, she stood up and

scooted away. They hadn't become lovers yet. Both wanted to wait until they were married. Their marriage was going to last forever so waiting a few months didn't seem that great a sacrifice.

Charlotte and Mac were going to build a separate cottage for themselves on Hannah's land. The property included three acres of woods behind the house. Their cottage would be secluded and private if they built it at the far end of the lot. It would leave another room empty at the bed and breakfast that could be rented out.

Charlotte was thrilled about the cottage. Newlyweds should have a place of their own no matter how small it was. They'd begin building it as soon as Hannah's was finished. She couldn't wait.

At the counter, she filled her cup with more coffee and her eyes took in the spring flowers blooming outside the kitchen windows. She'd been busy weeding and nurturing them for days. Hannah's gardens had never looked lovelier. The lilacs were delicate shades of purple and the fragrance was sweet. It reminded her of the other idyllic childhood summers she'd spent on the island with Bess and Hannah. Ah, those were good memories.

Today the weather was balmy and the bitter cold and endless snow of the past winter now seemed like a distant memory—a fading memory like Arlen Gofrey and the nightmare he'd put them through. His trial had been the previous week and he'd been found guilty of kidnapping, attempted murder and of Hannah's murder. He'd confessed to everything. Now he wouldn't have to worry about getting and

eping a job. He'd get three meals a day. He'd
ways have a bed to sleep in at night.

Charlotte had sat there in court with Mac and
ess and listened as the prosecuting attorney
scribed how Arlen had killed Hannah. As Mac
d thought, Arlen had drilled holes in the ice,
anted explosives and blown them up from the
ore with a transmitter. His receiver had used a
x-volt lantern battery. He'd made the whole
paratus himself.

It was ironic that he'd been clever enough to
ild bombs but not smart enough to hold a job or
ake his own way in the world. Perhaps Hannah
uld have been alive if he'd been able to do that
perhaps not. Arlen wasn't completely sane. He'd
ily believed he'd deserved all that Hannah had
vned and that he had the right to kill her to get it.
ier all, Arlen had mouthed off in court, *she was
ly an old woman. She would have died sooner or
ier anyway.*

Then again, there was another theory Mac held,
at Arlen might have murdered his own mother to
t her out of the way, so he could sell off her
ssessions and claim her house. Which wouldn't
ve worked out because there'd been liens against
already. There was no proof he'd killed her and
ice Arlen had been sentenced to life, and would
ver be eligible for parole, it didn't seem worth it
exhume his mother's corpse and go through
other trial. So Mac kept his theory to himself.

Arlen had gotten what he deserved.

But Hannah was still dead. That would never
ange.

Gazing out at the gardens, Charlotte suppos
Hannah would have liked what they'd done to h
house and that it was now a bed and breakfa
They'd left a part of her collections intact. The gla
pieces sat sparkling on the shelves in what was no
the bed and breakfast's new lobby, so everyone wh
came through could admire them. That would ha
pleased Hannah, since she'd loved to socialize ai
show off her pretty things.

Charlotte filled her lungs with sweet May a
The sun was warm on her face and she shook th
past off as she would a bad dream she'd awaken
from. She had wonderful things ahead. This was th
time for her to be happy, not brooding about wh
was behind her. As Hannah had always told he
"You're only alive once, so smell the roses and ki
the boys while you can."

Bess was snickering over something Mac ha
said and Charlotte was lingering over the windo
sights when the front doorbell rang.

"I'll answer it." She went to open the door. Ma
tried to capture and kiss her on the way out, but sh
evaded his arms and smiled as she danced by hir
"I'll get you on the way back."

When she opened the door, there stood Shaw
Sheahan.

She stared at him, unsure of what to sa
Dressed in blue jeans and an apricot color
sweater, he'd lost weight and looked older. In h
hands there was a bouquet of white lilacs.

"Well, Shawn, I didn't think we'd see y
again." She kept her voice down, but she couldn
hide her frown. What was he doing here? Hadn't I

rt her aunt enough?

"Hello, Charlotte. The people living next door Bess's old house said you'd moved here. They o told me that Hannah had died. I'm so sorry to ar that because she was a grand old lady. The ighbors said that she left you two her place. They id it's going to be a bed and breakfast. Is that ht?" His eyes had been empty when she'd first ened the door but they were slowly coming alive. glanced around her as if he were looking for meone.

"Yeah, it is." Charlotte waited, trying to figure t what she was going to do—slam the door in his e or let him in. She wasn't sure. After all she'd ed him as a person before he'd left, except for n being married. "We're opening in about four eks."

"Is Elizabeth here?" he asked timidly.

"She is."

"Can I see her?"

Charlotte thought about sending him away but e couldn't do that. She wouldn't interfere in ss's life like that. Her aunt could make her own cisions. Charlotte nodded. She stood aside so he uld come in. "She's in the kitchen with Mac."

"Mac who?" His expression became anxious.

"My fiancé. You know him. Maclean Berman? 's on the island police force." Charlotte had to gh at the way he sighed in relief at her words.

"No, Shawn, my aunt doesn't have a new yfriend. She still loves you, I'm afraid, and ways will. I don't know why after what you put r through. It's been terrible for her since you left.

But I think she's finally getting over you. She
been happier lately.

"So should I let you in or not?"

"You should."

"Are you going to hurt her again?"

"No," he replied simply, a hopeful sm
showing, and she let him in and led him to t
kitchen.

The shock on Bess's face before the lo
overshadowed it as Shawn walked in would ha
made a heck of a picture. She'd never seen so mu
love except on Mac's face when he looked at her.

Charlotte stood behind Mac and put her arn
around his shoulders. He took her hands and look
over his shoulder at her, a question in his eyes.

"He's Bess's one true love," Charlo
whispered in his ear, not taking her eyes off the tv
people in front of them. "He's just returned."

"I know who he is. Everyone on the isla
knows who he is," Mac whispered back. "Wl
does he want?"

Charlotte shrugged her shoulders.

Bess unsteadily came to her feet. "Shawn, wl
are you doing here?" The surprise was wearing (
and she was moving towards the man she'd lov
for twenty years.

"I came back for you, sweetheart." Shawn n
Bess half way across the distance and gave her t
flowers. Then he went to his knees. "Elizabeth A
Conners...will you marry me?" he asked in his Iri
brogue.

"You already have a wife."

"No longer." His voice was sad. "My wife, ble

her soul, died four months ago of cancer. I was a dutiful husband. I was at her side until the end. She died believing I loved her, as it should have been and as I did, as long as she lived. But I'm a free man now, Elizabeth, and I love you. I want to marry you. If you'll have me."

"What about your children?" Bess acted as if she still couldn't believe he was there.

"John's eighteen. He wants to remain in Dublin because he has a girlfriend and a job. Amy's sixteen and has asked to stay with her Aunt Ellen, for now anyway. Both John and Amy will come and visit later in the summer. I want us to be long married by then."

The rest of it came rushing out as if he were afraid she'd toss him out before he could finish. "My youngest son, Teddy, almost thirteen, is with me. He's at the Grand Hotel now looking about. Boss says he's got a job for him, helping take care of the horses. Teddy loves horses. I sold my home in Dublin and everything I owned except the clothes in our suitcases, but I'm not broke. I wouldn't come to you penniless. I got my job at the Grand back."

"I'm sorry about your wife," she said.

He accepted her condolences by nodding.

"I want to marry you." There was panic in his eyes since Bess hadn't answered, hadn't shown any emotion except the initial surprise.

"I heard you."

"I'm sorry for hurting you by leaving." His voice broke. "I had to take care of my family and honor my promises. I would have sent word but I wanted to see you in person. I came back for you,

Elizabeth. I love you and want you to be my wife. Please, will you marry me?"

Then, with a soft sob, Bess was in his arms, weeping and laughing at the same time. "Yes, yes, yes, I will marry you, Shawn Sheahan."

After the hugs and kisses, the two spent time catching up. They huddled beside each other and talked excitedly as if he'd never left. Charlotte had never seen her aunt so unconditionally happy.

Going into the other room to continue working, the younger couple left them alone.

"It looks like we're going to have two weddings this summer." Mac laughed. They were supposed to be painting walls, but were kissing and snuggling instead. They were taking a break, as Mac put it, inspired by Bess and Shawn.

"Theirs first, I'd say. I'm not sure they'll wait long. They'll probably run off tonight and get a justice of the peace to perform the ceremony. She's waited over twenty years to marry that man. I'll bet she doesn't wait much longer."

Charlotte was right. Twenty minutes later Shawn and Bess found them and asked if they'd take the rest of the day off to attend their wedding.

They didn't have to ask twice. She and Mac quit painting, cleaned up and dressed up.

Shawn had arranged for a short ceremony to be performed on the main porch at the Grand Hotel, which had reopened a few weeks before. They'd have a special meal afterwards. The ceremony at the hotel was part of Shawn's wedding present to Bess because she'd always wanted to have a wedding there. Their friends, called at the last minute but still

330

appy to oblige, gathered hurriedly to share in Bess
nd Shawn's joy.

Charlotte stood beside Mac as Bess and
hawn's simple but loving vows were exchanged
n the Grand's porch. Her eyes gazed out over the
ovely grounds covered in spring flowers. It was a
airytale and she was thrilled Bess and Shawn were
etting married there. They'd first met, had fallen in
ove and their love had flourished there. Yet
harlotte was sure she'd made the right decision
at Mac and she marry in Hannah's gardens. The
rand Hotel belonged to Bess and Shawn.
annah's backyard belonged to her and Mac. After
l that's where they'd first met.

Her aunt was prettier than Charlotte had ever
en her, in a pale cream lace dress with graceful
eeves. It was one she'd been saving for years,
ess had confessed to her as she'd taken it out from
s dusty box, for this occasion. It fit perfectly since
e'd lost weight. Her hair was swept up in a soft
un with wispy curls on the sides. Her smile made
er pretty as she married the man she'd loved for so
ng. Shawn, in a navy blue suit that looked brand
w, with the love he had for Bess all over his face,
as almost handsome.

His son, Teddy, was shy but polite and appeared
be happy for his father and welcoming of Bess.
e was a small thin child with big brown eyes and a
st air about him. He reminded Bess of Mac when
'd been small. Charlotte was sure living on
ackinac would change his wariness. The boy
ould need a bike. She remembered seeing a used
e in Hannah's shed. They could fix it up and give

it to him. It would be nice having a child around tl
house.

When Bess and Shawn kissed and we
pronounced man and wife, like a lot of other peopl
Charlotte cried. Afterwards, the guests, abo
twenty counting the hotel workers who knew tl
newlyweds, mingled on the porch and shared
lunch of tiny sandwiches, iced tea and coffee. Lat
they ate large pieces of a one layer but st
magnificent wedding cake baked by Gertru
Weaver.

Charlotte had to hand it to Shawn. He'd pull
off a beautiful wedding in an unbelievably shc
time. He must have had it planned.

At the reception Bess was radiant. She laugh
and joked with her guests. Charlotte smiled. Tl
whole afternoon was amazing. Everyone dance
socialized and ate the fancy food. The air was fu
of the honeyed scents of coming summer. Tl
island was alive around them. The water was
sapphire expanse beyond the hotel as the seagu
swooped along the shore. It was so lovely.

Life was getting better every day. Charlo
stole a look at Mac.

Soon Hannah's Bed and Breakfast would l
opening. Hannah would have been so proud.

She and Mac would build their cottage and g
married. They'd start their lives together; mayl
have children. He wanted a girl. She wanted a boy

Yes, she thought, the long deadly cold wint
was over, the ice had thawed and given up i
secrets, the island had enchanted, healed a
become their home forever and now all of them h

hance to be happy.

This was the way it should be. **THE END** ****
****

If you'd be so kind, I would appreciate it if you left a ef, but honest review of this novel on BookBub, azon, and Goodreads. Thank you. Also, if you liked s murder mystery...I have six other cozy murder steries, ***Winter's*** ***Journey*** *ps://www.amazon.com/Winters-Journey-Kathryn-yer-Griffith-*
ook/dp/B018IZ7G0U/ref=sr_1_11?keywords=Kathry Meyer+Griffith&qid=1570815406&s=books&sr=1-or http://tinyurl.com/nc6l9tl). *I also have five others ny best-selling cozy murder series, you might enjoy:*

And here is where you can find my five Spookie wn Murder Mysteries:

ıks to the other 4 sequels of the Spookie Town ırder Mystery series:

raps of Paper (Book #1): IS ALWAYS FREE!
Book #2 All Things Slip Away:
ps://www.amazon.com/Things-Second-Spookie-ırder-Mystery-
ook/dp/B00HUCNMDS/ref=tmm_kin_swatch_0?_enc ing=UTF8&qid=1563732561&sr=1-2 Tiny URL:
ps://tinyurl.com/y3nlcdhx) Now discounted.
Book # 3 Ghosts Beneath Us:
ps://www.amazon.com/Ghosts-Beneath-Spookie-ırder-Mysteries-
ook/dp/B010QW3VXE/ref=sr_1_5?keywords=Witche ımong+Us&qid=1563732639&s=digital-text&sr=1-5 ıy URL: **https://tinyurl.com/yxc5lgpa**)

~ (**Book #4 Witches Among Us**:
https://www.amazon.com/Witches-Among-Spookie-
Murder-Mysteries-
ebook/dp/B0718V6NN2/ref=sr_1_3?keywords=Witch
+among+Us&qid=1563732752&s=digital-text&sr=1-3
Tiny URL: **https://tinyurl.com/y4ud9h97**)
~ (**Book #5 What Lies Beneath the Graves**:
https://www.amazon.com/What-Lies-Beneath-Graves-
Mysteries-ebook-dp-
B07D1BT83S/dp/B07D1BT83S/ref=mt_kindle?_enco
ng=UTF8&me=&qid=1563733413 Tiny URL:
https://tinyurl.com/y4afpuqb)

And SOON, in 2020, there will be a Book #6: **All Those Who Came Before**.)

About **Kathryn Meyer Griffith**...

Since childhood I've been an artist and worked as a graphic designer in the corporate world and for newspapers for twenty-three years before I quit to write full time. But I'd already begun writing novels at 21, over forty-eight years ago now, and have had twenty-eight (nine romantic horror, two horror novels, two romantic SF horror, one romantic suspense, one romantic time travel, one historical romance, five thrillers, one non-fiction short story collection, and six murder mysteries) previous novels, two novellas and thirteen short stories published from various traditional publishers since 1984. But I've gone into self-publishing in a big way since 2012; and upon getting all my previous books' full rights back for the first time in 33 years, have self-published all of them. My Dinosaur Lake novels and Spookie Town Murder Mysteries (Scraps of Paper, All Things Slip Away, Ghosts Beneath Us, Witches Among Us and What Lies Beneath the Graves: soon, All Those Who Came Before) are my best-sellers.

I've been married to Russell for over forty-one years; have a son, two grandchildren and a great-granddaughter and I live in a small quaint town in Illinois. We have a quirky cat, Sasha, and the three of us live happily in an old house in the heart of town. Though I've been an artist, and a folk/classic rock singer in my youth with my brother Jim, writing has always been my greatest passion, my butterfly stage, and I'll probably write stories until the day I die...or until my memory goes.

2012 EPIC EBOOK AWARDS *Finalist* for her horror novel **The Last Vampire** ~ 2014 EPIC EBOOK AWARDS * Finalist * for **Dinosaur Lake**.

* Kathryn Meyer Griffith's books can be found here:
http://tinyurl.com/ld4jlow

*All her Audible.com audio books here:
http://tinyurl.com/oz7c4or

vels & short stories from Kathryn Meyer Griffith:
*il Stalks the Night, The Heart of the Rose, Blood
rged, Vampire Blood, The Last Vampire (*2012 EPIC
*OOK AWARDS*Finalist* in their Horror category),
tches, Witches II: Apocalypse, Witches plus Witches
Apocalypse, The Nameless One erotic horror short
ry, The Calling, Scraps of Paper (The First Spookie
wn Murder Mystery), All Things Slip Away (The
:ond Spookie Town Murder Mystery), Ghosts Beneath
(The Third Spookie Town Murder Mystery), Witches
iong Us (The Fourth Spookie Town Murder Mystery),
iat Lies Beneath the Graves (The Fifth Spookie Town
irder Mystery) and soon tehre will be a sixth, All
ose Who Came Before in 2020, Egyptian Heart,
nter's Journey, The Ice Bridge, Don't Look Back,
nes, A Time of Demons and Angels, The Woman in
imson, Human No Longer, Six Spooky Short Stories
llection, Forever and Always Romantic Novella,
ght Carnival Short Story, Dinosaur Lake (2014 EPIC
'OOK AWARDS*Finalist* in their Thriller/Adventure
tegory), Dinosaur Lake II: Dinosaurs Arising,
nosaur Lake III: Infestation, Dinosaur Lake IV:
nosaur Wars and Dinosaur Lake V: Survivors,
emories of My Childhood and Christmas Magic 1959.*
r Websites:
vitter: https://twitter.com/KathrynG64
y Blog: https://kathrynmeyergriffith.wordpress.com/
cebook author page:
ps://www.facebook.com/KathrynMeyerGriffith67/
cebook Author Page:
ps://www.facebook.com/pg/Kathryn-Meyer-Griffith-
thor-Page-
8661823059299/about/?ref=page_internal

https://www.facebook.com/kathrynmeyergriffith68/
https://www.facebook.com/pages/Kathryn-Meyer-Griffith/579206748758534
http://www.authorsden.com/kathrynmeyergriffith
https://www.goodreads.com/author/show/889499.Kathi n_Meyer_Griffith
http://en.gravatar.com/kathrynmeyergriffith
https://www.linkedin.com/in/kathryn-meyer-griffith-99a83216/
https://www.pinterest.com/kathryn5139/
http://www.amazon.com/-/e/B001KHIXNS

You can always E-mail me at rdgriff@htc.net I lov to hear from my readers.

The Ice Bridge

Made in the USA
Monee, IL
04 March 2022

92273898R00193